TAINTED FORTUNE

OF GOLD & BLOOD
BOOK SEVEN

Jenny Wheeler

Published by Happy Families Ltd
Copyright © 2020 Jenny Wheeler

ISBN: -978-1-99-117256-3 (Large print)
ISBN: -978-0-9951308-4-5 (Paperback)
ISBN: 978-0-9951308-2-1 (Kindle)
ISBN: 978-0-9951308-3-8 (E-Book)
ISBN: -978-0-9951308-3-8 (I Book)

OF GOLD & BLOOD SERIES

Poisoned Legacy #1

Brother Betrayed #2

Double Jeopardy #3

Tangled Destiny – A Christmas Novella and Prequel #4

Unbridled Vengeance #5

Hope Redeemed – A Spanish Novella #6

Book Bundle Of Gold & Blood Series One, Books 1 – 3.

Book Bundle Of Gold & Blood, Series Two Books 1 & 4 – Elanora's Story.

Tainted Fortune #7

Captive Heart – A Hawaiian Christmas Novella -#8

If you enjoy Tainted Fortune you may also like a Free Preview of Captive Heart, a Hawaiian Christmas Novella - #8.

They thought they knew the meaning of sacrifice. But the hardest choice is yet to come.

Details at the end of Tainted Fortune.

'Son, Observe the time and fly from evil.'
Ecclesiastes 4:23
Inscription on the clock tower of the Old Cathedral of St. Mary of the Immaculate Conception, 660 California Street, said to be a warning to men who frequented the surrounding brothels in the 1850s.

'When we try to pick out anything by itself, we find it hitched to everything else in the universe.'
Naturalist John Muir, *Nature Writings*.

One

San Francisco. Saturday night, July 9, 1870

Aristide Laurent stared at the girl—woman, he corrected himself, she was all woman—across the table from him, and his fluent tongue stuck to the roof of his mouth. His irresistible French charm had successfully romanced a dozen pretty girls, but tonight when he needed it most, it deserted him.

The voices of the 119 other guests who filled the cocktail bar at San Francisco's Occidental Hotel faded. He didn't hear the rattle of ice in cocktail supremo "Professor" Jerry Thomas's shaker as he turned out another gin fizz. "Gin, lemon juice, sugar, and ice," he advised his patrons. "Shake it until your arms fall off to get the proper fizz, then strain into a glass, top with club soda and a slice of lemon."

Aristide might have been on a deserted street corner, or a mountaintop, instead of attending the charity fundraiser for the Alycia Stockton Educational Trust with the cream of San Francisco society. The only thing he was aware of was the warning beat, low and soft at first, but rising, coming from deep within. That, and the caramel-skinned Hawaiian who sat a white linen tablecloth away. There it was again. A tom-tom flutter in his throat.

"Mr. Laurent? I believe we're both seeking Bully's good graces?"

Her dark brown almond eyes flickered to acknowledge the black-bearded giant who sat at his right elbow. Bully Pike was one of the city's most powerful and respected factor men, trading in everything from wine to sugar, from coffee to silk. Any enterprise wanting entry to the American Union's Pacific or Atlantic coasts sought out Bully's networks.

The man himself, knife dug deep into his steak, appeared deaf to Leilani Manolo's playful goading.

Her attention returned to Aristide. She'd half-extended her hand, though it was impossible to reach him across the table, and she drew it back again with a quick quirky grin, as if to say "Silly me." Beneath the sparkle, her dark eyes were quiet pools of reflection, watching, assessing.

When he didn't respond, she

continued, "Am I right in thinking that? You're into wine?"

Aristide was a spaniel emerging from a deep pond and shaking himself vigorously, all wagging tail and keenness to please.

I'm a Frenchman. Mon Dieu, I know how to charm women. I seem to have lost it with this one.

He drew his hands up under his rib cage, as if the gesture would quell an inner longing he couldn't recognize or understand.

"Yes, I am in wine. I run Sir John Russell's Vino d'Oro estate in Sacramento County."

He glanced to the neighboring table, where his boss sat with the night's senior dignitaries, including one of California's representatives in Washington, Senator Hector de Vile, and Alycia's bereaved husband, Basil Stockton, all of them shakers and movers in California's rising status as a powerhouse.

"We're looking for an agent to handle our exports to the East Coast and Europe." He hesitated. "I'm not sure I know what your interest is."

"Sugar. Some molasses, some pure cane." She glanced a couple of places away, where an Adonis of a young man with a warrior's stature and long hair tied neatly at the back of his neck was talking to Candy. "My brother Kaleo and I. We're hoping Bully will agree to import our family's sugar."

She gazed back at him, her deep brown eyes solemn.

"A lot of lives back home depend on it."

Candy Meadows wasn't so captivated by the Hawaiian prince beside her—he had to be a prince, she told herself, with those magnificent eyebrows framing sculpted cheekbones, the massive shoulders, the quiet grave dignity—that she didn't notice how mesmerized Aristide was by the prince's sister. What was her name? Leilani or something? Leilani Manolo. That was it.

Candy always liked to keep the competition well pegged. That was how she'd become her father's most valued confidante, and how Meadows Wines had become one of the most successful vintage houses in California, not only bottling their own wine but processing for a dozen other smaller concerns.

No one else would have noticed, but she spotted it immediately. Aristide's unusual quietness. The slightly distracted, mechanical tone to his responses, as the islander wittered on about the family's plantations. He wasn't taking much of it in, she could see that, but it wasn't because he was bored. Quite the contrary. He was enraptured.

Her ears burned. She'd put in a lot of work to lure Aristide and his boss John Russell and their Vino d'Oro business to her father's agency, and she wasn't about to see it threatened by some upstart who should be a steamship ride away on the other side of the Pacific Ocean. Aristide had worked for them for several years before he'd joined Sir John, and his departure still hurt.

D'Oro was one of the state's rising wine companies, and multi-millionaire Sir John was a powerful figure in industry and commerce, so it had been a great opportunity for Aristide. But it was humiliating for a woman desperate to secure the business relationship with a marital one. Create a wine dynasty, that's what her father wanted, with a charming, talented vintner filling the gap for the son he'd never had.

His move to Sir John had been a shock, but she wasn't about to give up yet. In fact, there were advantages to it. With Aristide now in control at d'Oro, he was perfectly positioned to bring one of the state's up-and-coming houses under the Meadows canopy. She couldn't imagine a nicer wedding present.

Her father had made an enticing offer for the d'Oro agency but, infuriatingly, she had no real sense of how close Aristide and Sir John were to accepting it. He was still dallying with Bully, trying to push through some special deal.

Well, good luck with that one.

Everyone knew Bully had an exclusive arrangement to represent the Buena Vista Cooperative, rumored to be linked to Hector de Vile, although the senator never openly acknowledged any connections. And Russell and de Vile never saw anything eye to eye, so that wouldn't be happening in the near future. She wished Aristide would admit he was chasing rainbows, and settle for the inevitable—the Meadows as d'Oro's official representatives.

She placed her left hand on top of Kaleo's right one, positioned by her bread and butter plate, and gazed up at his profile, angling to catch his full attention. He was breathtaking, no doubt about it. Cloakroom chatter reported he was some sort of water god too, one of the hallowed fellows who rode the surf back in Hawaii. Imagine that! Too bad she wasn't risking losing Aristide off her hook.

She glanced to where the winemaker sat, strangely isolated as the chatter flowed around him, lost in thought, and the anger bubbled deep inside. He hadn't even noticed her bid to capture the water god's attention.

"Misty told me you twins were coming to town. How is my little angel?"

Bully Pike leaned over Leilani. His lips grazed her cheek in a haze of whiskey and tobacco. The face she'd last seen shining with sea spray, fresh and tanned, was fuller, and flushed an unhealthy pink.

In the lull between dessert and coffee they'd found a quiet corner on a settee to catch up. Around them the other guests mixed and mingled, seeking out those they hadn't seen yet as they waited for the evening's formalities to begin.

Bully Pike was still a mountain of a man, but something about her Uncle Bo had withered since the long-ago days in Lahaina when he'd led her into the Maui waves, she an intrepid ten-year-old wanting nothing more than to learn how to surf like the boys. Silver glints showed in his straggly black beard.

His eyes peered out of wrinkled pouches. As he gazed at her fondly she noted a tightness, a tiredness, about his mouth.

But the midnight eyes she'd once believed detected every fib she'd ever told still flashed with black calculation. She knew better than to underestimate the man who together with Cyrus and Misty May had been her and Kaleo's closest "family" after her mother and then her father died. She'd been too young to remember either of them.

Bully was no blood relation, but he'd been a supportive "uncle" in the Hawaiian way. However, she knew his reputation when it came to business. He might still have a lingering affection for the orphaned twins of more than twenty years ago, but he'd be reluctant to make any concessions for old times when it came to profit.

And she needed concessions. The Civil War boom in sugar, when Hawaiian cane had been in high demand after the North refused Louisiana exports, had ended with the Peace, replaced by sugar tariffs which made it even more difficult for struggling island growers.

She brought her arms up around Bully's neck and returned his kiss, her lips brushing the smooth skin above the whiskery line of his beard, close to his ear.

"We've only been here a couple of days. I'm just getting over two weeks of seasickness."

She grimaced. "But we're great now, Uncle Bo. Kaleo's missing the surf, but he'll survive."

"What brings you to San Francisco? I thought you were so devoted to your grandpa you'd never leave Honolulu."

Leilani's heart gave a hollow thud. "Now that Grandpa's dead it's up to Kaleo and me."

"Yes, I was sorry to hear Archie had gone to Lua-o-Milu." The Hawaiian place for the dead. His fingers were warm on hers. "But why does that bring you to the Bay?"

Lani shot him a teasing smile.

"Intelligence not as good as it used to be, Bo? I thought you'd have heard."

Bully gave her a censuring tongue click and she laughed out loud.

"I'm not a baby any more, Bo. And you haven't ridden Waikiki in a long time."

Bully nodded kindly assent, and then his craggy face drew serious.

"I did hear whispers. Union Sugar bought by that New York outfit when Archie was hardly cold?"

His eyes softened as he gazed at her. "So what? Is Diamond changing the rules on you?"

"Changing the rules? Worse than that. They're dumping us. It doesn't make sense. They buy an agency and then get rid of one of their most profitable suppliers."

Her brow contracted in worried

ripples. "I don't understand what's going on, Uncle, but we have to find new agents if we want to sell into the United States. And that's the only place we can sell."

The hectic pink that flushed his cheekbones deepened to a warning red.

"I hope you're not expecting me to help, Leilani." He took in a big breath, as if preparing to deliver bad news. "I can't get involved. My arrangement with Diamond is exclusive. In return for not dealing with anyone else I get favorable margins for my clients."

Lani's breath hissed indignation.

"An exclusive deal?"

She glanced around and saw waiters were delivering coffee. Guests were resuming their seats. She plunged on.

"Who's behind Diamond anyway? We can't even find the right people to talk to. We get fobbed off by middlemen. It's been impossible."

Like a cloud looming up on a clear horizon, Bully's eyes darkened with what she could only interpret as guilt.

"If Diamond doesn't want your business, you can't do anything about it, Leilani. You'll have to find somebody else."

"What? What is it you're not telling me?"

Her voice was sharp, accusing.

Bully shook his head.

"Nothing. It's nothing. It's business, Leilani. I know you're a very accomplished young woman, but this one is beyond your fixing."

"Uncle Bo . . ." She hated that it came out sounding like a wail. "What's wrong? Is it something Archie did?"

Her grandfather, Archie Arnold, has

been a legend in the Hawaiian kingdom, adviser to three Kamehameha kings, a former missionary turned statesman and fix-it man who had been a steely power behind the throne for decades. It was inevitable he'd make enemies.

Bully's brow was shiny with sweat.

"I can't help, Lani. I won't intervene. It's not something I can fix. Simple as that."

Her jaw dropped and she gaped.

Too hard for Uncle Bo?

He got up to walk away and she stood up with him, reaching for his arm.

"But Uncle Bo, our family . . . Ani's getting old. She needs special care. And there's Malia's failing health and Kaleo's hopes of marrying. We need our sugar income to take care of everything."

"Archie should have thought of that a long time ago, Leilani." Bo's voice was gravelly and testy.

She became aware they were attracting attention. She'd grown taller since she'd last stood this close to him, or he'd shrunk. Maybe it was a bit of both, because she didn't have to look up into his eyes any more.

She dropped her hand from his arm, but she didn't step back.

They stood, shoulder to shoulder, two iron-willed people, their eyes shooting daggers.

"I don't even understand how this ancient thing got started." Her voice was a mournful whisper. "If only you'd give me a clue to what's going on."

"Drop it, Leilani."

His black eyebrows drew into a warning dark line, and his full lips curled up. Was he snarling at her?

"It's not my business to tell. It's your

grandfather's doing. But let me make one thing clear—you'll get no help from me."

He wheeled on his heel and strode away. A sharp acridness pierced the fuggy tobacco cloud he carried away with him.

If Lani didn't know better, she'd say it was the smell of fear.

But what Bully, ever the dominant male, had to fear, she didn't know.

The party was breaking up. "Professor" Thomas had replaced his cocktail shaker with a coffee machine, his ruby-ringed fingers flashing as he poured the thick black brew into tiny cups.

The murdered Alycia's husband, railway and real-estate magnate Basil Stockton, had made a speech thanking Senator Hector de Vile as a major supporter of the trust set up in his wife's name. More young men of modest means and good character would get the education or training they needed thanks to the trust's activities.

Appetites sated, thirsts quenched, the city's leading citizens had contributed their largesse, and were rising to go home with that satisfied sense of doing something for others while catching up on the latest gossip.

"What was up with Bully Pike and that girl? That didn't look good." Candy cast a sidelong glance toward Aristide with barely disguised glee. "Did you have a good night?"

"Fine, thanks." He knew he sounded a little short, but he couldn't be bothered moderating his tone. He had too much to think about.

He too hadn't missed the sharp

disagreement between the alluring Hawaiian and the big man. Hardly anyone had. And, like probably everyone else in the room, he didn't know what to make of it.

Outside the hotel he found Sebastian Russell, the middle of the three Russell brothers, six foot two of sun-browned outdoors man, standing tall with the bearing of the military man he once was. An engineer, he looked after Basil Stockton's business, as well as retaining close ties with Russell family interests.

Sebastian approached. "Just looking for you. The carriage is around the corner. John's gone home already. Pania needed to feed the baby." Sir John and his wife Pania, once a star of the San Francisco stage, idolized their new son, Robert.

Aristide and Candy followed

Sebastian away from the throng, around a corner into the hotel's side courtyard. The dark street was lit by a glimmer from the hotel kitchens, the slickness of light rain on the cobblestones picked up by the gas streetlamps.

Candy threaded her arm lightly through his, a safeguard against slipping on the wet pavement.

"Oh, no." She stopped abruptly and pointed.

He followed the line of her arm, and saw movement in the gloom. A brief glimpse of someone running. Maybe more than one person, vanishing into the darkness. And then others running toward them. No, not toward them, but toward the body of a man, spread eagled on his back, his form partly in darkness, a full dark beard catching the available light.

"Isn't that—?" Candy stared. "It's that woman. The Hawaiian."

Before Aristide had a chance to reply, a high-pitched keening rent the air. Candy was right. Leilani Manolo was on her knees in the street, bent over Bully Pike's mounded body. Standing over her was a second woman in a shiny red satin dress, her tousled black hair tumbling in disarray down her back. And it was she who was wailing, unintelligible words. He registered a lament in Louisiana French, but that was all.

Leilani rocked back on her heels and wiped at her right cheek. Even in the night gloom, Aristide could see her skin was smeared with blood.

"Oh my God! She's killed him."

At the sound of Candy's voice, Leilani looked around, her eyes glassy with shock.

"He said . . . He said to meet him outside. When I got here, he was bleeding."

She stared with wild eyes. "Bully was like a father to me. I'd never . . . I didn't do anything."

She struggled to get to her feet. Halfway through the movement she faltered.

In one stride Sebastian was at her side, catching her as she pitched forward, insensible to everything around her.

"Please. Step back everyone. Someone get a doctor."

In the bedlam that followed Aristide did what he could to assist. A doctor stepped forward. Leilani Manolo was carried inside. The doctor returned and pronounced Bully Pike dead. As Aristide helped Sebastian and a few others lift his draped bulk onto a gurney they were interrupted by a dapper, tweed-suited fellow with a pen and notebook in hand.

"Felix Duchamp from *Alta California.* I'm their French correspondent."

Alta California was one of the city's most-read newspapers. He paused and glanced around the circle, his eyes resting on Aristide for a few long seconds and then flicking back to Sebastian.

"Are you in charge here? What happened?"

Sebastian shook his head. "I'm sorry, sir. Not now. It's too early to say anything."

Aristide glanced to Candy, who was standing a few feet away watching.

"I'll be back directly," he said. Then with lowered eyes he took a corner of the gurney and guided the husk of the

man who had once been Bully Pike
inside, wishing with every step he could
escape from the grim cortege and
vanish.

Two

Kaleo draped a blanket around Leilani's neck. His hand lingered on her shoulder. "Are you OK?"

She glanced up at him through chattering teeth.

It was muggy and hot in the Occidental Hotel's luggage room but she was frozen to her core.

Kaleo drew her into his side protectively and glared at the man who stood over her.

"It's time I got her home, Russell. She's answered enough questions for one night."

He fixed Sebastian Russell with an uncompromising eagle eye. Officially

Russell was assisting the local police captain with investigations. He wasn't a sworn officer, although he'd acted as such in the past. However, he'd assumed direction of the crime scene with a natural authority.

"She doesn't know any more than what she's already told you. Can't you see that?"

Russell's mouth was a tight grim line as he shook his head.

"She's told me nothing. Apart from some garbled story about some boy telling her she was needed. And then Bully staggering up to her clutching his chest."

Kaleo let out a frustrated snarl. "Because that's what happened."

"And what was she doing out there anyway? What's this disagreement she had with the deceased?"

Russell stepped back, giving them breathing space. He tipped his head toward the door which led into the cocktail bar.

"A lot of people saw it. Your sister and the victim parted on bad terms, from what I've been told, not more than an hour before."

Kaleo made a dismissive sound in his throat.

"And you think she organized herself to kill him within an hour because of some ticklish business discussion? Bully's like an uncle to us."

His deep voice dripped with scorn. "What? She came prepared with a knife? Is that it? And where did she dispose of it?"

Her usually imperturbable brother was exasperated.

"Neither of us has seen Uncle Bo for

a decade. My sister had no motive to kill him. You're being ridiculous."

Lani snuggled into her brother's firmly muscled ribs and let his warmth flow into her, melting the ice inside, strengthening her. Then she cleared her throat and stepped out of his embrace.

"I've told you all I know, Mr. Russell. Bully was annoyed about something, but he wouldn't tell me what. Something from a long time ago. He said it was none of my business. I don't know any more than that."

She appealed to Kaleo with a flash of her dark eyes. "Neither of us do."

Her inflection was flat and her eyes strayed to where Bully's body lay, his feet hanging awkwardly over the stretcher end. They'd had a problem finding a trolley long enough to accommodate him.

"He was still conscious when I found him. He tried to say something to me, but I couldn't make it out."

Tears sprang to her eyes. She gathered the blanket more closely around her and crossed to the gurney with faltering steps.

"He looks so calm."

He lay on his back, a blanket drawn up over his bloodied chest. He was like of one of those antique marble busts she'd seen in picture books, like a general or commander-in-chief laid to rest after battle, his eagle profile strong and noble in death.

She ran her hand from his hairline down the side of his face. His thick beard was soft under her light touch. Someone, she guessed the doctor, had loosened the collar of his white dress shirt and his throat showed through, unlined and lightly tanned in the gap, as if he'd romped in Maui's breakers last week instead of decades ago.

She had another flashing image of the young Bully, like a human shark, all muscles and white teeth, the whale's tooth emblem at his throat shining through the salty foam.

Her heart stopped.

"Where's his whale's tooth?"

She glanced up at Kaleo, who had followed her and stood to the other side of the litter.

"His what?" Sebastian Russell's eyebrows contracted in irritation or confusion, she couldn't tell which.

"His whale's tooth pendant. He always wore it."

Kaleo loosened the shirt at his throat. "You're right. It was a sign of his rank. He never separated from it."

He widened the opening of Pike's collar, slipping his hand inside his fine cotton shirt.

His eyes went straight to Sebastian's closed face. "Look at this. He's got an abrasion like a rope burn mark on his neck here, under his ear."

Kaleo stared at Bully's throat.

"Someone has ripped his *lei niho palaoa*—that's what we call it, his ancestral necklace—off with force. They've rubbed against his skin and left a graze."

Sebastian moved to Lani's side and leaned over Bully's body to examine the spot.

"You'll have to explain. I can see there's a slight mark here."

He glanced up at the twins, his handsome face clouded.

"But it's nothing too nasty. Why do you think it's significant?"

Lani's voice was soft and tentative. "Bully's whale's tooth pendant was a rare family heirloom. His Hawaiian mother's family gave it to him when he came of age. Originally they strung it on human hair, but by the time it came to Bully it was threaded on woven fiber from the hala tree with some of the remaining ancient hair woven into it."

Kaleo interrupted. "It would never have broken. Someone's grabbed it with force."

He glanced to Lani. "It would take a man. A powerful man. And he would have wrenched it hard. Or maybe he cut it."

Sebastian raised his brows. "So if we find the pendant, we find who killed him. Is that what you're saying?"

Leilani nodded.

"Or someone who knows who did."

Three

"Who'd want him dead? It doesn't make sense . . ."

Lani Manolo dragged her hands down her face and twisted her mouth in frustration. Kaleo slumped opposite her in Cyrus and Misty May's sitting room, his long legs stretched out on a red velvet ottoman, arms behind his head.

This was their second home, and they'd been staying here ever since they'd arrived.

"Lani, you know as well as I do, Bully was no saint. He had his share of enemies, there's no doubt about that."

By the time Sebastian had released them from questioning and they'd got home, it was close to dawn and, exhausted as Lani was, sleep was impossible. Her nerves were on edge, her mind careening from childhood memories to wild searching for an explanation.

They'd made themselves a hot chocolate nightcap and were going round in ever-decreasing circles positing questions they had no answers for.

She could barely keep her eyes open, but hot irritation spilled through her at her brother's languid sprawl. Didn't he understand she'd come close to being arrested for murder tonight? That Russell brother still regarded her with suspicion, just because Bully had died in her arms.

Her head pounded like a sharkskin drum played with a heavy hand.

What was it Bully said? It was a

whisper, a few words expelled on a wraith of breath before the man who'd been so unavoidable in life had expired like sea spume. One moment he was a mountain, the next he was tumbleweed on the sand hills. She wasn't sure of those last words, which was why she'd mentioned them to no one.

"Oh for goodness' sake, Kaleo!"

She spat out the words, but Kaleo barely registered her frustration.

He lifted one brow—his scarred right brow, the brown arch broken by a clear diagonal mark, souvenir of a flying surfboard—and continued as if she hadn't spoken.

"It could be a jealous husband. It could be a business enemy. It could be—"

Lani spoke over the top of him. "Honestly? What could he have done to get someone so furious they'd want to kill him? No one's mentioned any public feuds."

Kaleo shrugged.

"Let's face it, Lani. We haven't had anything to do with Bully for years—not since he came here when we were twelve. A lot can happen in ten years. We have no idea what he might have gotten into."

He lurched forward, his elbows on his knees, a quizzical look on his handsome face.

"And we might be riding the wrong wave entirely. It might go right back to the old days. You know a lot of bad juju went down around the time we were born. Maybe it's the Manolo curse."

"Oh, be serious, Kaleo."

His face showed no sign of humor.

"Serious? I *am* being serious. You

don't take the old ways seriously enough, that's your trouble."

An icy trickle ran down Lani's spine.

What had got Bully so angry at dinner tonight? Maybe Kaleo has a point.

She mirrored her brother's stance, leaning forward in her chair and gazing up at him, eyes bright with determination.

"Kaleo, it's today we've got to be concerned about. Not some ancient vendetta. Who will buy our sugar? How will we take care of Ani and Malia?"

Her heart panged as she saw her *haina* mother in her mind's eye, her once erect carriage stooped and wasted, her sight almost gone. Precious Ani, who'd been a protective angel when Grandmother Cornelia had died.

At the thought of her wise, deeply

grooved face, the one-time sparkle in eyes now clouded with cataracts, a riptide of fear washed through her. Would they even see her alive again? First Archie, now Bully. If Ani was next, Lani didn't know how she'd bear it.

She pushed to her feet, unable to sit any longer, determination surging in to replace the fear.

Malia, their gorgeous, irrepressible adopted sister, could be relied on keep Ani's spirits buoyed up while they were away.

Malia was as impossible to rein in as a Waikiki curler, but she adored Ani as much as Lani and Kaleo did.

They were both relying on her and Kaleo to patch up the disaster that had broken over the family following Archie's death. Their nearest and dearest were depending on them. One in the shadow years of life, the other blinded by childhood measles which limited her opportunities if not her joyous spirit.

"We can't stand around talking any longer, Kaleo," she said abruptly. "We've got to do something before we lose everything."

Four

"You're looking dreadful, Aristide. Anything I can do to help?"

"Nothing. But thanks for asking."

He gestured her to the breakfast table. "Help yourself to croissants, Sis."

His eyes, usually sparkling with good humor, were dull, ringed by smoky shadows.

"Things went from bad to worse last night, that's all."

Madeleine dropped into the empty chair beside him. They had already used two settings at the small gingham-clothed table because Sir John and her husband Caleb Stewart had risen early and were out and about on their joint business.

It was after ten o'clock, so she and her brother were starting late. The sheriffs had kept Aristide until the early hours making a statement about that man's death. She knew that. And she was enjoying the luxury of a few sleep-ins, pampering herself after discovering she was in the early stages of coming motherhood. She'd wed only three months ago, and at thirty she was old to be having her first child, so she was digesting the news for a while.

She'd sensed this morning was no time to be sharing the happy event with her younger brother, although he'd greet the news with enthusiasm.

"A terrible business last night. I'm sorry you were anywhere near it."

He stopped in mid-pour, the coffee pot poised above his half-filled cup, and stared up at her, his eyes troubled.

There was a long silence.

"You're all right, aren't you, Aristide? It must be upsetting, a violent murder and all, but it's nothing to do with us, is it?"

He shook his head and finished pouring his coffee without speaking, before passing the pot to her. He hesitated before the plate which held several fresh croissants oozing strawberry jam, his usual appetite notably lacking.

"Now that shows me there's something seriously wrong, when you don't look happy about croissants," she joked.

He had the grace to give her a weak smile.

"Sorry, Maddie. I'm not very good company today."

"Why don't you tell me about it?"

Ten months ago, he'd been a rock when she'd endured terrifying blackmail threats from a murderous ex-husband who deserted her years before in France and whom she'd assumed was long dead.

"You were an anchor in the storm for me this last year. Let me return the favor now."

She reached out her hand and gave him a brief touch. "It can't be that bad. I mean you didn't have anything to do with his death."

A dart of pain darkened his handsome features.

"Something is wrong, isn't it? Tell me, Aristide."

"That girl. Woman. The Hawaiian. Leilani Manolo." His words were coming in short, pained bursts.

Croissant-laden hand poised midair,

he paused to take a deep breath.

"She had a public spat with the man who was killed right before it happened. It just feels as if something's not right. I'm not saying she killed him. Although Candy's not so willing to give her the benefit of the doubt."

"Candy?" Madeleine couldn't help the doubtful tone that crept into her voice. She didn't like Candy Meadows, the princess daughter of a powerful California wine merchant, who'd suckered herself onto her brother like a tick on a Bordeaux deer. "What would she know about it?"

Aristide shrugged. "Nothing, Madeleine. You're quite right. Not a thing. But she's certainly got it in for her."

Madeleine choked on her coffee and broke out coughing.

"Well, it's not hard to see why that would be. She's not too fond of competition, as far as I can make out."

"I'm in a stew about it, that's all. I was putting a lot of hope in a special deal with Bully to get our wines into the Golden Gate Symposium."

He paused to finish his croissant.

"We need an official export agent to show we're ready for the big time. Winning the right to have our wines on the menu at the famous places—Delmonico's in New York, or Le Café de Paris—would set us up for international sales. It'd be an announcement that we'd arrived. There'd be no more battling the terrible reputation of California wines."

Madeleine took in her brother's pale drawn face, and wondered if finding an agent was all that was bothering him.

"Bully Pike's death is bad luck. I can see that. But surely you've got other options. One in particular staring you right in the face."

"You mean Ramsden Meadows?" He put his coffee cup down with a bang.

"That's who I mean, yes. Candy's father. Isn't it obvious?"

"Too obvious, if you ask me."

His eyes flickered with uncertainty. "Honestly, Maddie, I get the feeling more strongly all the time that they think this is a package deal. They take over Vino d'Oro sales, and in return Candy and I tie the knot. They're expecting a family as well as a business alliance."

"And you don't want that?"

"Firstly, I'm not convinced Ramsden can handle the wines the way I want him to. You know how fanatical I am about protecting them from adulteration or tampering. That's what's giving California wine a bad name. The practice is far too easily accepted here. I'm insisting we have security from any possibility of adulteration."

The energy returned to his voice at this topic, one of his pet hobbyhorses. He'd seen too much evidence of lax practice among California wine merchants and exporters to trust his precious drop to anyone.

"This is my first big chance to make something of myself, Maddie. I don't want to be like our father, all big dreams and hot air. I want to do it right." He paused, reached out for a refill.

"And the rest? The alliance? You're not sure about that either, are you?"

His face took on a reluctant, guilty expression.

"I'm not."

He shot her a weary smile. "Terrible, aren't I? Candy is smart, beautiful, comes with the promise of a substantial inheritance as the sole heir. She's been trained to manage it all after her father goes . . ." There was a painful silence.

"But?" Madeleine was flooded with warm relief at her brother's discomfort. Thank goodness he'd had the sense to see through Candy's scheming.

"But I've got cold feet. I'm not convinced her father is trustworthy. That's important, isn't it?"

Madeleine eyed him with bubbling humor.

"That's not the whole story though, is it? It didn't escape my notice that you seemed more than a little enchanted by Miss Hawaii last night—and that Miss Meadows wasn't impressed."

Aristide shot her a sheepish grin.

"Was I that obvious?"

She shook her head, laughing.

"Only to a sharp-eyed sister who loves you dearly. Don't worry. I'm sure everyone else was too engrossed in the food to notice."

"Well, I guess I can be thankful for small mercies."

He pushed his chair back from the table and gave her one of his lopsided grins. "You caught me red-handed."

He hesitated, hands resting on the back of the chair.

"But Maddie. What if she did have something to do with that agent's death? How stupid am I to even think of getting involved?"

"Is that what you're doing?"

His eyes momentarily couldn't meet hers. She sensed him steeling himself to confront her gaze.

"Yes." He straightened his shoulders.

"Yes, I am. It's fool's talk—pure *la folie de l'amour*, I know. But I can't let this one go. She—" He shook his head as if he couldn't believe what he was saying. "She's different from any woman I've ever met."

He wiped a hand across his tightly screwed eyes.

"Please God let her not be mixed up in murder."

Five

"Misty, you know about Bully's business. You worked for him for ages. You must have a pretty good idea of what was going on."

Lani leaned her elbows on a chair back, watching Misty May prepare breakfast at the kitchen bench in the Mays' elegant Victorian. Bright California light poured in through expansive arched windows, picking up the kaleidoscope of fruit—yellow pineapples and bananas, vermillion oranges—displayed on the sideboard. Through the hallway, columned archways and an opulent crystal chandelier reminded Lani of the pictures of Napoleon's palaces she'd seen in their children's books.

This was how they lived in the prestigious part of Folsom Street, close to Mansion Row where the real-estate kings, bankers and silver-mine shareholders chose to reside.

It was Sunday morning, so the Spanish housekeeper had the day off. Misty stood with her back to Lani, chopping pineapple with fast and fluid wrist movements, the curved knife she was using similar to the ones used to trim sugar cane. It tapped out a regular rhythm on the wooden chopping board.

Misty was still the willowy elegant woman Lani had adored as a child, her blonde fall of hair framing high cheekbones, green eyes and an ivory complexion. Even now in her middle years her beauty was arresting, but her appeal wasn't due to appearance alone. She reminded Lani of Hawaii's tranquil Nene goose with its beautifully barred gray-and-white form.

She had an unattainable allure, an inner serenity that seemed indifferent to seduction. She was the calm at the heart of things, always flying ahead of the eye of the storm. After their mother's death, Ani gave them her fierce protection, but Misty gave them a secure place to stand.

Like the godmother she was, Misty kept chopping as if Lani hadn't spoken. That was another thing about her. She wouldn't be hurried or rushed by anyone or anything.

"Misty? Who would want to do something like this? Did Bully have any enemies?"

Misty's hand movements slowed,

then stopped. She turned sideways on to the bench, fixing Lani with her unflinching gaze.

"Enemies? There were folks who didn't get what they wanted from him, but enemies? I don't know of any."

"What about a jealous husband?"

Bully's first wife had died years ago and he'd never remarried, but that didn't mean he denied himself the pleasure of female company. Over the years he'd had a string of "companions"—high-class admirers, wealthy widows, desirable socialites, who saw him as a challenge—but as soon as they got their claws into him he detached and moved on. That's what Lani had always believed, anyway.

Misty's jaw tensed at the suggestion.

"Not a chance. Bully was careful about that kind of thing. And besides . . ." Her voice trailed off and she turned back to the chopping board.

Lani moved to stand beside her.

"Besides what? Was he involved with someone?"

Misty stopped the knife's movement and her eyes narrowed.

"No. I think you're barking up the wrong tree."

Lani leaned back from the chair and crossed her arms over her chest in frustration.

"Then what *is* going on here, Misty? People like Bully Pike don't get stabbed in the chest in the street in the middle of town. Outside the Occidental, for goodness' sake."

Her hand flew to her mouth as a thought struck.

"Maybe it *was* a random attack. A

robbery. Maybe some vagrant was attracted by his pendant."

Misty's already pale face went chalk-white and a light sheen of perspiration rimmed her top lip.

"His pendant? What are you talking about?"

"Oh, sorry. Didn't I mention it? His whale's tooth pendant is missing. You know how he valued it. Looks like it's been ripped from his throat. Kaleo noticed it. You could see the graze on the side of his neck where it had been pulled away."

Misty clutched her waist. She bent over abruptly with a low moan.

"Misty! What's wrong?"

"Sick. I feel sick."

She stood again, one hand covering her mouth, her words distorted.

She stared at Lani with hollow eyes—

as if she was seeing something far removed from the quiet kitchen. And then she dashed for the bathroom.

Six

"Aristide! Come in! How are you after that dreadful scene last night?"

Ramsden Meadows widened his arms as if to greet Aristide like a long-lost son, but halted his advance mid-stride, moments before he grasped his shoulders, as if sensing the younger man's resistance.

Candy tensed as she watched the two most important men in her life circle one another like wary dogs, unsure of whether the bone would be shared or guarded.

"Fine. I'm fine, thanks."

His face looked more gaunt, his cheekbones more pronounced than last night, but the French winemaker's warm smile still made her heart beat faster. He stepped in to peck her gallantly on each cheek in the chic way that was second nature to him. Then he spoiled it by drawing his hand over his lightly bearded chin with a distracted air, dismissing her without even being aware of it.

"Still a bit shook up, I admit," he said. "But I've got to move on."

Her father gestured him through the hall into the sunroom and turned to Candy. "Can you organize coffee, sweetheart? Then come join us."

She tamped down a mild annoyance at being dismissed on domestic duties, but graciously obeyed. With her mother's death when Candy was twelve, she'd had years to grow into the role of her father's right-hand man but, being female, she would also always be his prime hostess.

"Your usual, Aristide?" There was the hint of flirtation in the query, and she affected a languid pose against the door pillar as she awaited his response.

When he'd worked for her father as the Meadows Estate winemaker, Aristide's preference for black coffee with the consistency of tar had been the subject of friendly teasing from the other workers.

He nodded quick assent and turned back to her father.

Dismissed twice in as many minutes. That was too bad. She'd make sure she did something about it.

When she returned she carried a tray of coffee and some hot-from-the-oven madeleines. Their cook had made them at her request, shell-shaped part-cake, part-cookie treats, all lemony and crumbly, the way Aristide liked them. The men were already deep in conversation when she returned, and as soon as she crossed the threshold she sensed they were at cross purposes.

Her father's face had the pinched look it got when his wishes were thwarted. Aristide ran his hand through his hair, as if at a loss for a solution.

"I'm not willing to take the risk, Ramsden. We've been over this a dozen times."

They'd got straight into arguing the question of who would represent the Russell wines—who would take care of export documents, freight details, all the aspects of distribution for which a winemaker did not have the expertise or connections.

Ramsden Meadows was certain it

should be his business, yet Aristide still seemed to hesitate.

"Let's face it, Laurent, Bully's gone and goodness knows who will be taking over his business—if anyone. There's no obvious successor. You're plumb crazy to keep knocking, as I've tried to tell you."

"Ramsden, I appreciate your experience. I do. It's just . . ."

He glanced from father to daughter with a self-conscious grin.

"Frankly I want to put them into the Golden Gate Symposium and try and crack the nut that way. If d'Oro won that competition and got into places like Delmonico's, we'd be halfway up the ladder."

Ramsden gestured irritably to Candy to put the tray down on the occasional table.

"Listen to him! You'd think he didn't trust us."

"It's not a matter of trust . . ." Aristide hesitated.

"Ramsden, I don't expect you to understand. Put it down to the weird ways of the foreigner." He flashed a weak grin in Candy's direction, an appeal for her support in calming her father's temper.

But Ramsden rose to his six-foot-tall frame, his frustration boiling over, and paced behind the settee set at right angles to the one Aristide occupied.

"There's a lot more than a shipment to New York involved here, Aristide. Why don't we get it all out in the open?

"I don't know why you're so fixated on getting Vino d'Oro wines into Delmonico's anyway. There's dozens of French restaurants on the East Coast we could sell wine to. What's the rush? I've always made it clear. Meadows Exporting is willing to take all you can produce and sell on your behalf. We understand the business. We've been doing it for years. You're an excellent winemaker, Aristide, but you don't understand the business here in California. It's different from France."

He paused mid-stride and gestured to Candy.

"Let's face it, this isn't only about New York. It's about whether you and Candy are joining forces. Whether Meadows Estate is expanding as a family concern. Why don't we face facts?"

The coffee pot lid rattled as Candy's hand shook and she abruptly set it down. Heat rose up her neck and into her face.

Curse you, Father, for your Good Ole American Boy brashness.

"Father, that's quite enough!" she snapped. "You're entering territory where you've no right to go."

She rose from her seat, powered by equal parts indignation and humiliation.

How could he?

Aristide's legs were frozen. He was the only one left sitting.

Then with a deep calm he summoned from the depths of his embarrassment, he too stood.

His voice when he spoke was unwavering.

"Ramsden, I owe you the humblest apology. I mean it. You've offered me nothing but kindness. You gave me a job, taught me so much about the local scene..." He hesitated and glanced to Candy. "Allowed me to escort your beautiful daughter . . . I've been honored to be counted as an employee, and, I hope, more recently as a colleague and friend."

He gestured to the coffee tray.

"Your hospitality has been without peer. And I'm afraid I must appear the most ungrateful of fellows to decline your kindness."

He looked from father to daughter and his self-assurance faltered. He sank back down to the settee and gestured to Ramsden.

"Sit down, Ramsden, please. Sit down. You too, Candy."

He fiddled with the handle of his now-cold coffee.

Candy huffed, the quiet puff of warm air defrosting ice.

"That will be about set solid; would you like a fresh cup?"

Her attempt at defusing the tension was pathetic, but he shot her a wry grin.

"I'm fine, Candy. Thanks. . ."

He steepled his hands and expelled a big sad breath over them.

"It's not easy to explain why New York means so much to me. It just does. My father…" He let out another uncertain sigh. "As a boy I vowed I would never be like my father. Never."

His deep bass echoed with a fierce edge.

"He was a man who dreamed big dreams but never did a thing to achieve them. He barely fed his family, but he was always jawing on about what he was *going* to do. Buy this. Win that. It made me sick. I don't know how my mother tolerated it."

He blew through his fingers and

dropped his hands to his knees.

"It probably sounds terrible to you, but the last thing I ever want to be is, as we say in French, *tel père, tel fils.* Like father, like son. The very last thing.

"I've got big dreams, you know that, of making my name as a winemaker, of putting Vino d'Oro up there with the best of the best in California wines. Sir John has trusted me with a lot and I'm not letting him down."

He ran his hands down his face, then rallied his attention.

"It's as simple as that, Ramsden. As simple as that."

He stood abruptly. "I'm sorry. I have to go. I've got another appointment."

He made an apologetic sweep with one hand. "Candy, thanks for the coffee and everything. I know my way out. We'll talk again soon."

And with that he was gone, without even a perfunctory farewell kiss.

And he hadn't touched the madeleines.

Aristide sank onto the oak bench seat in the Montgomery Street coffeehouse and inhaled the aroma of hot chocolate that pervaded the place, a legacy from the Ghirardelli factory down the street. For a few moments he allowed himself to sink into its velvety fragrance, basking in brown, consoling blankness. Then a punishing anxiety spiked through him. He was ready to admit it. He was rattled.

Head rested in his hands, he took deep breaths, willing the tightness in his shoulders and chest to ease. He was oblivious to the hubbub around him— the bank clerks and bookkeepers, power brokers and politicians—who frequented Monties to share the latest business intelligence over their coffee and cake. Monties was the dealmakers' hub in downtown, the place to pick up commercial tips and money-making gossip.

"Can I get you anything, sir?" A beanpole of a waiter with a spotty complexion and nervous eyes stood before him, perilously angled tray in hand.

Aristide's thoughts slipped to Candy and her jest about his taste in coffee. He recalled the coquettish tilt of her head as she'd teased him. The familiarity had a heavy-handed desperation.

Had he led her on? He'd never viewed the many women he'd romanced as anything more than a means to an end, as pleasurable playthings. He was gallant, he was courteous and entertaining, and then he moved on. He'd assumed they'd understood.

The young attendant waited patiently.

"*A choca, s'il vous plâit.* I feel like a change from café noir."

"Mocha or java blend, sir?"

"Mocha."

Just the antidote he needed. He ran his tongue around his mouth, anticipating the creamy mix of coffee, hot milk and chocolate. He was punch-drunk from bad news and the *choca* had been a French favorite for more than a century, Napoleon's choice, so an apt consolation.

He counted the blows. First Bully's death. Then the beautiful Hawaiian covered in blood, possibly incriminated.

And that damn Duchamp . . .

Did he recognize me? Remember where we met last?

He hoped not. Shivered at the thought.

He heard the thud of closing cellar doors in his head. He was running out of chances for entering his wines in the contest that could make his name. He wasn't going anywhere without a reliable agent and distributor, there was no question about it.

Ramsden had never spelled out the options as blatantly as today: working with him meant marrying Candy.

Aristide had rocks in his stomach. Why hadn't he seen where it was all heading?

He was in the ring, flat on his back, and the referee's count was closing.

Six . . . Seven . . . Eight . . .

The young attendant slapped down the foam-topped ceramic mug and Aristide gulped down the first hot, reviving mouthful, awaiting the clarity it would bring.

His options for finding a capable agent, one with integrity, were shrinking. Should he settle for Meadows after all? He knew the business. He had connections, networks, experience. And Candy was a desirable, intelligent woman.

Two days ago, he'd seen it as tempting. He admitted it. The end justifies the means, see it all as a business arrangement.

But now? The weight on his chest lightened. He had other choices.

His body warmed at the memory of Leilani Manolo, the challenging sparkle of her eyes, the flashing white smile.

And the lingering frangipani fragrance from the flowers in her shining dark hair. He couldn't make any commitments to anything but d'Oro now, but . . . in the future? He hoped it would be different.

He massaged his forehead between thumb and forefinger, smoothing away a dull ache.

Another image came to him—Madeleine in her wedding gown, her face glowing with eager anticipation at the future she and Caleb had chosen together.

A fierce longing clutched at his insides, catching him off guard. He wanted that. A family. A sense of his own place, his own people.

He'd been feeling the stirrings of this sea change within for a few months, but now it was roaring like a riptide.

He had to get himself moving. Settle on the agent. A man of integrity. Had to be.

And when he'd got the wines set up, then he could satisfy this hunger to find a mate. Set up a home.

He cast his mind back to the previous night, and all the people he'd met. He thought of the Hawaiian consul to California, Cyrus May. He'd surely be a man with the right connections? He must have known Bully Pike well if they'd grown up together. Hawaii wasn't that big, especially back then. He might know who was likely to take over Bully's business, or have other ideas about who to target as an agent. Maybe he'd be able to give a pointer on the man's enemies.

Leilani Manolo was staying with the consul and his wife, wasn't she? He seemed to remember someone had mentioned that last night.

Yes. For the want of any better idea, that would be his next step. Search out Cyrus May. Offer his condolences at his friend's death, and ask his advice. Who would he recommend? While he was at it, he could query him on Bully's business and see if there was a likely successor. Maybe there were still possibilities with Pike Consulting.

He drained the last of his *choca*, savoring the faint clove aroma that lingered in the dregs, and stood to leave.

He'd be killing two birds with one stone. Find an agent and have an excuse to see the charming Hawaiian again.

A noisy group of stockbrokers at a nearby table who'd interrupted his musings with rowdy speculations on ways to corner the precious metals market—gold, silver, or tin—pushed back their chairs at the same time. A burly fellow whom the others had deferred to tossed the daily news sheets his way.

"Take a look. We've finished with them."

Aristide sat down and considered the crumpled sheets. Alongside an account of a Lick House bar brawl between a well-known pugilist and his "friend" in which the loser was left "profusely covered in claret" and a review of the British Blonde Burlesque Troupe's "charming rendering of Rossini" at MacGuire's Opera House last night, there was a single column heading that caught his eye.

SENATOR'S FRIEND MURDERED
Prominent San Francisco import-export dealer Bully Pike was struck down outside the Occidental Hotel last night, where he'd been attending the Alycia Stockton Educational Trust dinner with other prominent citizens, including California Senator Hector de Vile, Mrs. Stockton's husband, real estate king Basil Stockton, mining magnate and Vino d'Oro owner Sir John Russell, and San Francisco's Hawaiian consul, Cyrus May. Guests who'd been at the charitable event, including Sir John's French winemaker Aristide Laurent, rushed in their formal dinner attire to assist the popular San Francisco businessman, but he died at the scene.

Police could not say if the incident was a random strike by footpads or a planned attack. Mr. Pike, a well-respected local businessman, was a close colleague and long-standing friend of Senator Hector de Vile through their Hawaiian connections. No arrest has been made.

Well. There's your answer as to whether Dupont recognized you.

Aristide's knees turned to water. He needed another coffee, but this time it had to be café noir.

Seven

"Who in the hell would want Bully dead?" Hector de Vile took an angry pull on his cigar and glared at Cyrus through a cloud of gray-blue smoke.

His old friend stared straight back, his face blank, crow's feet prominent at the corners of his eyes. He gave a slow shrug.

"I don't know, Hector. He was unlucky, I guess. The wrong place at the wrong time. Met up with some thugs who were after easy pickings."

He took an answering suck on a Cuban.

"Although why they would pick on a big man like Bully is hard to fathom. I suppose it could have been any one of us. They probably heard about the dinner and thought they'd try their luck when the guests were leaving."

Hector raised a skeptical eyebrow.

"You think so? And they picked out one of the biggest brutes there?" He let the question hang. He knew from experience that uncomfortable silences often prompted fascinating admissions. Though why he suspected his old friend had anything to add to the incident, he wasn't sure. Still, Cyrus was incapable of dissembling.

De Vile had known him since his mariner days in Hawaii and he'd always considered him a jovial, honest fellow. It had surprised them all when he'd married Misty, the femme fatale to Cyrus's teddy bear.

An elegant, brooding blonde with an

eagle wit, she only told you what it suited her for you to know. While he'd got Cyrus's measure at their first meeting in a Honolulu tavern, de Vile had always found Misty unreadable and unpredictable. Sometimes even shocking.

Hector stubbed out his cigar. "I'm not at all convinced it was random. And if there's something smelly going on here, I want—need—to know about it. It will be a sensitive few months leading up to the Senate election. It's not as if anyone knows how much business Bully and I were doing together. You know I like to keep my financial dealings separate from the public ones. But if Bully was involved in anything murky, I need to know about it. I don't like nasty surprises."

He gestured around the Mays' sitting

room, where the capacious, maroon-studded leather sofa he occupied was set off by light-green botanical-print wallpaper and white paintwork. Fresh flowers and a large green potted plant by a stacked bookcase added a feminine touch. He got to his feet and paced to the bay windows and back, stopping abruptly in front of Cyrus's chair.

"Do you know of anything about Bully's affairs that should worry me, Cyrus?"

"Affairs? Literally? You mean women?"

Cyrus's tanned face had turned gray.

"Women. Business deals. Anything." De Vile's neck prickled in irritation. Cyrus could be obtuse sometimes.

"Oh. Sorry. I mean, we all know he liked the ladies . . ." Cyrus turned a weak grin on him that soured when de

Vile didn't respond.

"He liked the ladies, Cyrus, but he always had his safety net in place. He chose carefully. You know the type. The society matron wanting someone to partner her to the opera while her bored husband played poker. The wealthy widow seeking a bit of fun and no complications—certainly not wanting to lose control of her money."

"She won't."

"She won't what?"

"Lose control of her money. They've changed the law on that."

"For goodness' sake, Cyrus. Don't be so literal. She might still have her own bank account, but if she marries she has to give him a say, doesn't she?" De Vile's temple set up a dull pulsing thud.

"I'm just saying, it seems unlikely to be woman problems."

Cyrus nodded vaguely. "Sure. Right."

"Who was he seeing recently? Anything serious? He squired a lot of ladies as a friend. It's hard to know."

Cyrus steepled his hands and blew against his fingers, lifting the silvery cowlick that hung over his dark brows.

"No one that I know of. All pretty normal so far as I know."

De Vile plopped down in a chair. "So has Misty heard who's taking over?" He glanced around, listening for any movement in the quiet house. "Where is she, anyway?"

"She's sleeping. Neither of us got much rest last night. Naturally she's upset."

Misty had managed Bully's office for years. De Vile recollected that whenever he called in she'd been the "queen of all she surveyed" at Pike Consulting.

Cyrus sat in silence, contemplating the carpet for a minute, and then seemed to spark up, reconnect. "Oh, about the office. There's this young chap, Will Davenport. I referred him on to Bully. He called on me when he arrived from back East. He wanted contacts and I thought he might be useful over at Bully's.

"He's got good foreign-trade experience in a family firm in New York, but wants a new start out here. He's been working for Bully a few months now and I believe he's settled in well. I guess he can hold the fort, at least in the interim."

He glanced up at de Vile, eyes screwed in uncertainty.

"Elizabeth Wenderhoven is Bully's executor, I understand. Did you know that? She'll be handling his will. With no wife or children, I'm not sure what he's done with the estate."

Charles Wenderhoven's widow. The Countess?

The low ache in de Vile's head grew more persistent. "Really? Is she still alive?"

Cyrus chuckled and de Vile got the strong conviction it was the first time during this whole conversation his friend had relaxed into his usual easygoing self.

"Oh yes, alive and kicking, sharp as ever. She's a bit of a social recluse, but she still seems to keep up with what's important."

"How do you know that?"

"Misty sees her when the women get together. About the only thing she goes to, I gather. They have this Hawaiian luau thing for the women occasionally.

Talk about who's got grandkids and who's died. You know the story."

De Vile held out his brandy glass.

"Time for a refill, Cyrus. I'm parched here."

Ellie Wenderhoven. An ancient, gnawing grief clawed in his chest at the name. Abigail, Ellie and Misty were an inseparable threesome back in the Honolulu of his youth. Three gorgeous young women, so different in appearance and character: Abigail midnight-haired and willful; Elizabeth statuesque, regal and oh-so serious-minded; and Misty—well she was already an ice-cool femme fatale at seventeen . . .

Cyrus got up to retrieve the decanter and sat down again.

De Vile murmured appreciatively. "What a long time ago that was." A siren's call rang in his head.

"That girl at dinner last night—the one who I understand had some sort of disagreement with Bully. Who was she?"

Cyrus's hand jerked, slopping brandy over his hand.

"Girl?" His eyes wondered vaguely to the windows. "The young woman at his table, you mean? Leilani Manolo?" He paused to suck up the liquor from his dripping hand.

De Vile nodded, his eyes glittering with interest.

"She's here from Honolulu with her brother Kaleo. They've got interests in sugar, I believe."

"Manolo? Any relation to the Maui Manolos? She's easy on the eye . . ."

"Yes. Vaguely related, I think."

"And what's her interest in sugar?"

"I gather she and her brother want a better deal."

The tension was back in Cyrus's shoulders.

"Deal? Where does their sugar come from? Who's their agent?"

"They're with Diamond, I believe. Or were. Not sure."

"And the disagreement with Bully? What was that about?"

Cyrus's eyes once again wandered the room as he took his time to answer.

"According to Misty she wanted to talk with Bully about their sugar, but he wasn't interested. Probably not a big enough client."

Cyrus couldn't meet de Vile's eye. Something was off here.

Cyrus is a terrible liar. He should never try it.

De Vile changed tack. "What about

the Frenchman? Russell's man. He was greasing up to Bully too."

"Oh, Bully is—was—always in demand."

Am I imagining it, or was there a bitter edge to that remark?

"He's looking for someone to handle Russell's wine exports."

Cyrus gurgled back a draught of brandy, as if reminded it was there.

"He doesn't want to join the Co-op, though. He got put off cooperatives back in France. And he's picky about wine tampering. He thinks Californian growers are too slack on it. Can be vocal about it."

De Vile snorted in derision.

"Well, he's keeping the right company then, isn't he, with his 'broomstick up his behind' boss. Good luck to them. They won't get far outside the Co-op. Ramsden's got it sewn up."

He sensed he'd got all he could out of the reluctant consul. He never was a man for gossip.

"Do you ever think about the old days, Cyrus? When we were all happy chaps together? You, me and Bully?"

Cyrus shot him a sharp glance. "Not really. All too long ago."

"I suppose…" De Vile savored the brandy, which was excellent, and calculated his next move.

"Well then. To the present. If you hear anything about Bully—anything at all—I want to be the first to hear. Any hint of trouble. Understood? And while you're at it, it wouldn't hurt to do whatever you can to compromise Miss Manolo and the Frenchman.

"Start with the woman. Isn't she under suspicion as far as Bully goes?

See if Misty can find something. Anything. It doesn't need to be true."

Cyrus shifted uneasily.

"Hector. I am the Royal Hawaiian Consul to San Francisco. I can't get involved with your intrigues." His voice trailed off in protest, and he bit his lip.

"Cyrus, talk sense. The sooner the lawmen get an arrest, the better it will be for all of us. You. And me. Can't you see that? And who's to say she's not up to her elbows in it? Now's not the time to be squeamish."

As he strode the few blocks back to his Russ House suite his mind flicked back over the afternoon's conversation.

There was definitely something Cyrus wasn't telling him, he sensed that, but he wasn't too worried.

Cyrus was always a man who liked to stay on the high road. De Vile didn't mind detouring to the low road now and then in the interests of business.

First, he'd see whether he could tempt the Frenchman into an alliance, despite Russell's objections.

And then he'd call on that Will Davenport, and see if he was willing to pick up where Bully left off.

One thing was for sure. He wouldn't stand by and let things get out of control.

Eight

"Mr. Laurent, Hector de Vile. Sorry we didn't have an opportunity to meet at Basil's fund-raiser, but glad we're making up for it now. Do sit down."

Aristide had a strong sense of "pinch yourself to see if this is true" as he sat with one of California's two sitting senators in the Lick House bar and billiards room on the corner of Montgomery and Sutter Streets.

It was an appropriate setting for the man who many said ran California even though he spent a good deal of his time in Washington. Lick House was considered the finest hotel west of the Mississippi, a three-story-high and two-blocks-wide masonry pile with a 400-seat-dining room modeled on one James Lick has seen in the Royal Palace in Versailles.

Aristide fleetingly wondered if this was the same bar where the boxer Tommy Chandler had beaten up his friend Ned a couple of nights before, and then chided himself to concentrate on the matter at hand. Senator de Vile was an important man.

"You're managing d'Oro for my good friend Sir John, I understand. I'm sorry he wasn't available to join us."

"He sends his apologies," Aristide said. "He's devoting more time to his family these days. He has returned to the vineyard to be with Pania and their new baby, Robert. However, he's still closely involved."

De Vile's manner was genial and

expansive, but he shook his head in mock dispute.

"Fickle thing, wine. He's brave." He raised his eyebrows quizzically. "You're both brave."

"I don't know about that," Aristide demurred. "Truth is, wine's the only thing I know."

"Really? So you grew up with it? Your father was a vintner before you?"

"Yes. Yes, he was."

"And how long have you been in California?"

"Eight years. I've been fortunate to learn from some of the pioneers. I've worked in William McPherson Hill's Zinfandel winery, and then with my fellow countryman Isaac de Turk."

"Ah yes. De Turk. He's going for those newfangled bottles instead of the oak casks, isn't he? What do you make of that?"

"Oh, I fully approve, Senator. California wine will never have a good reputation outside of the state until we stop the widespread adulteration. So many of the growers do it. And storage in casks makes it that much easier to cheat. To water down. To tamper."

Aristide's heart was beating faster as he got launched on his favorite topic.

De Vile watched him through cool, hooded eyes.

"And you've recently been with working with Ramsden Meadows, I understand? At Meadows Estate?"

"That's correct. You're well informed."

"I make it my business to be."

A waiter arrived with two wineglasses and a bottle on a tray. A second attendant followed with a cheese and charcuterie board with prosciutto and empanadas.

"I took the liberty of ordering some of your elixir. You can critique it for me."

Aristide had the impulse to shift nervously in his chair. Was the man making fun of him?

"I wouldn't presume—"

De Vile waved his hand in dismissal and picked up the bottle, turning the label toward him so he could read it. *Vino d'Oro Zinfandel. California, 1869*.

"Let's see what you make of this," said the senator, raising his glass in salute.

They made their leisurely way through the wine and food while the senator quizzed Aristide on his impressions of California wines. What was their future internationally—or even across the continent in New York and Boston?

Aristide thought they were getting along swimmingly, and then the senator said: "So what is your ambition, Mr. Laurent? What do you want to achieve in your life?"

His eyes were piercing, and Aristide prickled with a sense that he'd loaded the seemingly innocent query with hidden meaning.

"Me? I want to make Sir John's d'Oro wines some of the most successful in California. I want our wines to win gold at the Golden Gate Symposium and to be found on the menu lists of the top restaurants in the top cities."

De Vile raised his eyebrows again, this time in admiration.

"Big goals. I approve. It's always

good to see a young man with high ambition. And how do you plan to achieve those big dreams?"

Aristide hesitated. The last thing he wanted was to sound like his father, all hot air and no practical steps. He shivered, momentarily struck by the loathing that rose within him whenever his father came to mind.

Sensing his equivocation, de Vile rallied. "Come now, don't be shy. You must have a plan. It wouldn't be John Russell's enterprise if there was no plan."

"As I indicated, I aspire to rate well in the Golden Gate Wine Symposium that's coming up. I'm preparing our entry at present."

"Really?" The senator's tone was querulous. "I had the idea that entries close in a few days. You'll need a proven agent and distribution network. Didn't you say you'd been hoping Bully would provide that? You haven't got that signed off yet?"

The senator's interrogation was unnerving. A big hollow space yawned inside Aristide.

"You could always go with Meadows, I suppose." De Vile stilled like a cobra about to strike.

"But then you'd also need to be members of the wine cooperative."

He fixed Aristide with a calculating stare. "The Buena Vista Wine Cooperative. I believe the Symposium is changing the rules so only Co-op members can enter. Did you know?"

Aristide froze in his seat. The "hail fellow well met" charade had vanished. Instead, he was staring into the face of a remorseless hunter.

He cleared his throat. "No, Senator, I can't say I did. Is that very recent?"

"Very. They're announcing it in the next few days, I believe."

De Vile rubbed his hands together, as if anticipating a pleasurable outcome.

"I can assist with getting you entered. No problem at all. You might even have a good chance of winning. But you'll need to be in the cooperative."

"I see." Aristide drew the linen table napkin from his lap, crumpled it into a ball and put it on the table beside his appetizer plate.

"You'd understand I would have to consult with Sir John before we made such a momentous decision, but thank you for your advice."

De Vile shrugged. "Happy to oblige. I'm merely an interested bystander, you understand. I've nothing at all to do with the Co-op, except I hope it succeeds. I think it will be a good thing for the industry to have everyone pulling together."

Aristide hesitated. "We'd certainly be a lot happier if we could see any evidence the Co-op was willing to get to grips with some of the bad management practices.

"I know Sir John feels like I do—we don't want our reputation damaged by being linked to dirty practices. You'll never get into the doors of a place like Le Café de Paris if your wines are questionable."

"Oh, I agree. Fully agree." Hector de Vile was back in his role as the magnanimous booster for the California wine industry. Except Aristide couldn't miss the cold triumph shining from his dark eyes.

"Oh, and one other thing, Mr. Laurent. I am bound to mention it. You and your little companion. The one you 'helped' on Saturday night when Bully died in her arms. I'd be careful how you proceed there, if I were you. A warning to you, as a friend. I have a feeling she'll end badly. Might be as well to keep your distance."

Aristide's jaw dropped. And as if de Vile had to underscore the last word by leaving first, the politician stood abruptly, consulted a pocket watch he drew from his expensive jacket and shook his head in dismay.

"I have to be going. Got to see the governor." He fixed Aristide with a gimlet eye. "Our chat has been most instructive for me, Mr. Laurent. I hope it has for you too. And don't forget my advice."

Aristide stumbled to his feet as a courtesy as the most powerful man in the state turned and strode from the room, turning heads in his wake.

Nine

Hector de Vile's son Alex and Will Davenport, the pipsqueak upstart who was temporarily running Pike Consulting, were warm buddies within minutes of shaking hands. The senator sat watching through narrowed eyes as they chatted on about Will's experiences in New York, and Alex's involvement with the diverse de Vile business interests, as if he wasn't present. He'd been sidelined, a rare experience for him.

He had brought his reluctant heir along with him because he hoped he'd get inspiration from meeting a young man of a similar age to himself who was already winning plaudits as an energetic and innovative operator.

Will Davenport was unobtrusive, a pale, quiet chap who could be overlooked. De Vile wasn't fool enough, however, to miss the shrewd glint in his gray eyes, the quick resolution in his jaw, even as he took a back seat, ever the quiet observer who recorded and stored away every word. These two young men both had gray eyes, but that's where any resemblance began and ended.

In contrast to Davenport's reticence, Alex had a dashing appeal. With his shock of dark hair and buoyant personality, he stood out from the crowd. He'd inherited it all—the looks, the vivacious temperament—from his Spanish father, the virtuoso photographer Rafael Castellanos. Of that Hector was certain, though he'd never known the man—or even seen a daguerreotype of him, for that matter—but he'd heard the stories.

Alex had been separated from his family by a catastrophic accident as a small boy, and Hector had adopted him in a convoluted process, believing him an orphan. He hadn't asked too many questions, and he'd never regretted the decision.

Since Cyrus's mention of Davenport he'd asked around and discovered the entrepreneur was universally liked and widely respected as an up-and-comer who worked all the hours God made, was quick to build networks and happy to help others solve problems.

Outward appearances could be so deceptive. Will Davenport, who could so easily be undervalued as a mouse, was a clever powerhouse when it came to business.

Alex, who looked as if he was born to run a corporation, had no talent for business at all. He was popular wherever he went, but he had no killer instinct. His sole ambition was to be an artist, a photographer like his long-dead sire.

De Vile didn't know how Bully's will disposed of the Pike estate, but he was already giving serious consideration to financing Will Davenport into Bully's business—if he needed it—as a shrewd future investment.

The admission left him with his recurring problem. What to do about Alex? His son was conscientious but uninspired in business. He tried hard to please, but the senator was recognizing what he'd long tried to deny—business was not Alex's passion or vocation. It was something he applied himself to with fastidious attention to please his father, but his heart lay elsewhere, in his damned photography.

"You didn't!" Will Davenport was now gazing at Alex de Vile in open admiration, as the younger man told him the story of how he'd rescued historic photographic plates from a studio fire, only to later discover they were of his long-lost mother (now dead) and sisters (still both very much alive).

De Vile shifted one buttock and then the other in the easy chair he occupied in Bully's comfortable study, which doubled as a parlor for entertaining visitors. Davenport had brought in coffee and almond biscuits. Not a man for hard spirits, apparently.

De Vile craved a stiff Scotch, and he

bit down on an impulse to ask for something stronger. He sensed that Davenport wouldn't join him, and he wanted to preserve the illusion of congeniality.

He'd satisfied himself on one count. Davenport was a gifted manager and a creative businessman.

But is he biddable?

"I'm most impressed to see how well you've settled into Bully's chair," de Vile said to the sandy-haired clerk. "You've only been in California a few months and you've picked it up remarkably quickly."

Will's expression was bland, his eyes fixed on the plate of biscuits. "The work is much the same as I was doing back East," he replied. His accent carried the cadence of Brooklyn. "It required that I get an idea of who's who out here. And

Bully and Misty both were very helpful."

"I see," said de Vile. "And your family business—what sort of commodities were you dealing with there?"

"Oh, sugar, coffee, manufactured cotton, spirits, tobacco—all sorts of stuff. Anything where there's money to be made. As long as it's legal, of course. We drew the line at the slave trade."

"I see. And your father is still alive?"

Will's face clouded, and his eyes lifted to the wall as though he was taking in a distant view.

"My father died a long time ago. My older brother runs the company now."

His gray eyes darkened to the color of thunderclouds. He sat for a long minute, reflective, not moving, and then seemed to rally.

He rose from his seat with a determined thrust. "Enough of this chat. Let me take you on a tour. Down to the warehouse and around about. It's not the only warehousing we have, but we tend to keep the finer articles on the premises and leave the bulk goods down at the wharves."

He turned to Alex. "We've even got some cameras you might be interested in."

An hour later when they'd completed the tour and even the young men had grown quiet, they settled at the parlor table for a second coffee.

De Vile cleared his throat. "I don't know if Bully ever mentioned it, but we were close friends and business colleagues for a long time. A lifetime. I suppose you could say he knew my secrets and I knew his."

What a liar you are, Hector. There's a lot he didn't know about you. And a lot, no doubt, that you don't know about him.

Will looked up, a keen interest lighting his face. "Really? What sort of secrets?"

"Oh, where the bodies are buried, that sort of thing."

Was it his imagination? Will seemed to flinch at the joke. His jawline set hard.

"Just kidding, of course. But we were together in Hawaii when we were about the same age you and Alex are now. Friends you make at that time in your life tend to stick, I've found."

Will Davenport gazed at him, waiting.

"Anyway, I'm hoping we might grow to be as close—in a business relationship—as Bully and I were.

Nothing formal, you understand. An exchange of intelligence and business favors now and then?"

"What sort of favors, Hex?" asked Alex. "Sounds interesting."

"Well, one example. Right now, the state's winemakers are working hard to get a cooperative off the ground. They're banding together in their efforts to get Californian wines more widely recognized. It's a battle to get our wines into the best restaurants in New York or Washington or Boston—and even harder to be taken seriously in Paris."

"Okay," said Will, dragging out the second vowel. "Sounds reasonable. And what can we, Pike Consulting, do about it? The wines, I mean."

De Vile cleared his throat. "You're already handling the shipments for some California growers. I'd ask you to restrict your arrangements to companies that are members of the Buena Vista Cooperative. Same goes for sugar imports. Take guidance on whose sugar to handle and whose to leave alone—with good cause, of course. Nothing sinister. It's not as if we're blacklisting people for no reason."

Alex frowned. "That sounds a bit cavalier, Hector. Why would you want to block genuine traders?"

De Vile toyed with his empty cup.

"Bully had an exclusive deal with one agency. Diamond Sugar—have I got that right, Will? His customers get a favorable price in return for Bully handling a limited exclusive list. Had he told you about that?"

Will nodded, but he'd lost his sunny demeanor.

"He did, Senator." He frowned. "Though I must say I have my reservations about it. Comes close to contravening fair business practice, I'd have thought. Doesn't sit well with me."

"You'll follow his practice, though?"

"Let's say I will take it on a case by case basis."

There was an awkward silence.

"I see."

De Vile stood and turned in a slow circle, surveying the room.

"And how much longer do you expect you'll be here in San Francisco, Mr. Davenport?"

Will shrugged. "Nothing's ever permanent, is it? I'll take it day to day."

"That's good," said de Vile. "Because who knows? After Bully's will has been read there mightn't be a job."

He allowed another calculated pause.

Alex glanced at Will in consternation. "I say, Hex, that sounds a bit rough."

Will shrugged, unperturbed. "He's quite right, Alex. Nothing is forever."

"Of course," said de Vile smoothly, "there's always the possibility of a financial backer putting money in and setting up a partnership. Do you have that sort of money, Mr. Davenport?"

"What? To buy Bully's business, do you mean? I guess that depends."

De Vile was suddenly irritated by the cat-and-mouse game he'd initiated.

"Depends? Depends on what?"

Will shrugged. "On how badly I might want it, for one."

He flashed de Vile a bland smile that showed nothing of his true feelings and thrust out his hand. "So very good of you to call on us today, Senator."

He turned to Alex and with a note of

genuine pleasure added, "And you, Alex. Do hope we have the chance to talk again sometime. I'd love to see some of your daguerreotypes, when we can."

He stepped back and considered de Vile.

"All the very best with your re-election campaign, Senator. You can't afford to be anything except squeaky clean with that looming, can you?"

He took another step away, as if subtly distancing himself. "Let's hope they find out who killed Bully soon. The longer it lingers unsolved, the more chance there is for scandal. And I'm sure you wouldn't want that."

De Vile stared at him, disbelieving.

The cheeky pup. Is he insinuating he knows something about Bully that I don't? And if so, what?

He picked up his hat as the younger man gave a slight bow and walked out. The senator had been dismissed.

After Bully's will has been read there mightn't be a job.

What a creep!

Will Davenport sat on the windowsill of Pike Consulting and gazed out to the busy port. Immediately below him were the offices of Goodall Nelson and Perkins, a local steamship company; beyond that was the evangelical spire of the Seamen's Bethel "Mariner's Home," and then his eye hit the Bay, and the docks and main wharf where the Oakland ferry disembarked. Away out to his right, the tall chimney of the Bay Sugar Refinery on Union and Battery belched black smoke into a duck-egg blue sky.

This place was growing on him by the day, but he couldn't forget his real purpose in being here.

A puff of breeze heavy with the smell of salt water and docks dusty from unloading holds of flour and tobacco and coffee . . . He rubbed his face with both hands, forcing himself to concentrate.

He was quite right of course. Bully's will hadn't yet been made public, and who knew its intent.

He braced his shoulders.

Whatever the outcome, it didn't matter.

He was here for one purpose only, and he'd fulfill that or die in the attempt.

Ten

"Mr. Laurent!"

Leilani Manolo's mouth dropped open in surprise as she stood, one hand poised on the front door handle of Cyrus May's residence. In her other hand she held a bunch of flowers, freshly cut, it seemed, from the garden.

She flashed Aristide a mischievous smile. She was wearing a loose-fitting smock in reds and yellows imprinted with a swirling Pacific pattern— something he guessed must be common dress in Honolulu. No trace showed of the distraught young woman from two nights ago.

"Well, I'm sure you're not here to

see me," she quipped. "Not after Saturday."

She straightened, her eyes solemn. "I do want to say thank you for your help the other night. I never had time to say. Too much going on. It was ghastly."

Aristide dipped his head. "It was nothing." He stood, hat in hand, uncertain of how to continue.

"You haven't had any further news? From the police, I mean. No arrests?"

She shook her head. "No. All still a total mystery."

She opened the door wider. "But come on in. I'll see if either Cyrus or Misty is up to seeing anyone today. They're both still cut up about Bully's death."

Aristide surveyed the sitting room she led him to while he waited. A tiled fireplace, a handsome mantelpiece clock, walls hung with a California landscape, of Yosemite if he wasn't mistaken. A place of serene seclusion decorated in light green and white. He suspected Cyrus used this room for official meetings.

Leilani returned a few minutes later with the consul on her heels.

Dark eyebrows framed an open, tired face, more pronounced because they were topped by snow-white hair worn slightly longer than was fashionable. One unruly lock hung over his face.

Leilani gestured toward the older man. "Cyrus will see you now."

Aristide jumped up and shook Cyrus's extended hand. It was cold and dry to the touch, an old man's hand.

"We met on Saturday, yes?" Cyrus said. "At the dinner?"

"Yes. That's how I knew where to find you. You gave me your card and invited me to call, if you remember. With the shock of everything, I'm sure it's the last thing on your mind."

Aristide's voice trailed off uncertainly and there was an awkward silence.

Leilani filled the gap by dipping her head toward Cyrus. "Would you like me to bring coffee, Uncle Cy?"

Cyrus looked questioningly at Aristide, who shook his head.

"No thanks, I've had one." He grimaced. "Well, two, actually. But water would be most welcome."

Cyrus gestured him to the sofa.

"We're fine, Lani. A carafe of water and a couple of glasses and then go and check on Misty for me, will you? There's a good girl."

With a swing of her slender hips that

sent the loose tunic swishing around her, she turned and left. Aristide experienced her disappearance as a rumbling disappointment that reached to his toes.

Really, Laurent. What's wrong with you? This murder has pushed you off balance.

Lani was back in a couple of minutes with the water, then away again.

With effort, Aristide focused his attention on Cyrus.

"I'm sorry to intrude on your grief unannounced like this, but I'm hoping you can put me on the right track. With Bully gone I'm not sure who to turn to next. Sir John would have some ideas, but he's back home with Pania and the baby. He's happy to leave the call to me."

He outlined his dilemma: needing an

agent and distributor to ship their wines as a necessary part of putting an entry in to the Golden Gate Symposium; his dashed hopes of fitting into Pike's respected supply chain.

"You don't want to deal with Ramsden Meadows? He'd be an obvious choice."

Beneath his bushy dark eyebrows Cyrus's pale blue eyes were penetrating.

"Is there a reason you don't want to use Meadows?"

Aristide shrugged. Tried to appear nonchalant. "Call it Frenchman's instinct. I suspect it's more than rumor that some of the wines he sells are adulterated. He denies it, but I've got an unsettled feeling about it. It likely is the supplier's fault, and he's got nothing to do with it, but it leaves me with questions. The most important thing for us—myself and Sir John—is the security of our product. That's why we're not interested in joining the cooperative either. We want control of the whole chain."

Cyrus nodded. "I understand. I've heard the same thing about Meadows, so if that matters to you, you're probably wise to give him a wide berth."

He gulped some water from the tumbler as he reflected.

"There is a young chap I put onto Bully a couple of months ago. A fellow by the name of Will Davenport. He came to see me seeking contacts. Newly arrived from New York, where he'd worked in import-export in a family business. Had a recommendation from a mutual friend, and seemed to be a very capable chap, from what I saw."

He banged the glass down. "I understand Bully gave him some work." He glanced around, momentarily distracted.

"That's what Misty said. She's not here to confirm that." He glanced around again, as if uneasy.

"What will happen with the business now, goodness only knows, but you could give him a try. He's familiar with the New York scene, anyway."

Aristide nodded. "Thank you. I will follow him up." He paused. "What do you think will happen with Bully's business? Has he got family to take over from him?"

Cyrus's face darkened, as if the question annoyed him.

"No family," he said abruptly. "He was married once, but he liked to play the field."

"Oh, I see. A sensitive subject. Sorry I asked."

Cyrus shrugged. "He was always like that. A bit of a player. Don't know how his wife Marjorie put up with it."

Aristide stood to go, uncomfortable at the direction the conversation was taking.

"Well, I suppose it will give the police something to work on."

Cyrus had looked at him blankly. "Pardon me?"

"I mean in investigating who killed him. Maybe it was a jealous husband."

Cyrus wiped a hand across his face, as if he was suddenly tired or unwell.

"Oh, I see what you're getting at. You could be right."

Aristide made a slight bow. "Don't let me disturb you any longer. And as I said before. Sorry for intruding at a time like this."

He backed out of the room quietly, glad to make his escape.

Is it just me, or was there something that struck a false note here too?

Out in the street, he glanced back at the house and allowed himself a long sigh of relief. It sounded as if there were likely suspects for Bully Pike's death other than Leilani Manolo. Not that it was any of his business.

Aristide was descending the Mays' stairs when a hack drew up and a dumpy, bald man in an elegantly cut, light-colored suit stepped out, a tortoise-shell-handled cane tight in his fist. He paid the driver and turned to gaze up at the house, eyes screwed up against the late afternoon sun.

Then he spotted Aristide, and a grin lit up his face.

"Why, the very man I was hoping to catch. Aristide Laurent." He allowed for a dramatic pause, tapping the cane once or twice on the pavement, his expression like that of a cat with a mouse to torture.

"How are you?" His mouth drew back in a tight line. "You're working for Sir John Russell now, I believe. I found that a little surprising."

He gave the words a sarcastic flourish.

"Does he know about what happened the last time you managed a vineyard? He's such a model of rectitude."

Aristide's legs locked. He couldn't move his feet or his tongue.

A long silence hung between them.

In the garden leading up to the consul's front door he noticed for the first time the Hawaiian flag—a bright array of red, white and blue horizontal stripes with a Union Jack in the top left-hand corner—hanging limply from its flagpole. An irrelevant detail, of course, when the man beside him held his future in his hands.

"I've got something a little more urgent than a Frenchman with a murky past to deal with right now, Mr. Laurent, as I'm sure you appreciate. But when I've completed my inquiries into Bully Pike's unfortunate death, I'll come for you. A friendly warning."

He whirled on his one-inch-heel tan patent-leather boots and began a laborious climb to the front door, wheezing as he advanced.

Aristide realized that up until this minute he'd been worrying about how he would put d'Oro wines at the top of exclusive wine lists.

A peculiar vibration rattled in his chest, as if his heart had stopped pumping while Duchamp had been talking and had now remembered to get back on the job.

It pulsed through his jacket. His cheeks were warm, as if the blood was returning to them too.

He'd been consumed with getting his wines into Delmonico's and Le Café de Paris.

He hadn't understood that he should have been worried about keeping his job.

Eleven

Lani heard the front door click shut as she entered the sitting room with a vase containing the flowers she'd picked to brighten things up.

"Oh. Has Mr. Laurent gone?" Her insides contracted, as if the room were depleted of oxygen.

She glanced at Cyrus. He was flopped like a deflated balloon in the corner of the leather settee.

"Are you feeling okay, Cyrus? You don't look well."

His complexion was like putty. His sagging cheeks reminded her of a hound dog.

He stirred, straightening up.

"I'm fine, Leilani. Just tired. I will have that coffee now, if you don't mind. Might help me keep awake."

He winked, a hint of the old Uncle Cy in the gesture.

"I'll get it straight away." She hesitated. "Everything go all right with the Frenchman?"

She knew she was fishing, but she couldn't help herself.

"Yes, yes. He's only recently left. He's got a bit to learn."

"Oh?" Before she could ask anything more, the doorbell chimed.

Cyrus scowled. "Now what?"

"Maybe Mr. Laurent forgot something. I'll get it."

She had to restrain herself from skipping to the front door. She composed herself and opened with a flourish.

A paunchy, middle-aged man stood on the doorstep, the buttons of his smart jacket strained across his belly. He peered at her through pince-nez glasses.

"May I inquire if the Honorable Cyrus May is receiving visitors?"

He leaned his cane against the doorframe and drew a flat silver box from his jacket pocket. With surprising deftness he flicked it open with fat fingers and presented Leilani with a visitor's card.

"Felix Duchamp at your service." He frowned. "Please tell Mr. May, Mr. Felix Duchamp is here to see him."

When Leilani returned with the hot coffee Cyrus had requested ten minutes later, the two men were sitting glaring at one another from opposite sides of the sitting room. The atmosphere was frosty.

"And I am telling you, Mr. Duchamp, that I know nothing of Bully Pike's death and I have nothing more I can say on the subject."

"But you knew the man well? You were old friends?"

"We were old friends, yes, but what's that got to do with it? Senator de Vile is an old friend too, and I'm sure you're not harassing him." He caught Leilani's eye and gestured irritably to the table. "Leave it there."

As she bent to follow his instruction, Duchamp leapt from his seat with unexpected agility.

"Well, well, if it isn't Miss Manolo, the centerpiece of Saturday night's little drama."

He was acting as if he hadn't already seen her on the doorstep. He thrust out his hand to shake hers, but Lani backed away in shock.

"Centerpiece, Mr. Duchamp? I'd say Bully must occupy that place."

She turned to leave but he grabbed her wrist to stop her. "Not so fast, young lady. Not so fast."

He pointed at a nearby chair. "Sit there."

She glanced at Cyrus, unsure if she was supposed to acquiesce or not. He shrugged as if to say "Better you than me," so she complied.

"I understand from the constabulary that you're still a person of interest in this investigation, Miss Manolo. What do you have to say to that?"

Her eyes flew wide open and once again her eyes slid to Cyrus for some lead on how to respond. He was glaring at her, as if he too wanted to hear her answer.

"Say, sir? I have nothing to say, apart from what I told them on Saturday night. A small boy pulled at my skirts at the Occidental as I was on the point of departing and told me I was needed.

"I followed him down the street not knowing what was happening or where he was leading me, and then Bully appeared out of the darkness and collapsed onto me. That's it. That's all I know."

"And do you always follow small boys who tug at you in the street?"

She heard the accusing tone in his voice, saw his eyes had a malevolent shine. He was enjoying this.

She sought a cue from Cyrus, and again he avoided giving any.

"I don't, Mr. Duchamp, but I know Teddy. I'm friends with his mother, and

I thought Mamie might be in some kind of trouble."

"Mamie? Are you referring to the streetwalker who hangs out near the Occidental, hoping to lure in wealthy men?"

"I think you've got the wrong Mamie, Mr. Duchamp. The woman I know, Mamie Bilouxie, is a seamstress who numbers some of the Occidental staff among her closest friends. So naturally she's at the hotel occasionally. That's all."

"Tell me why I shouldn't conclude you lured Mr. Pike to his death. Say you set it up with her. Got some lumberjack lover of hers to rob him. And you helped in covering up a monstrous crime with your 'innocent as milk' act."

Lani jumped up, outraged. "Uncle Cyrus, this is ridiculous. It'd be laughable if it wasn't insulting. I'm not listening to another word."

Cyrus stirred from his cushions. "The man's got a point, Leilani. Answer him."

For the first time since the exchange began she gazed into Cyrus's face. His eyes were hard.

"Answer him?" she faltered. It was the last thing she would have expected him to say.

She stared from the man she'd considered a kindly uncle to the worm of a newspaperman.

She rose to her full five feet ten inches and put her hands on her hips, defiant.

"Mamie would never hurt anyone. And Bully was like family to me. I'm bereft that he's died this way. Neither of us had anything to do with his death, apart from being unfortunate witnesses."

"And what about that Frenchman who was here when I arrived? I suppose he knows nothing about it either?"

Leilani was on the way to the door to escape, but his words brought her movement to an immediate stop.

She whirled to face him, furious now, her face heating with anger. "Mr. Laurent? No, he does not. He wasn't even there."

"But you were." Duchamp sounded triumphant, as if he'd caught her out in a lie. "He's already been mixed up in suspicious deaths before, you know."

One corner of his mouth curdled, as if he was enjoying a malicious private joke. "Or didn't you know that?"

Lani put her hands over her ears. A weird buzzing in her head blocked out whatever this dangerous madman said next.

As he turned back to Cyrus, his mouth kept moving, like a goldfish in a bowl, with no sound coming out.

And Cyrus sat and did nothing.

Twelve

"Cyrus, Lani's upset. She's crying in her room. What's going on?"

Her husband was in his favorite padded office armchair, facing out to the street, a tumbler of brandy at his elbow, his white hair tinged yellowish from cigar smoke.

Misty took a deep breath. This room was the only place in the house she permitted him to indulge in the foul things, and from the warm fuggy air she knew this one wasn't the first he'd smoked today.

She crossed to stand by his chair and heavy red blotches under his eyes told her this wasn't his first drink either. His face always turned a mottled color when he overindulged.

He acknowledged her presence with a belligerent glare and took another pull on the cigar.

"How should I know? Maybe she's upset about Bully."

He kept staring out to the street. She followed his eyes. There was nothing out there to see. At this time of day the residential part of Folsom Street was quiet. The only pedestrians were likely to be a mother pushing a pram or an office manager coming home loaded down with his briefcase. Right now the street was empty.

She banged the arm of the chair to get his attention.

"Of course she's sad about Bully, but that's not it. There's something else—something new—that's bothering her."

He stared out the window, a mulish, sullen cast on his face.

"How am I supposed to know? You're the one with all the feminine intuition."

She stepped back, assaulted by the vehemence in his voice.

"The *what*? What are you talking about?"

"Isn't that right? Women are the ones who are supposed to feel things most deeply. To understand the heart of man."

"Cyrus, you're not making sense. What is wrong with you?"

"This will end badly, Misty. You know that, don't you? We should never have agreed to have her or Kaleo here. Never should have allowed it."

His speech was slurred, but his eyes as he stared into hers were steady. "I saw de Vile yesterday. He hasn't got a clue about what's gone on. But if he ever finds out, we're done."

Misty sank to the carpet at his feet, gazing up at him. "We didn't have any choice, Cyrus. That was years ago and we've always got through. Always stuck together. We can do that again this time. Stick together."

He rolled his eyes, as if she was talking romantic nonsense.

"You don't understand. He's on the warpath to get a quick resolution to Bully's death and he doesn't care who gets lumbered with it. Even if it's an innocent like Leilani."

Her hand came to her mouth in involuntary shock. "What are you talking about?"

"He's worried that if this crime remains unsolved it will hurt his re-election chances. He's worried Bully's been involved in something that might end up smearing him. He wants it tidied up. Lani is already under suspicion. He wants me to help give it a nudge or two."

"What are you saying, Cyrus? For crying out loud, this is worse than madness. It's plain wrong."

"So are you the one who'll tell him?"

Thirteen

"Ari, you're blind. Don't you see? He wouldn't do the business with her sugar so she got mad and killed him."

Candy turned on him, seeking his agreement. When none was forthcoming, her eyes brightened with a new thought.

"Or maybe he tried something on and she hit back. Called her outside on some pretense and then tried to force himself on her. He's got a reputation."

"Not for that," Aristide retorted.

His cheeks flamed at the besmirching of a dead man's reputation. He knew what it was like to be the target of false gossip.

"Just because he liked the ladies, there's no reason to blacken his name like this. Quite the opposite."

She reached over and stroked down his face, curving her soft hand down his jawline in an intimate gesture. "You don't want to admit it because you fancy her."

He caught her wrist and held her still. "Candy, we're not doing this. I told you."

He stood and moved to the corner table where the decanters stood. "Another one?"

She held out her glass to him, pouting.

He crossed to where she lounged on the sofa, her feet tucked up under her voluminous orange skirts, her soft indoor shoes discarded on the rug that covered the parquet floor.

"You're no fun any more," she said in a little-girl whine that set his teeth on edge.

Imagine the self-possessed, straight-talking Hawaiian resorting to this.

He couldn't.

He reminded himself why he had come here. He'd wanted to finish things with Ramsden and his daughter on a good note. Explain to them why he would not give Meadows Estate the d'Oro account. To end things as friends. They would see each another around about at wine events. It was a gossipy industry. Crossing paths was inevitable.

And maybe there was a bit of self-pride mixed in there as well. He rated himself as an honorable man. He didn't relish leaving a mess behind.

He spread his arms wide in a gesture of helplessness. "I'm sorry. It's hard to be fun with the day I've had."

She gazed at him over the rim of her glass. "Oh dear. What went wrong?"

"What went *right* might be a better question. I guess mainly, though, it was bumping into an old enemy from my days in France."

He settled back on the sofa some distance from her and took a sip of the warming liquor.

"An enemy?" She slipped along the sofa edge, closing the gap, leaning into his space. "Who?"

"A guy called Felix Duchamp. A French journalist working for one of the papers. I suspect he'll cause a shipload of trouble before he's finished. He was around at Cyrus May's this afternoon, asking questions about Bully's death."

Candy sat up smartly. "Isn't he the one who did the report in the *Alta*

California? The one who was there on Saturday?"

"Clever you. That's him."

"So why are you enemies? What happened?"

He glanced to the doorway, aware of oncoming footsteps. Ramsden had arrived.

"Oh, that's a long story, Candy. Best left for another night."

At the sight of them nestled on the sofa together, Ramsden Meadows scowled. Aristide's stomach reacted, skittish with butterflies. How was he going to present the news Ramsden already suspected? He didn't want to make enemies of them.

The older man turned away. "Dinner is served."

They were dipping into crème brûlée when Aristide suggested they try a drop of last year's Late Harvest Zinfandel: "It's got a hint of cherry that should complement the brûlée beautifully."

He was especially proud of the vintage. *And if there's one thing I can say about Ramsden, he knows his wines.*

Meadows had been withdrawn through the meal and let him know he wasn't enthusiastic about opening the extra wine, but Aristide insisted. He'd given Ramsden half a cask to try weeks ago. He was sure he'd be impressed.

"You can be an utter bore sometimes, Aristide. You know that?"

Candy shot her father a look that mingled exasperation and alarm.

Aristide sighed inwardly. She was always protective when it came to her father. She hated to see him upset, which was why she usually let him get his own way.

Mrs. Mellsopp, the housekeeper, brought in an already-opened bottle and Ramsden poured three glasses.

"You've already tried it." Aristide's eyebrows were raised, but he wasn't asking a question. "What did you think?"

"We'll save that till you've tasted it," Ramsden said with bad grace, raising his glass to the light.

The moment Aristide lifted his glass to sniff the anticipated aroma, a blend of sweet candy and sour cherry, he understood Ramsden's reluctance. He'd tampered with it. No doubt in his mind. What was it he'd heard John Russell say when he was betting on a sure thing? That's right, he would wager "Pompey's Pillar to a stick of sealing wax" or "All

Lombard Street to a China orange."
They had tampered with it. And both
father and daughter knew that he knew
it.

Fourteen

As Aristide trudged up Montgomery Street to the Occidental to seek out Will Davenport, he mused over the nightmare threatening his future. The glaring reality had kept him awake most of the night. He'd gone from being set to conquer the wine world and thinking of starting a family to attracting a Who's Who of prominent enemies.

As he brooded on their names he caught the steamy whiff of musk and lavender from the Turkish Baths on Dupont Street, but it failed to soothe.

Number One: Senator Hector de Vile, with the power to lock Vino d'Oro out of the Symposium.

Number Two: Ramsden Meadows, who had resorted to adulterating his wine. He'd kept his cool and not challenged Meadows last night, earning a curious stare from his host as he quit the house, pleading his need of an early night.

Number Three: Felix Duchamp. His stomach cramped at the thought of the portly newspaperman. A man with the power to ruin his life in California altogether, probably guarantee he'd never get another job in the wine industry.

And what had he done to earn such opprobrium? He couldn't believe it was punishment for being outspoken about standards.

Pike Consulting's front door was ajar, as if Will Davenport was inviting callers, so he plunged on in and approached a receptionist seated at a heavy oak table.

"Can I help you?" Soft blonde curls framed an elfin face and light hazel eyes that skittered away nervously when they met his. He saw she was ill at ease, possibly new in the job, her set jaw at odds with her mild, courteous expression.

He waited until she'd focused back on him. "I hope so. I'm here to see Mr. Davenport. I don't have a prior appointment—I was hoping to catch him between meetings."

"He has someone with him. I'll check when he might be clear. Could you give me an idea of your name and business?"

"Certainly. Aristide Laurent from Vino d'Oro. I'm wanting to tap into Mr. Davenport's expertise in relation to wine distribution. See if we might do business together."

She nodded compliantly. "Take a seat, Mr. Laurent. I'll be back shortly."

She gestured to a straight-backed corner chair and vanished through a door in the wall behind the oak table.

Aristide could hear faint echoes of conversation from further down the hall. She returned almost immediately.

"Mr. Davenport is finishing up this appointment and then he'll be with you. Shouldn't be long."

Aristide was nodding off—the sleepless night finally taking its toll— when his senses surged to high alert, the resulting jerk in his legs nearly lifting him out of his chair. He heard the unmistakable lilt of a woman's voice, with a softer musical inflection than the brassier native lingo.

The door behind the receptionist opened and a sandy-haired, bespectacled man, probably younger than he was, ushered Leilani Manolo through.

Her hands flew to her mouth at the sight of him. "You! I thought . . . Oh, I beg your pardon!"

The normally composed Miss Manolo was *dérangé*. Knocked off her perch.

He covered the distance between them in a few big steps. "Is something wrong, Miss Manolo? It's nothing unusual. I'm here probably for very similar reasons to you."

She glanced at the man at her back—Aristide assumed it was Davenport—and then back to him, pushing her long dark hair off her face with one hand as she did.

He proffered his hand. "Mr.

Davenport, I presume? I'm Aristide Laurent. Thank you for taking the time to see me."

Davenport shook hands and turned to his other visitor for the accepted farewells, but she stood her ground.

"Mr. Laurent, I wonder if I could have a few words with you privately?" She glanced to Will Davenport. "Is there somewhere we could speak—very briefly?"

If Davenport was surprised at the unusual request he didn't show it. "Certainly." He turned to the receptionist. "Sarah, could you take our visitors through into the small meeting room. And arrange some coffee for them perhaps?"

Leilani shook her head. "Thank you, but that won't be necessary. This won't take long."

"Then maybe get some ready for Mr. Laurent and me. Say ten minutes?"

Davenport backed through the open door and disappeared.

Ushered into the small meeting room by the receptionist, Aristide studied Leilani Manolo with undisguised interest.

She was as beautiful as he remembered—perhaps even more so. Almond-shaped brown eyes, a luxuriant fall of midnight black-blue hair which today hung loose down her back, and a wide expressive mouth. She tucked a loose lock behind an ear which bore a flower-shaped mother-of-pearl earring not unlike the flowers she'd worn in her hair on Saturday night.

But the thing that struck him most was how quickly she assumed control again, when minutes ago she'd been upset. She might be young, but this woman was used to giving orders and having them followed. She would not be deflected easily once she had set her mind on a goal, he was sure of that.

She nibbled her lip as she regarded him with equally candid interest.

"I asked to see you, Mr. Laurent, because of what occurred after you left Cyrus and Misty's house on Sunday."

His heart turned over. "You're referring to Felix Duchamp's visit, I presume?"

She raised one eyebrow in surprise.

"I know he called on the consul," Aristide explained. "I bumped into him on the way out." He gave a quick grin. "Not literally, of course. I don't want to go within ten feet of the man. In the sense that the *Anglais* use—our paths crossed."

She returned his smile, though he

sensed an underlying tension in the way she held her hands clasped in front of her.

"I can confidently say the feeling is mutual. About the crossing paths, I mean. I'm afraid he didn't have too much good to say about you. I thought you should be warned."

His heart did another bounce in his chest. "Really. Do tell. What did he have to say?"

She glanced around her as if concerned about being overheard. "He seems to believe we are both implicated in Bully's death, simply on the basis of being at the scene."

She paused and chewed her bottom lip again. He knew there was worse coming.

"And he's under the apprehension that you've been responsible for other deaths. In the past."

Anxious lines showed around her eyes, waiting for his denial.

He shook his head, not in denial, but in sadness that his worst fears were confirmed.

"What did he say to you, Miss Manolo? Tell me exactly."

"He said exactly that. You'd been mixed up in suspicious deaths before. I think those were his words. He refused to say any more, but I got the impression he was getting ready to write a new report about Bully, and he would add that into the mix."

She stared at him, as if reading every fleeting expression in his eyes, his face, trying to discern his thoughts.

He remained silent, gazing back at her. She was an exceptional woman. No hysterics or tears, even though he could see she was under heavy stress.

"It's not true, is it? He's trying to make us both look bad, and if he's got something incriminating on you, it will pull me down in the dirt too. Please say it isn't true."

Finally he spoke. "It's not true, Miss Manolo. Not one word of it. But it's also complicated. It will be difficult to convince people of my innocence. Given the circumstances, very difficult."

She shot to her feet, as if the strain of containing herself had finally crumbled. "Then explain it to me. Try me first. See if I believe you."

Her cheeks were flushed a light pink, her eyes bright. He hadn't seen her more beautiful.

He stood also. "I am more than prepared to do that, Miss Manolo, but—"

She held up her hand in a quick urgent salute.

"Lani, please. Call me Lani. That's what my friends and family call me."

"Lani, then. The story I have to tell is long and complicated, and now is not the time. I don't want to keep Mr. Davenport waiting any longer—and we shouldn't be in this room alone any longer, either. Perhaps I can call on you later today? If you are worried your name will be somehow mixed up in this, then obviously it is urgent."

He gestured with his arm for her to precede him out. "Till later? Then I promise I will tell you the whole sorry story."

Fifteen

"Miss Manolo left with her equilibrium restored?" Davenport's query had an edge to it that made Aristide's hair stand on end.

"Quite happy." He considered the factor man coolly. "Why do you ask?"

"She was my visitor. I want to make sure she wasn't upset."

Aristide rubbed the prickling sensation at the back of his neck.

"And I am nothing if not gallant. The last thing I would wish is to upset Miss Manolo."

Davenport was even younger than Aristide had gauged on first meeting, but there was a steeliness in the gray eyes framed by gold-rimmed glasses. Although he looked like a mild-mannered clerk, Aristide saw the iron in his soul. He'd be a force to be reckoned with if occasion demanded it.

Aristide rubbed the side of his face, wanting to break the tension and restart the conversation.

"I'm sure you've heard. Miss Manolo and I had the misfortune to attract attention through Mr. Pike's death. Thanks to a nuisance of a newspaperman it's proving inconvenient for us both."

He shifted in his chair, attempting to regain his sense of momentum, as Sarah arrived with steaming coffee. A good strong java, by the smell of it. He let out a grateful sigh as he took the first sip.

"Thing is, Mr. Davenport, I seem to

be making powerful enemies. I'm just a vintner—I like to think a good vintner, but a new immigrant to this state, grateful for the opportunity to work in d'Oro. Building a future for the cellars and myself. And all hell is breaking loose. Take Senator de Vile, for starters. I've never met the man until this week, and yet I'm already off-side with him."

Davenport chuckled easily. "Some folks might consider that a badge of honor."

Aristide scratched behind his ear. "Really? Are you one of them?"

Will Davenport's brows drew into a serious line. "I'm publicly neutral. What I might think privately is something I don't talk about."

Aristide nodded. "It's no secret that the senator and d'Oro's owner, Sir John, don't see eye to eye, though Sir John never says anything publicly either. But I suspect that's the reason I'm making hard work of getting an agent for our wines."

Davenport nodded, searching Aristide's face with those deceptive eyes, as if divining secrets.

"It's urgent. We need a recognized distributor, someone familiar with the finer points of international trade, freight forwarding, tariffs and duties—all that stuff. We need them by Friday. That's the deadline for entry into the Golden Gate Symposium."

Will Davenport nodded slowly. "And you want to enter that competition why?"

Aristide put his cup down and brought his hands up to his lips in a prayer position.

"Mr. Davenport, the wines we are

making at d'Oro, some of them, are exceptional. They deserve much wider appreciation, a place on the wine lists of the top restaurants in New York and Paris, sampled in courts and clubs the world over. One instant way of getting known is to win an international contest like the Golden Gate, where you're up against the best in your field."

His voice was getting louder, his words speeding up. Whenever he started on this topic, he always got excited.

He reined in his enthusiasm. "Sorry. I don't mean to be a bore. I hope you can see my heart on this. It's my one dream in life. To excel as a vintner, to repay Sir John for the trust he's placed in me. To produce wines we can be proud of. He's given me my big break and I don't want to let him down."

Will Davenport eased back from the desk, subtly creating distance between them. Aristide realized he'd also been leaning in, desperate to communicate his passion.

"What about Ramsden Meadows?" The agent's face was bland, but once again there was a sharp hook in the enquiry. "I understand you used to work for him. Meadows Estate is probably bigger than d'Oro when you add in all the smaller vintners they represent. And forgive me for getting personal, but you've been squiring Mademoiselle Candy all over town. Ever the gallant? Is that it?"

Aristide's mouth went dry. "And you've only been here a couple of months? You've developed impeccable sources."

Davenport lifted one eyebrow. "I

make it my business to know what's going on. In this job you want to avoid getting caught up in something unpleasant."

"Then you'll also be aware that statewide we have a pressing problem with wine-tampering. Owners or distributors adding this and that. It's difficult to track down who's doing what, but they're breaking good winemaking practice and cheating on business.

"When I worked for him, Ramsden never asked me to do anything like that. Never. He knew it's something I find *méprisable*—despicable. But I'm not sure he was as conscientious with other winemakers. I'm not comfortable using his services as an agent. Any wine I supply will come direct from d'Oro so we can be sure it's not contaminated.

"Sir John wouldn't want to be

involved in anything like that and neither would I."

Aristide's eyes appealed for understanding. "Please bear with me. This is a very long reply. Miss Meadows is an attractive and intelligent young lady, but I've come to the conclusion there's no future for Vino d'Oro with the Meadows Estate.

"Sir John and I both want d'Oro unsullied by the dirty practices which are unfortunately widespread in California. And I'm getting a reputation for speaking up against the practice. I've even begun to get jumpy at the idea some of our competitors might try to adulterate our wines to shame us. We'll have to be particularly careful."

Davenport leaned back in, elbows on his desk, nodding. "That was rude of me. My apologies. I like to be sure."

The ironic gleam in his eye told Aristide he was anything but sorry for the jibe. He enjoyed prodding.

"Mr. Davenport, Senator de Vile has already told me d'Oro has to be a member of the Buena Vista Co-op—the group the industry is putting together—before Pike Consulting would take us on as a client. Bully indicated the same to me on Saturday."

He folded his arms across his chest and appraised Davenport's cool exterior. "Is that the way things are? Has anything changed with Bully's death? And what the heck does the senator have to do with it anyway? I thought he was just a politician."

Davenport rested his chin on his hands and his eyes glinted behind the frames.

"Senator de Vile is many things, Mr.

Laurent, but you should know right now you'd be very foolish to dismiss him as 'just a politician.' Many a man who's done that has ended up with a knife in his back—literally or figuratively. Quite possibly, Bully among them."

Sixteen

"Well, I'll be blowed. Since when did you start smoking those filthy things?"

Leilani poked her brother with the parasol she disliked lugging around with her. He took the smelly cheroot out of his mouth and blew her a blue smoke ring.

"Since I could." He glanced around him. Fashionably dressed people of the most respectable classes frequented the Occidental's long facade, busy going here and there or simply loitering like Kaleo, enjoying the street scene and people watching.

"It's pleasant loafing around here with nothing to do but watch the hordes," Kaleo said. "Ready to go home?"

"Not yet. I've got shopping to do." She glanced back to the hotel where the City of Paris Drygoods Company nestled into a street-level store on the Occidental's frontage. She pointed.

"How about I meet you at the coffee cart in Union Square in twenty, maybe thirty minutes?"

His strong black brows creased in doubt. "Misty said not to let you go about alone."

"I'll be fine. It's only a block or so."

Before he could quibble any further, she made for the store entry.

From the day it had opened nearly twenty years before, the City of Paris had been in demand as one of the premier suppliers of everything from exotic foods to French wine, brandy to bonnets, Persian shawls, cotton and woolen stockings, petticoats, laces, perfumes, patent medicines and postcards.

Misty had told her that the first cargo the Verdier family unloaded in the Bay sold before they made it to shore. The citizens of San Francisco surrounded the ship with rowboats and purchased everything the silk merchant brought from France before it could be unloaded. Felix Verdier went straight back home for another shipment, and the family's popularity had ballooned in the years since. The place bustled with activity.

She ignored the fabric counters with their rainbow offering of silks and velvets and made for the basement where an array of foods and freshly baked goods overwhelmed with mingled luscious aromas. With so much to choose from, it was hard to decide, but within twenty minutes she was back outside on Montgomery Street weighed down with two bags of delicious food.

Now to find Mamie. She strode confidently into O'Farrell Street, west of the now respectable Union Square, into a more questionable area edging the Tenderloin District, where Mamie operated as a seamstress from a cubicle that was barely bigger than a cupboard in the back corner of a Chinese laundry.

"Mamie! Stop work and talk for a few minutes!"

Leilani held up the two heavy brown paper shopping bags, marked with the store's Latin motto, *Fluctuat nec mergitur*—"It floats but never sinks"—taken, the store clerk had proudly informed her, from the City of Paris's coat of arms. "I've brought something for you."

Mamie's feet stopped working the floor treadle machine. She jumped up and enveloped Leilani in an excited hug.

"Miss Leilani! What are you doing here?" She glanced behind her, as if expecting someone else to shadow the doorway. "You didn't come alone?"

"Mamie, it's the middle of the day and Kaleo isn't far away. I'll be fine. I wanted to talk to you."

A froth of white satin billowed from under the needle foot. "Another wedding dress?"

"Yes, good for me. Brides pay well."

Lani parked the bags on the top of a corner cupboard and Mamie dug into them, excited at every new item. She was a well-built woman, muscled and fit, but not doughy, with lively dark eyes set in a careworn, walnut-colored face.

Leilani knew from an earlier chat that

she'd come to the coast from Louisiana with her Creole husband who died soon after they arrived, leaving her with sole responsibility for her eight-year-old son, Teddy. The boy was an energetic, streetwise hustler who offered to act as her guide the first time she and Kaleo came downtown.

It was Leilani's gift and her passion to notice the people others did not see, the caregivers and hostlers and servers, the humble grafters, who keep the world's wheels turning and never get any recognition for it. She paid attention to people that others saw right through.

Within a short time Teddy had been talking merrily about his mother, and her sewing machine, and his dream of one day working as a porter in the Occidental, rubbing shoulders with the rich and famous. He'd taken her to the seamstress's premises, where a peeling painted sign on the street announced:

New Garments Made

Old Ones Repaired

Come In

He led her down the narrow path and through the steamy laundry gaily chattering to his new best friend: "Lots of famous people stay at the Occidental, Lani." (She'd told him that was her name.) "Ma has friends there and they're always telling her about the people who are staying."

On that first day she discovered that Mamie kept herself and her son alive after her husband's death by taking in washing and then expanding into sewing. That afternoon she'd commissioned a dress that Mamie was still finishing.

"How are you?" Lani asked after

Mamie had recovered from the excitement of the food delivery. She was perched on a wooden crate, a few feet from Mamie's sewing chair. "You haven't been bothered by anyone?"

Mamie frowned. "The police, you mean? No, Miss Lani. Thanks be to our Lady Mary."

Her hand strayed to fondle a large pewter cross that hung on a long chain between her ample breasts. "Long may it remain so."

"Amen," said Lani. She shuffled her feet, wondering how to break her bad news.

"I wanted to warn you. I've been bothered by a French newspaperman. He's short, bald, and has a big stomach." She drew air mounds in front of her own. "If he turns up here, play dumb. Pretend you don't understand him. He's trouble."

Mamie nodded, as if nothing surprised her. "Sure thing."

Lani frowned, watching. Mamie's eyes were guarded.

"Mamie, had you ever seen Bully Pike, the man who was killed, before Saturday? Did you see him around the hotel? I mean, his offices were in there, in the hotel. He would have been coming and going from this part of town often. Did you see him? Know anything about him?"

Mamie's eyes fell to the rough board floor. She didn't reply.

"Mamie? You heard what I asked?"

Mamie reluctantly lifted her dark eyes to Lani's. She simply nodded, her eyes glittering.

"Mr. Bully, he was good to the girls around here."

She gave a wan smile. "He wasn't good, if you know what I mean. But he was generous. He wasn't mean. Even when he was drunk, he didn't beat them."

"Oh. I understand. But he did visit them?"

"Only when he'd been drinking. Otherwise no."

"Did he have any particular favorites? Anyone special?"

"Oh no. Not like that. Not on the streets. He had the one in his office. They often went off in a carriage. And the Countess."

"The Countess? Who's that?"

Mamie shrugged. "A rich lady. She used to work at a mission down here in the Tenderloin. She knew a lot of the girls, and she was an old friend of Mr. Bully's. They often had coffee together.

She doesn't work around here anymore though. Hasn't for a long time."

"But you think Bully still saw her?"

"I expect so. They talked a lot. They were like brother and sister. Or husband and wife."

"And he didn't see her when he was drunk either?"

Mamie had picked up a piece to resume work, and she nearly spat a pin out of her mouth.

"Never!" Her mouth fell open.

"Funny thing. For the last six months or so Mr. Bully was telling the girls he might be moving to Washington. The girls thought he was working for the senator, but he never actually said. When he was drunk he'd go on about it. When he was sober, he never mentioned it."

"And what about the lady in the

carriage? You mentioned a lady from the office. Do you know her name?"

Mamie shook her head. "No. She was a bit highfalutin. With whitish-blonde hair. He made a real fuss of her, he did."

Mamie wrung her hands together, an anxious pull on her lips. "Miss Lani, I have to get this dress finished today. I can't do any more talking."

Lani jumped up. "I understand, Mamie. You've been especially helpful. Can I ask one more thing?"

She gazed across at Mamie expectantly, and the dressmaker frowned but nodded.

"Where did the Countess go when she left here? Have you any idea where I could find her?"

Mamie shook her head, as if suddenly frightened.

"No! I don't, Miss Lani, I really don't. And I don't like the idea of you poking around in that man's business. Please. I've got a feeling. . . The girls say—"

She shook her head. "No, I'm not saying any more. But it's dangerous, Miss Lani. See what happened to him. Leave it alone. Please."

She found Kaleo and they sat in the Union Square gardens with their afternoon coffee. She told him everything Mamie had said, reliving it as she did.

Kaleo was quiet for several minutes after she finished talking, watching a bird on a nearby tree, then turned to her and said, "The obvious person who fits Mamie's description is Misty."

He gazed back into the tree. Birdsong and the buzz of wagons hummed around them.

He reflected for a while in silence. Then he switched his attention back to Leilani. "By the holy jumping mother of Moses, it *can't* be Misty, can it?

"Because if it is, there's a good chance Cyrus is our killer. Or Cyrus knows him."

Seventeen

The Countess picked up the silver coffee pot with an enameled coat of arms on the lid and held it aloft. "Can I freshen your cup?"

The voice was velvet and well-modulated, her wrist as she offered refreshment was poised at the appropriate elegant angle, and yet there was no stiff formality about the gesture.

Leilani thrust the bone-china cup and saucer toward her, momentarily forgetting her manners in her thirst for more.

She had been in Elizabeth Wenderhoven's Queen Anne villa on Nob Hill for less than an hour, but she already felt as if they'd known each other for years.

Approaching up the broad front steps she'd swallowed nervously at the house's grandeur. The big round tower on one corner, the wide front gable, expansive verandas and iron-fretted roofline gave it an exotic Eastern air. But inside, the playful opulence relaxed into understated elegance.

As her hostess poured the coffee, Lani snuck a look around the big room. The paneled walls were painted a restful olive green; the light oak floors were covered in Oriental rugs, whose jewel-like colors echoed in the glazed tiles around the fireplace and the stained-glass mullion window on the end wall.

An iron candelabra heavy with cold, dripped wax sat on the mantel, and the faint vanilla scent of beeswax hinted that it wasn't there just for show. The Countess enjoyed simple things.

Lani relaxed back into the sofa and covertly appraised the older woman. She must be a similar age to her own mother, she reflected. They'd probably met. She did a quick calculation. The twins' mother had died before their first birthday, so if she was still alive and here today, she'd be in her mid-forties, maybe forty-five.

The woman pouring coffee looked younger than that.

Elizabeth Kalama was from an elite Maui family, married to Charles Wenderhoven, a Boston blue blood with links back to the Austrian royal house. They'd met and wed when Wenderhoven visited Hawaii as part of a diplomatic delegation from the US Secretary of State's office.

Wenderhoven's diplomatic career had taken them to London and Paris as well as Washington, but when he died young, leaving his wife independently wealthy, Elizabeth had settled in San Francisco, shunning the city's burgeoning social scene for a life of charitable works and hosting a private arts salon.

Charles had playfully nicknamed her the Countess because of the regal composure that came naturally to her, but Maiden Lane's diseased and destitute folk usually called her the Rich Widow. It hadn't been difficult to track down the reclusive benefactress once Leilani heard about her from Mamie.

With Kaleo as escort she'd returned to the Occidental Hotel dining room later the same day. Seated for an early supper of Hawaiian chicken—she'd discovered the chef traveled to the islands and made a lot of friends there—she dawdled over her plate and waited for her opportunity.

When a waiter she recognized as a friend of Mamie's appeared to clear plates from a neighboring table, she signaled to him, as if requiring service.

And when he'd leaned over her to courteously inquire how he might assist she'd handed him a note for Mamie's common-law husband Sam Morley, the Occidental's Big Kahuna of service, who ensured that everything ran like clockwork behind the scenes.

"Could you ask Mr. Sam if he could spare us a few minutes downstairs when his shift finishes? We'll be waiting at the coffee cart in Union Square."

And Sam, as she thought he would, knew exactly where the Countess lived, because she'd helped many a mission woman with dislodging a blackmailing bailiff or a drunken boyfriend from her doorstep. The Countess had the resources to see that kind of job got done quietly and effectively.

"I can tell you how to find her—but you mustn't share it with anyone," Sam said, his eyes darting over her shoulder to check who was within earshot. "She arranges miracles for the girls sometimes, and their pimps don't like it. No one wants to see her suffer for it."

"Mr. Pike's *lei niho palaoa*—you say it was stolen?"

Elizabeth Wenderhoven spoke over the cup poised before her lips, the question inflected with gentle empathy.

Hot tears threatened as Lani gazed into the matron's deep brown eyes.

Understanding eyes. She'd barely had time to remember her Uncle Bully in the furor following his death. First she'd faced the awful accusations from that woman Candy and then suspicion from Sebastian Russell. The final straw came with Cyrus's betrayal when she'd needed him most. And now her grief had caught her by surprise from behind.

In this tranquil salon with its teal-blue sofa highlighted with hot-pink cushions, seated with this refined, measured woman, she was more grounded than she had felt at any moment since Bully had fallen bleeding into her arms. The realization dawned. She wasn't some piece of flotsam tossed hither and thither on dangerous seas, with no safe shore in sight.

She was Leilani Kamamalu Lilolilo Manolo, daughter of Apialaki Kamamalu

Arnold. She was Kaleo's twin, and with him joint preserver of her family's fortunes. She had done nothing wrong and had nothing to fear. She couldn't explain how a woman she'd not known before today had infused such deep peace into her spirit. And she'd done it without once making any direct reference to her distress.

Lani had come here seeking answers, but she wasn't sure she even was asking the right questions. How well did the Countess know Bully? Did she have suspicions about who might have killed him? Did she know of any enemies? Might he have been involved in a love triangle, and fallen victim to a jealous husband bent on revenge?

The questions had tumbled out, while the Countess—Leilani could see after five minutes in her presence why the name had stuck—sat with her hands quietly resting in her lap, listening as though she was drinking in every word, absorbing every gesture, giving herself wholly to Leilani, seemingly unaware of the long-haired Persian blue that curled in a wound-up ball asleep on the sofa beside her.

When Leilani's flood of stress and confusion slowed then finally ceased, Elizabeth Wenderhoven gave her a gentle sad smile, raising her hands in a graceful gesture of "who knows?"

"So many questions, Miss Manolo. And at this time, so few answers. But it will not always be that way."

"Please, Mrs. Wenderhoven. Call me Lani. That's what my family calls me."

"Lani." She breathed a musicality, a longing, into the name. "Short for Leilani, is it not? Before we get back to

Bully, tell me about you. Why are you here in San Francisco?"

Another flow of confidences tumbled forth. Archie's death, Diamond Sugar's perfidy, the family back home who were relying on her.

What was it about this woman that loosened her tongue?

"I'm a twin. My brother Kaleo and I were born to Abigail and Matthew Manolo at Lahaina, Maui in September 1847. We never knew our father—he was taken by a shark, and our mother also died when we were young, but we've been very fortunate.

"They raised us in the Hawaiian way with shared family. First with Archie and Cornelia, and then with Ani, our *haina* mother at court. We have a wonderful extended family."

Lani had been gazing absently at the

sleeping cat as she rattled off her family history. She glanced back to where the Countess sat like a regal monument, gazing at her with sad eyes.

"Is something the matter, Mrs. Wenderhoven? Have I said something wrong?"

The Countess let out a long, slow dying sigh. "I confess I haven't been entirely open with you, Leilani Kamamalu Manolo."

Lani's heart turned over. "How . . . How do you know my mother's family name?"

"I know her family name, my dear, because I knew your mother. I knew her well." Elizabeth Wenderhoven smiled wistfully. "We were very close friends for a regrettably short time. I admit from the moment you stepped through the door I guessed you were

Apialaki's—Abigail's—daughter. The resemblance is striking. I wanted a little time to digest the news, and to get to know you a little."

She flung her arms open wide. "You can't imagine the pleasure it gives me to meet you after all these years. You must stay for lunch."

Long after they'd lunched on Charles' favorite midday snack—salmon salad with mayonnaise, anchovies, gherkins and hard-boiled eggs, nestled in lettuce—and Lani Manolo had departed, Elizabeth stroked the Persian blue and let the memories flood in.

Leilani Manolo was a perfect delight. She wanted to adopt her on the spot. The young woman showed the same brilliance and good humor as her mother, but she radiated a disciplined purpose which had always eluded the free-spirited Abigail.

A heaviness settled around her heart as she reflected on the twins' birth, and their mother's death in a measles epidemic.

"She has no idea," she whispered to Artemisia, the purring Persian. "No idea at all. When Hector finds out—and I can hardly believe he hasn't already winkled the story out of Cyrus or Bully by now—there'll be all hell to pay. But I can't be the one to tell her, can I?"

Artemisia regarded her with baleful violet-black eyes and purred.

Eighteen

"Kaleo, what are we going to do? Tell me!"

"Do about what, Princess? About the sugar? Getting us an agent? Or about Cyrus being happy to throw you to the wolves?"

"All of it!"

They were once again sitting in Union Square, sipping coffee-cart café au lait, and the sharp inflection in her response turned heads. Lani's hand went to her mouth, as if silencing herself, and she dipped her head in apology to a woman sitting on a nearby bench with a sleeping baby in her arms.

"Sorry," she mouthed and dug her

elbow into Kaleo's ribs with her free arm. "See what you made me do? Stop being annoying."

The visit to Elizabeth Wenderhoven had raised so many questions. Remarkable as it was to discover Elizabeth's past link with her mother, she hadn't found many satisfactory answers to the questions worrying her today.

She was more at sea than ever when she finally departed Nob Hill, and the sleepless night that followed underlined her dilemma. She had more questions than answers, and no real sense of who she could trust.

Bully's death revealed cracks in relationships she'd thought as safe as houses. Take Misty and Cyrus, surrogate parents in her early years before Cyrus's appointment as consul a decade ago. They'd chosen to talk here in a city park rather than back at the Mays' house because she didn't want their conversation overheard.

Kaleo moved closer to her and lifted his scarred eyebrow, a mischievous glint in his eyes.

"Sorry, Princess. Now go over it all again. At a pace I can handle—slowly. Very slowly. You know I'm not a sharp-witted creature like you."

"Kaleo, you always play at not being the brightest light in the harbor, but you don't fool me. You want someone else to do the work."

She gave a soft laugh. Suddenly, the tension in her shoulders eased.

Everything will work out. It has to.

She resumed her report from her visit of the previous day, her frustration ebbing away as she went through the facts as told to her by Elizabeth Wenderhoven once again.

"She doesn't seem to know much more than us about who killed Bully. She shook her head when I asked about Misty. I don't think she was telling me everything, but I couldn't get any more out of her on that topic. She had a lot to say about that Senator de Vile, though.

"For starters, he knew Mother, and Cyrus and Bully—all that crowd—when they were young. Knew our venerable guardian Archie too. It sounds like de Vile had some sort of row with Archie. The Countess confirmed my suspicion from Bully that they didn't get on, anyway.

"And she said Senator de Vile was a lot closer to Bully than you might think, with him being in Washington a good part of the year and all. De Vile has business connections everywhere that are never publicly declared, with Bully and Cyrus as well as lots of other people.

"She hinted that could be the reason Bully seemed edgy that last time we talked. Why he got upset when I pushed about the sugar. Maybe if the senator had a vendetta against Archie from long ago, that's the problem."

She took a final gulp from her coffee and took Kaleo's hand in hers. It was a big, tanned man's hand, his palm twice the size of hers, but with long, slender fingers. A workman's hand with an artist's fingers. A warm sense of security flowed into her from holding it.

"The Countess was pretty straight on it. She told me not to approach de Vile directly, without someone to negotiate for us. She said he'd make mincemeat of us. And she said not to tell him about our mother. She said if he knew about Archie being our grandfather we'd be sunk."

She gave his hand one more squeeze and then let go, swallowing at the sense of loss. She gazed into his black eyes, the sensation of being on eye-level with him giving her a happy lilt in spirits.

"So what's it to be, oh brother mine? Are we confronting the lion in his den, or playing it safe as the Countess instructs?"

Kaleo gave a deep rumbling laugh and his eyes gleamed. "As if there was even a question about 'if.' The only question is 'when.' Isn't that it?"

He stood, gathered her into his arms and swung her around in an embrace.

Lani squealed. The baby started crying.

"Now see what you've done! Really, Leilani, you can't help it. You're trouble."

He bowed to the frowning woman, his best version of the athletic sportsman he was, and she gazed at him, eyes shining.

"Sorry, ma'am. We're just going."

And they walked away, Kaleo blissfully unaware he'd made another effortless conquest.

Nineteen

Leilani's slim figure showed to perfection in the scarlet silk dress trimmed with jet beads she'd chosen for the occasion. Even Kaleo had surpassed his usual sartorial efforts, with a three-piece suit—trousers, waistcoat and thigh-length sack coat—in the same smoky-gray wool that set off his olive skin and dark eyebrows. She doubted there was a better-looking couple taking lunch in the Occidental's increasingly familiar dining room.

And thanks to invaluable intelligence from Sam, they'd timed their visit perfectly. As they swept past Hector de Vile's disbanding lunch party, intent on nothing more than a late nibble on the hotel's lunch special—Dungeness Crab on ice with shallots, mayonnaise and Worcestershire sauce—she ensured that she caught the senator's roving eye.

He wasn't a ladies' man, she sensed that. But he was one of those men who was always searching over shoulders to spot someone more important, more influential, more enticing, who might be of more benefit to his advancement than the person he was talking with.

And as she and Sam had planned, they took their seats at their reserved table, right next to where de Vile was farewelling his departing guests.

As easy as attracting bees to a honeypot. She would get an audience with him, and she had made a special effort to ensure it.

Kaleo made a show of contemplating

the wine list for several minutes before they agreed they'd satisfy themselves with Vichy Springs mineral water and the crab for their late lunch.

Their table attendant was pouring the mineral water when a second tray-carrying waiter arrived and bowed. "Senator Hector de Vile requests," he said, handing Kaleo a note. With a nod to the neighboring table, he departed.

Leilani followed his head movement and saw de Vile, seated alone and nursing a café noir. Kaleo handed her the note:

Senator Hector de Vile requests your company over coffee.

Plainly penned by the man himself, black fountain pen on Occidental stationery in a confident, flowing hand.

Leilani held up the note, fluttered it between her fingers, and with a faint smile inclined her head.

Don't look too eager—or nervous.

"Delighted, I'm sure," she said. "Please do join us."

They discovered over the next half hour that when the senator turned on his charm he was delightful company. He hinted at his wide-ranging business interests, referred modestly to his coming election chances and then turned his attention to them.

"I confess I spotted you briefly at our charity dinner on Saturday night. I believe you were sitting at Bully's table. Is that right?"

He tapped the top of his cane with a perfectly manicured index finger. "Such a dreadful business, that." He paused, as if giving Bully his minute of silence, and raised his eyes.

Lani saw their icy determination. The

charming man of the people had vanished, replaced by an iron-willed inquisitor.

Right. Now we're getting down to business.

"You were on familiar terms with Mr. Pike?"

'More than familiar. We are—were—almost family."

De Vile's eyebrows arched. "And the unfortunate disagreement with him, was that just a family thing? I saw you together," he said, smooth as cream.

Lani held her silence. Two could play this game.

"So what was that about? I prefer to know if there's the danger of a snake in the grass."

Lani smiled her sweetest smile, while her heart banged against her ribs. "No snakes, Senator. We don't have snakes in Hawaii, I assure you."

She glanced down at the remnants of her meal, a few crab tails and limp lettuce leaves, equally calculated in her response.

"It was a little perplexing, actually." She shot a winsome smile at Kaleo, as if seeking his endorsement.

"He was our Uncle Cyrus. No blood relation, you understand, but we were close. He was a father figure for us back in Honolulu. Our parents died when we were young, you see, and we were brought up in the Hawaiian way in the extended family. Bully was always available if we wanted to go swimming or riding. Anything out of doors, he was up for it. Isn't that so, Kaleo?"

Kaleo nodded. "Yes. He was a special figure in our lives."

"And then he came here, and we

didn't see him any more. But we thought he'd be pleased to see us. To help us."

She let the words hang, adjusted her expression to one of melancholy.

"Sadly, it seems things have changed in the last ten years. He said it was impossible, he couldn't help us. And when I asked why, he got angry. I don't know why."

She reached out and took Kaleo's hand, as much for her own comfort as for the effect.

"We're bereft. We've lost the man we thought we knew. And now we have no way of asking him what was wrong."

When she gauged they'd spent enough time paying tribute to Bully's passing, she peered at de Vile through long black lashes. "I believe you started your impressive career in the Pacific,

Senator. Hawaii in particular? I imagine you knew Bully in your younger days?"

De Vile took a sip of his lukewarm coffee and his eyes flicked around the nearly deserted room, as if seeking more amenable company.

"I knew him, yes. And naturally we've seen a bit of each other here in San Francisco. He was hard to avoid if you do business here."

"Then I wonder if I can ask you one of the questions that's been bothering me ever since Saturday night."

Lani challenged de Vile with her eyes, imagining herself for a moment as Elizabeth Wenderhoven, regal and in command. "Have you any idea what it is?"

"None whatsoever, Miss Manolo. No idea." Clipped. Final. Uninterested.

She watched his fingers tighten on

the top of his cane. The manicured tips were pink from the tension.

"Do you want to know?"

He suddenly smiled, as if enjoying the game. "I'm sure you will tell me, Miss Manolo, whether I want to hear it or not."

"Let's say it's something a man who is concerned about snakes in the grass might want to know."

She glanced at Kaleo, who was signaling his glowing approval with his eyes.

"Such a man might want to know why Bully appeared to fear taking on our sugar business. And why he was unwilling to tell us why.

"He might have had perfectly good reasons. Who knows? Big, muscular, bruiser Bully. He was frightened of something, Senator de Vile. I knew him.

I saw it in his eyes. And then an hour later he was dead."

Hector de Vile squeezed his eyes shut in an attempt to banish the picture he could not get out of his mind.

That beautiful, brazen Manolo girl. If that was her true name, which he doubted.

The challenge in her dark flashing eyes as she'd dared him to take her on.

First Will Davenport and now this. Two youngsters in as many days who challenged him, undaunted by his rank and power.

But that wasn't what bothered him the most.

When he closed his eyes he was back in the Lahaina of his youth, when it was the biggest whaling port in the Pacific. He heard the hiss of retreating waves, saw again the fern-bedecked dais where he had stood, a froth of native hibiscus around his neck, and been wed.

Why did this insolent chit of a girl, who claimed to be here to sell her benighted sugar, take him back to that day?

And her brother? He'd barely spoken, but he too had a familiarity about him, some fleeting reminder in stance and gesture rather than facial expression, that took him straight back to those days in the 1840s when he was a young man on the make, desperate for a break, fighting with every fiber of his being to fulfill his father's expectations and earn his inheritance.

He'd come so close.

She was right about the snake in the grass, but he didn't think it had anything to do with sugar.

He sifted back through the years, reflected on the choices he'd made, and for the first time in many years fear licked at him. Bully Pike wasn't the only one haunted by ghosts.

Who *were* Leilani and Kaleo Manolo. And what, if anything, did they have to do with him?

He leaned back in his chair and watched a spider on the curtains, climbing up and then falling, sustained by the thinnest of gossamer, before alighting on a new surface and beginning the climb all over again.

It wasn't falling in love that had been his big mistake. He would never regret the sweetness, the delight, the breathtaking joy of it.

It was what he'd done afterwards. When the doors had closed on him once and for all.

What he'd done then might still cost him all he'd won.

And he couldn't allow that to happen.

Twenty

"Here it is. With one day to spare. The d'Oro 1869 Zinfandel that will get the world talking!"

Aristide presented himself before Will Davenport with a self-mocking flourish, like a courtier making a presentation to the king. "I hope you haven't changed your mind about representing us in the last two days."

He carefully lowered the crate containing a dozen bottles onto the front office desk and took a step back. "Hot off the Central Pacific and the Oakland ferry. Specially freighted from Sacramento under the eagle eyes of one of our cellar men. I can guarantee this consignment is contaminant-free."

He straightened up from discharging his load and instantly saw he'd badly misjudged Will's mood.

His normally bland fairness was marred by a dark frown. He had a smear of black ink on his chin, probably from the news sheet dangling in his right hand.

The factor man lifted the paper and waved it in front of Aristide. "I'd say contamination is the least of your worries right now, monsieur." His tone was heavily ironic.

"And the only thing that the wine world will be talking about is this." He rattled the paper in Ari's face a second time.

Ari snatched it from him. Occupying the same front-page position as the earlier *Alta California* story about Bully's death was Felix Duchamp's follow-up.

Wine Company's Shocking Secret

Respected mining magnate Sir John Russell's move into wines masks a dreadful history—his French winemaker Aristide Laurent's entanglement in the Poisoned Alcohol scandal in Bordeaux eight years ago which left ten dead. Laurent presented himself as a rescuer in the death of Mr. Bully Pike on Saturday, but the French winemaker's past contains a deadly secret. He left the family firm in France after he was blamed for the deaths of ten guests at a wedding party in his home village.

Aristide's insides cramped. He'd known Duchamp was working on something like this, and now the worst had happened. He'd tried to ignore the warning bells. Avoided seeking out Duchamp and giving his side of the story. And now it was too late. No one would believe him, and no one would drink wine he'd had a hand in producing.

"I can explain."

"I think it's a bit late for that. Read on."

Davenport's face was grim.

The French winemaker has been vocal in criticizing California winemaking practices since arriving on these shores several years ago, but he kept quiet about his entanglement in a terrible tragedy involving contaminated wine. Alta California *understands from eyewitnesses who knew him in France that he left the family firm in disgrace after the tragic event.*

Aristide's knees gave way and he grasped at the desk for support. His sides heaved. His throat was raw and dry, and when he spoke next his voice cracked.

"This is not true. It's just not true!"

Will Davenport searched his face as if he was trying to read his innermost thoughts. Then he shrugged. "I warned you. There's more than one way to get knifed in the back." He turned toward the interconnecting door.

"Will!" Aristide's voice was loud, plaintive, demanding. "I can explain."

"It's not me you need to explain this to, Laurent. You need to explain it to your boss, and the people of San Francisco. Right smart. Or there will be no d'Oro wines made by Aristide Laurent to taste."

Twenty-one

The young man with a disbelieving stare had not committed the heinous crime of which he stood accused. Sir John Russell trusted his inner senses when rooting out falsehood.

He glanced at the paper under his hand, one he hadn't shown Aristide Laurent yet. A telegram from Ramsden Meadows advising him of a proposed rule change for entries to the Golden Gate Wine Symposium, to be voted on early this week, before the first round of blind tasting. Only winemakers who were signed up members of the Buena Vista Cooperative would be eligible for entry.

That both Meadows and Hector de Vile had been quick to leak the smear story under the guise of sharing a sympathetic confidence when he'd seen them at a Wine Board meeting shored up his certainty of Laurent's innocence more than he was willing to let on to his young vintner right now. The man deserved to stew for a while yet.

"So. Start from the beginning. When did you become aware of Duchamp's presence in the city? And, more importantly, him of yours?"

Laurent let out a huge sigh. "Saturday night. A week ago. When I went to the aid of Bully Pike. Duchamp showed up like a blowfly on rotten meat in the crowd that gathered. But I wasn't sure at that stage whether he remembered me. I only had the briefest of dealings with him back in France. He covered the story of my father's trial. My father always had an illegal still going with cheap alcohol he added to his wine to fire it up and keep it cheap. His firewater was a favorite in the village because it packed such a punch. You didn't need much of it to get drunk.

"I was always telling him he was playing with death. That he'd get caught one day. And he mocked me. Told me I had no imagination. That I wasn't a visionary like him.

"But then it all went wrong at a game of boules. They charged him with the deaths of ten people. He and his lawyer had it all worked out. They banded together and blamed me. Said I was the one doing the illegal brewing. I could either stay and face the music, or I could run. He gave me no choice, really. I thought it was either me or him for the hangman's rope, and I wasn't about to die for his sins, so I ran.

"Then at the trial they produced false witnesses who testified that I'd been the one responsible and he got off on all charges. So neither of us swung, but I was left with a heinous record when I was totally blameless."

Russell held up his hand to signal a pause in the confessional outpouring.

"Is there anyone who could back you up on this? I know it's a very long shot, but it's worth asking. Anyone at all?"

Aristide sank his head into his hands and his chest heaved.

"Well, Gavonnier. The guy they called in as a false witness. Theoretically. I have no idea where he is, or even if he is still alive. My father is long dead so I guess there aren't any recriminations for him."

The young vintner's face creased into worry lines.

"But even if we could find him I've no idea if he'd be willing to do it. I mean, what's in it for him? And finding him would take months. And we only have days. The preliminary judging for the Golden Gate Symposium is next week. The first round of the blind tasting is Tuesday. We have to be in that if we are to make the final."

Russell released the slip of paper under his thumb and pushed it down the table to Aristide. "Take a look at this."

The vintner reached out and took in its contents with a quick glance. He shook his head, not wanting to believe it.

"Various people have hinted to me about this—de Vile, Will Davenport. I suppose it's no surprise it's happening."

He glanced up at Russell, and the

wine owner could see a glint of hope in Aristide's eyes for the first time since they'd entered this discussion.

"Dare I say, Sir John, but it's all a little too neat, isn't it? Blackening my name. Blocking us from entering."

He fiddled with the edges of the telegraph form. "I said to Will Davenport that I seemed to have made a lot of influential enemies without even trying. I was joking—it seems so unlikely I'd even rate a mention."

He glanced up. "It's almost . . . Well, I wonder if it isn't shaping up as an organized campaign. To shut us down. Maybe it isn't just about me. It's a campaign against Vino d'Oro, isn't it? It's an attack on you as patron too."

Russell screwed up the telegram and threw it toward the fireplace. It bounced on the hearth.

"It's a campaign against your integrity, Aristide. You've been talking about the contamination issue far more than some of the men behind the Golden Gate Symposium like. If they can attack you on that weak spot— make it appear as if you are protesting so loudly because you're as guilty as sin—they discredit you and people will dismiss the issue. The Golden Gate show will shine as white as snow.

"I'm glad you came racing back here to the farm today, even if it did take you half a day to get here. Tomorrow we visit the state governor in his flashy new office. I think it's about time I tried pulling a few favors with the governor.

"Goodness knows if I'll be successful, but it's worth a try."

Twenty-two

California was run from the Sacramento Capitol building, a domed masterpiece modeled on Washington's White House, where Henry Hunt, the current governor, had sat down to business for the last few years, as completion of the construction continued around him.

It was an immense building, three lofty stories in Roman Corinthian style, set in the center of four city blocks of park traversed by granite walks, native tree plantings and flower beds, still being terraced and planted.

The Vino d'Oro principals proceeded up granite steps through the imposing rotunda, seventy-two feet in diameter and rising through the height of the first dome. The governor occupied elegantly furnished offices, past the statues of Washington and Lincoln set in wall niches, on the south-west corner.

Aristide's insides were jumping at the prospect of the audience that lay ahead of him, but when he and Sir John presented their credentials, Hunt's secretary directed them with a broad wave to the extensive gardens.

"Governor Hunt is devoted to the region's agriculture and he likes to check out progress in the experimental greenhouse. We're growing a lot of the plants we'll be using on site, did you know? I'll show you the way."

He led them past teams of gardeners working on paths and borders to a large greenhouse near the corner of Tenth Street.

"You'll find him in there, consulting with the gardeners. He likes to check in with them every day at this time." He gave a significant nod to a nearby terrace, paved in marble, and furnished with a pretty wrought-iron table and chairs.

"He conducts his meetings on the terrace if he wishes to sit down." As he strode away, Sir John touched Aristide's arm to halt his forward motion.

"Let me make the introductions. You can take over once we've got him engaged."

He lifted his hat and resettled it on his dark hair, already damp and flattened from the heat of the morning sun. "Take heart, Laurent. He's as unhappy as we are about the rogue operators in the wine industry. He wants it cleaned up as much as we do."

He gave his hat one final tug. "We can play that to our advantage." He glanced around him. "I'll make sure we do."

The Democrat governor was a short, stocky fellow with a jutting jaw obscured by a neatly trimmed, sandy bristle of beard. He was standing by beds of grape cuttings, raw newly planted sticks, talking with a bulky sideburned fellow who was leaning on a spade, a wheelbarrow at his hip. He turned at the crunch of their boots on the gravel and broke off his conversation when he recognized Russell.

"Sir John! Delighted to see you, old man! To what do we owe the pleasure?"

He glanced at his hand and chuckled. "Forgive me if we forgo the customary handshake... Hand's soiled with natural

245

labor, wouldn't you know. Come and see. You're the man I'd like to hear from."

Sir John drew his arm inclusively toward Aristide. "Allow me to introduce my winemaker, Mr. Aristide Laurent. You might not have come across him before. Aristide, Governor Hunt. As you can see, Aristide, the governor is already well-versed in our business."

The governor's eyes widened momentarily in surprise at Aristide's name, and then he regained his statesmanlike calm.

Aristide tensed as he made a slight bow. So he too had read the *Alta* hate piece. It hadn't vanished without trace. That had been too much to hope for.

They gathered in a semicircle to examine the specimens the governor had been investigating when they arrived.

"These cuttings are from the stock Agoston Haraszthy donated to the state. From a range of varieties he rescued from a nursery back east which was closing down."

Haraszthy, a Hungarian noble and major grape-grower and landowner, was known throughout California as a prime mover in establishing wine as a commercial commodity.

The governor stepped back to allow Aristide and Sir John to get a better view of the slips. "They're already putting forth good growth, though they haven't been in long."

Aristide reached down and read the plant labels that hung from several of the specimens.

"Muscat of Alexandria. Ah yes, also known as White Tokay? Golden Chasselas. Yes, that one makes quite a potable, dry, fruity white. And good for table grapes too.

"Very interesting. I see Mr. Haraszthy is pushing hard with his conviction we need to move away from the Mission grape if we are to produce anything memorable. And he's right about that. Some of the local wine publications have picked up on it too."

John Russell stood with his hands behind his back, scanning appreciatively around him, and the two men fell into companionable silence.

"We were wondering, Governor, if you could spare us a few minutes of your time. Something's come up we'd appreciate your input on."

Hunt's brows lifted in mild surprise.

"Certainly, Sir John. Anything I can do. I'll arrange for cool drinks to be brought to the terrace. Join you there in a few minutes."

"It wasn't a wedding, Governor. It was a drinking session the village men got into after a game of boule. One of them believed my father owed him a debt he wasn't repaying. They took it out in liquor—helped themselves to a cask in my father's cellar that they shouldn't have touched.

"That doesn't make it any less tragic," Aristide said. "I understand that. It should not have been sitting there, topped up with wood alcohol to give a faster hit. But it was not a deliberate act on my father's part. That's some consolation.

"No, the deliberate act came next, when they discovered where the wine came from."

Aristide's face flushed with shame. Even under the canvas awning erected to compensate for the lack of any big trees in the developing gardens, he had the urge to loosen his collar and tie. He squeezed his eyes tight to block out painful memories.

"My father was a delusional fool. Full of bombast and lies, making grandiose claims he had no means of fulfilling. Sorry to speak ill of the dead, but these are the unpleasant facts of my birth. He was an embarrassment, ridiculed village-wide because of his cock-a-doodle-do fantasies."

He rubbed his eyes, and glanced over the governor's shoulder, unwilling to meet his eyes.

"When the village realized where the wine came from, who was responsible, they howled for blood. And *mon père* took the easiest way out. He blamed me. Oh, he gave me due warning. Told me what he was about to do and told me to run for it. I was young and could start over, he said. He couldn't. That's more or less it. He had some drunkard lined up to back his story with a false testimony that he'd seen me doctoring the barrel. That it was all my fault.

"So that's what I did. I had no choice really. I was eighteen years old and I'd been under his thumb my whole life. I did what he told me to do. I ran."

He raised his eyes to the distant park, unwilling to see the disgust, or worse, maybe doubt, on the governor's face. The sun was dazzling, beamed right in his face. He rubbed his eyes and focused on the path leading up to the terrace.

Two people were making their way

toward them, gravel crunching under their feet as they came closer, a man and a slender woman, leaning into the man as if requiring protection and help.

Her form had rounded in the years since he'd last seen her, but her hair was still a sparkling blonde halo against the glittering sunlight. Her eyes as she raised them to meet his were the same piercing, periwinkle blue. Beside her hurried Governor Hunt's secretary, his hands fluttering, his voice high-pitched and remonstrating.

"Really, sir, you need to wait—"

Aristide couldn't breathe. He half-rose and stared at the approaching group, unable to speak.

He sensed rather than saw Russell and the governor glancing up, wondering what the interruption was.

"Governor, I'm sorry, but this man

insisted—" The secretary was out of breath. Beads of sweat shone at his temples.

Felix Duchamp, ever the confident dandy in an orange sack coat and wide-legged trousers, stepped out in front. He made a sweeping bow toward Henry Hunt.

"French correspondent Felix Duchamp at your service, sir. And this is Mademoiselle Belle Gaston."

He paused dramatically, puffing lightly from the exertion of walking through the garden.

"She has a very interesting story to tell. One I'm sure you will find most enlightening."

Twenty-three

Henry Hunt frowned, and straightened up with a formality that came naturally to a politician who'd been a practicing lawyer.

"I am aware of your work, Duchamp. However, why you'd think it appropriate to interrupt a private meeting I can't fathom."

He sniffed with irritation. "Haven't you heard of making an appointment?"

Before he could continue Duchamp jumped in.

"I can explain everything, Your Honor."

Hunt's frown deepened. "I'm the California governor, man. Not a

Supreme Court judge."

"My apologies, Governor. A little cultural misunderstanding, *n'est-ce pas*."

He turned to the secretary. "Can you find a chair for the mademoiselle?"

Hunt irritably waved his consent.

The scene unfolded before Aristide's eyes like a dream. He could not believe what he was seeing.

Belle Gaston. Never in his wildest imaginings had he expected to ever see her again. Not this side of the Great Divide, anyway.

His social mortification was complete. His throat closed up. He had difficulty swallowing. He couldn't take his eyes off the face he'd known so well.

The dew had dried on the rose, no doubt about that. She was still attractive, but her fair Norman skin was tired, with traces of fine wrinkles around her eyes and mouth.

She was simpering to Duchamp, while he'd always treasured her fresh, natural manner.

But she was nearly a decade older than she'd been the last time he saw her, and she'd suffered dreadful loss.

He caught a glint of steely hatred in the periwinkle eyes. It was gone in a flash, but he hadn't mistaken it. The pale blue of her floaty chiffon dress drained color from her already washed-out complexion. A woman past full bloom who still saw herself as an ingénue.

She offered her hand to him in a languid gesture. "Mr. Aristide Laurent. Still playing the gentleman vintner, I see." She left a significant pause, hinting at some underlying contradiction. Was she casting doubt on him as a gentleman? Or a vintner?

Her English was charmingly hesitant and accented but fluent, indicating time spent in an English-speaking country. He wondered how long she'd been in California—if that was where she'd been—and he'd not known of it.

After a moment's hesitation he accepted her hand and brought it to his mouth, barely brushing his lips across the papery skin.

His stomach heaved, but the return of the secretary saved him from having to garble any response. Two workmen with him carried extra chairs.

As soon as they sat Felix Duchamp took over. "I owe you a full explanation, Monsieur Governor, and I am confident you will find it most instructive." His lips curled in a smug crescent.

"Miss Gaston presented herself to my office following the story I wrote about the tragic death of Bully Pike. She was curious about my mention of our compatriot here, Mr. Laurent, because she'd known him in their home village. A very interesting story about him she had to tell, too."

Duchamp gauged their receptiveness. The smugness faded, but he plunged on.

"Yes indeed. A tale of an innocent miss, in the bosom of a loving family, courted by her one and only beloved. And then the fires of Hell burned it all up in one afternoon. Her father and only brother dead in the space of a few hours. Her mother dying of grief soon after."

Her mother too?

The nausea returned, and he fought

to keep his expression calm and somber.

My father will face a reckoning, for sure. But it's not my sin.

Duchamp continued, relentless. "This lovely lady, Belle Gaston, deserted by all she loved in death and in life, because her beloved had been the very devil who had wreaked this destruction."

As Duchamp related his dramatic tale, Belle drew a lace-edged handkerchief from a reticule on her wrist and delicately dabbed the corner of her right eye, adding soft gasps at critical points in the story.

When Duchamp finished there was a long, awkward silence. Aristide's shoulders bowed with a guilt not his own, but still he could not bring himself to speak. It would not be right for him to do so. He'd never been more certain of anything. The wronged deserved to be heard, even if he was not the one who had committed the transgression.

Finally the governor spoke. "Mr. Duchamp, you relate a very sad state of affairs, but one of which—in the main telling—we are already aware."

He glanced at Belle and his face softened to fatherly concern. "Mademoiselle Gaston, I offer my sincerest condolences."

The silence lengthened. A gentle soughing breeze lifted the branches overhead. The soothing cooing of the pigeons that strutted the lawns carried on the air, as if nature grieved with Belle.

The governor's voice broke the spell. "I'm sure you're aware, along with your countryman, of the sentiment expressed by one of your great dramatists: *Plus l'offenseur m'est cher, plus je ressens l'injure.*"

Belle's eyes flickered with confusion, and then her lips set in a tight line.

"In English we would say with Racine, 'The more dearly I hold the offender, the more strongly I feel the insult.'"

Her back straightened into a defiant rod.

Henry Hunt continued in a quiet, calm bass, "Life has asked you to bear the unbearable, my dear, and I am sorry for that. But I am satisfied from all the accounts I have heard of this terrible business that Mr. Laurent is also an innocent party, just like you. You must be aware that his father is the guilty one. And in a Protestant country like the United States, 'The son shall not bear the iniquity of the father.'"

Duchamp leaned his head toward Belle and repeated Hunt's remarks in a subdued voice. *"'Le fils ne portera pas l'iniquité de son père.' Comprenez-vous?"*

For moments Belle sat, rigid and unyielding, the stiffening line of her body the only sign she'd heard the governor or Duchamp. Then her hand darted to the reticule on her lap at the same moment as she leapt to her feet. The blue eyes held a wild light not of this world.

"Ah, monsieur, I understand now."

Her hand dug deep in the reticule. Her face had a fierce, implacable cast. *"Mieux vaut amie en voie que denier en courroie.* A friend at court is better than money. *N'est-ce pas?"*

She whipped a small handgun—the sort they called a pocket pistol—from her bag and pointed it at the governor. "How much has he paid you?" She tipped her head in Sir John's direction. "Because they have bought you. Obviously."

In her fury the lilting accent had disappeared, replaced with pure venom.

Duchamp jumped to his feet in protest. He put out his hand as if to disarm her. "Mademoiselle, no, this is not what we agreed."

She backed away from him, her voice hard and sneering. "What we agreed . . ."

She spat on the ground, but her hand did not waver on the gun.

"I know it was not Aristide who killed my family. But someone has to pay. His father, coward that he was, escaped too easily. He died in his bed. Still, *someone* has to pay!"

Her eyes flickered to Aristide, though she wasn't really seeing him. She was captured by her past.

She steeled herself. "And he should not have left me. He is a coward like his father. His actions prove it. He deserves to die. But before he does, it's time for all the lackeys who've protected him to face up to judgement. Starting with you."

Again she leveled the gun at Henry Hunt.

At last Aristide found his voice. He spoke out now, sure of what he had to do, his words soft and slow, digging up memories of how things used to be.

"No, no, my little dove, *ma petite colombe*, don't do that. You don't want to harm the governor. Take me. I'm the one you want."

Echoes of the teasing games they'd

played when they were no more than children seemed to register through her madness.

Aristide raised his hands in surrender. "I will go with you, *ma belle*. Take me to the sheriff."

He glanced to her gun hand and saw that the ruffles of her sleeves mostly concealed the barrel.

She stepped close and pushed the gun into his ribs while encircling his waist with the other arm.

"*Allons-y*," she said. "I've been waiting for this moment a long time."

Twenty-four

They stumbled down sunny N Street, heading for the waterfront where the police building was located, like a love-drunk couple who'd celebrated too enthusiastically. But the iron circle of the barrel in Aristide's ribs was a persistent reminder that this was not a journey of love but of desperation and madness.

Two thoughts penetrated his raddled mind and kept him focused.

The first was a prayer sent to heaven that none of the companions he'd left behind would attempt an ill-advised rescue. He had no wish to die in a hail of bullets, nor did he want to see the damaged butterfly at his side crushed on the sidewalk. Because that was what she was, insane with years of unrequited grief.

The second was that if there was one thing he wished to do for the young woman he'd once loved, it was preserve her life.

As they walked, he talked, a flow of reminiscences and stories to distract her from pulling the trigger before they got to their destination.

They were on the Capitol Walkway, where N Street and L Street on the other side ringed Capitol Square. And as could be expected for such a salubrious address, merchant mansions that would not be out of place in New York or Philadelphia faced onto the thoroughfare. Aristide had been in the Golden State long enough to know some of the stories, and the rest he made up.

He told himself he was out on a summer's day walk with an old friend. He tried to ignore the iron in his side. Anyway, he thought, maybe Belle was right. She'd had poor compensation for her collapsed world. Maybe someone did need to pay. Maybe he had been a coward to run. A coward like his father.

He'd linked his arm lightly around the back of her waist to keep her from falling and fumbling the trigger. He tried to slow the cadence of their steps for the same reason, saying to her as he did, "I understand, Belle. We asked you to do something that was too hard."

His steps dragged, slowing them down further. "But you're wrong about one thing. I'm not like my father. I never wanted to be like my father. Never."

She halted her steps and gazed up at him.

"I'm not a brave man, I don't pretend to be. But neither am I a coward."

She gave a brief hiccup, as if returning from a far-off place, then resumed her walking as if he hadn't spoken.

Near the corner of N and 8th Streets he pressured her to slow down again. "Now this one you *must* take a look at. The mansion of Leland Stanford, one of the Big Four, the quartet of men who made California."

He'd assumed the playful patter of the fairground barker, and a tiny smile lit her lips. They paused and gazed at the massive brick-and-plaster mansion set in park-like grounds. The driveway was wide enough for half a dozen carriages.

"Inside they've got gilded mirrors and carved ceilings," said Aristide. "But that didn't stop it from flooding something awful a few years back. Mr. Stanford had to attend his 1861 inauguration as governor in a rowboat."

Belle's eyes widened in surprise and for a second she was the girl he'd once known.

"*Mais oui*. He had to climb out a window and get in a boat."

She stared for a few more seconds, confusion chasing across her face. Then the shutters slammed down.

"*Marche*," she ordered. "We've not here for stories."

A grocery store, a tobacconist's, a telegraph office and then a bakery replaced the fine houses as they got closer to the waterfront.

Belle's breathing was rasping in her

throat. The longer they walked, the stronger her list to one side became.

"We don't have to go so fast," he said. "If it's too far."

"It's not too far." Her mouth creased into a scowl, as if she'd discovered dog waste on her shoes.

She loosened her grip on him and pushed the barrel into his ribs with a vicious poke. "I told you, I've been waiting a long time for this."

Her pupils had shrunk to tiny indigo dots, swimming in a white sea. Pedestrians flowed past in a constant stream, blind to the drama playing out right here outside the New York Bakery.

Aristide thought this was the day he most likely would die. He could smell the warm, yeasty promise of the bread rolls. He could see Chelsea buns in the window, smell their cinnamon and mixed spice, rounded seashell whorls lined up in trays for the next hungry customer. Not him.

He took a breath, was searching for the right words, something to distract her from her deadly intent, when her body stiffened against his. He grabbed her wrist and jolted the arm holding the gun skywards at the same moment as he heard a deep voice from behind them.

"Stop! Police! Don't move!"

Belle reacted as if she'd been shot, twisting for the trigger. The bullet roared skywards.

"Stop it, Belle! Stop it!" Aristide hissed. "You'll get us both killed."

He fought to keep hold of her, but she wrenched sideways from him and broke free, turning with blazing eyes. "Do you think I care?"

She swung at him and he pitched forward to avoid the line of fire. As he hit the ground a searing shoulder pain overwhelmed him, whether from a bullet or the hard pavement he couldn't tell.

Then a third sharp blast reverberated, and the breath was crushed out of him by a body falling on top of him, hot and smothering.

He got a mouthful of hair and tasted blood.

He struggled to free himself, but he was too feeble to rise.

"Take it easy, sir. Take it easy."

Until that moment he hadn't realized he'd shut his eyes. He opened them at the touch of a hand at his throat, pressing against his jugular. Checking for his pulse. A rough hand, at the end of a uniformed arm.

The policeman stood and hauled the smothering weight from his chest. And then came the words he'd never wanted to hear.

"I'm sorry, sir, but the lady's dead. She's taken her own life."

Twenty-five

Delighted laughter came pealing down the hallway as Aristide stepped into Pike Consulting's reception area. Sarah's desk was unoccupied, but someone was here, and having a jolly time, by the sound of it. A wave of deep fatigue washed over him. Would he ever laugh like that again? Like he didn't have a care in the world?

Every breath in his bruised ribs reminded him of Belle's barrel. His left arm hung in a tidy sling, the shoulder hit by Belle's bullet cleaned and bandaged and pronounced a mere flesh wound. But the desperate lethargy in his soul when he saw the bloody mess she'd made of her once-beautiful face? He didn't think any medicine could fix that.

He banged the bell on the counter with his right hand and waited.

Will's head peered around the doorframe down the open hall. "Oh, Laurent. I wasn't sure we'd be seeing you again."

He stepped back and Leilani Manolo appeared.

So that was the cause of all the happy mirth. Enjoying business a little too much?

The sour jolt that shot through the low growl of his listlessness, his soreness, brought him up short.

Mon Dieu, man, what's wrong with you? You're a grumpy old man before you're thirty.

The Hawaiian sugar merchant was

magnifique, he had to admit. She wore a prettily patterned blue paisley walking dress, its deep neckline filled with a finely pleated cream under-blouse with a high collar.

A dimple he hadn't noticed before showed as she smiled. "Good afternoon, Mr. Laurent." She faltered as she took in his battered condition. "Whatever have you been doing? You're all banged up!"

He tried to deflect her with an offhand smile. "Another very long story, I'm afraid, Miss Manolo. For another time, perhaps?"

Will Davenport's cool demeanor told him he had already heard of Monday's disaster.

Leilani accepted the brush-off without any check to her serene good humor. "I'll leave you to your business then,

Will. Thank you for your help. Either Kaleo or I will be in touch."

She turned, and in one fluid movement disappeared.

There was a pregnant pause. Neither man spoke. The light frangipani fragrance that seemed to follow Leilani everywhere evaporated.

"I wanted to make sure you were still on board with us." Aristide hesitated. "Well, I hope you are with us. Things were left a little unclear when we last spoke." His words trailed off, and still Will Davenport did not speak. He was searching Aristide's face with those cool gray eyes again, seeing into his soul.

This must be what it is like to be in God's searchlight.

An ancient schoolboy memory came back, from his days of Brother Francis and the convent school.

"Sharper than any double-edged sword, it penetrates even to dividing soul and spirit, joints and marrow; it judges the thoughts and attitudes of the heart."

That's what it felt like when Will Davenport looked into you.

The agent relented on the wordless inquisition as sharply as he'd begun, signaling the change with a gesture toward his office. "Come and sit down. You look like a man who needs somewhere to perch."

He stepped aside to give Aristide space to precede him.

"And you're quite right. I have heard a garbled version of yesterday's events. But I'd very much prefer to hear your version."

Twenty-six

"I cannot believe what you've told me. Oh Aristide, I am so sorry."

His heart flipped at her use of the familiar, and he chided himself again for not being able to control his response to her.

They were sitting in an open-air café near the Occidental, as the tide of passersby turned subtly from businesspeople to a fashion parade. From mid-afternoon through to evening San Francisco's fairest liked to strut their stuff, showing off the latest in dresses. The new short-length walking gowns which allowed a glimpse of ankle were prominently displayed, but amid the promenade Leilani Manolo's fresh simplicity in blue paisley shone like the morning star.

"I mean, Mr. Laurent." Her hand went to her mouth, and she smiled from behind slender fingers, as if amused by her gaffe.

"Ooh la! *Excusez-moi, monsieur.*" Her chin lifted in a playful tilt.

Mon Dieu! Was she flirting with him? After what he'd told her?

"Please. Call me Aristide. And I'm surprised you want to finish your coffee with me after that ghastly story."

He gave her a rueful smile. "I'm afraid there is nothing I can say in my own defense. It was horribly upsetting."

He'd found her loitering awkwardly outside Will Davenport's office, waiting—as he soon discovered—for a boy to deliver a parcel.

The street urchin, who couldn't have been any older than eight or nine, had arrived at much the same moment as he did. Leilani Manolo's eyes were bright and dancing as the skinny, grimy-fingered lad skidded to a halt, making breathless apologies for being late.

"Ma had a customer who took too long." He thrust a brown paper parcel up at her. "But here's your dress."

Leilani bent down and picked up two City of Paris carry bags.

"And here's something for your mama," she said. "I hope they're not too heavy for you to carry, Teddy."

The boy hopped from one foot to the other in a frenzy of anticipation. "Oh, Miss Lani. Ma says thank you. Thank you so much. And course I can carry them."

He tipped his cap and picked up the bags with a grunt.

"I'll be going then. Oh."

He dropped the bags, and hopped from one foot to the other, as if he'd forgotten something important. "Ma says if the dress needs any alteration, get in touch."

He picked up the bags and in a whirl of dust he was gone, leaving the smell of a healthy small boy—a mix of horse and dog and yeasty bread—in his wake.

Aristide had hung back, watching the encounter from a few paces away, but as Leilani hugged her parcel to her chest and prepared to walk on, he stepped in.

"Nice afternoon for a walk?"

She whirled at the sound of his voice. "Oh, Mr. Laurent." She gave her light, musical laugh. "Yes. Catching up with one of my friends."

One of her friends. The bone-weariness that had been there since yesterday lightened even as he smiled down at her.

"How about a coffee before I take you home? I owe you an explanation."

Now her hand hovered uncertainly on the tablecloth, her dark eyes somber.

"Utterly awful. I can hardly guess how much so."

Her lips framed an uncertain pout. "Can I ask you, did you love her very much?"

She spoke quietly, almost wistfully, but he was stunned at her boldness.

"Well, Lani, there was a time when I was young and foolish when I thought I did love her. Yes. When I thought I was heartbroken to be forced to leave her in the way I was, by my traitorous father.

But I've realized in the years since that it was a first love. Not all first loves are destined for permanence. And my life has taken such a drastic turn since then . . ."

He sighed deeply, searching his heart to be as honest as he could be. "When I saw her yesterday I understood my nostalgia was for a time before my father betrayed me so absolutely, not for any one person. Belle had become someone I did not know or understand."

Lani nodded, as if satisfied. She took a sip of coffee, as if to signal a change in the subject. "And you're happy now with your dealings with Will Davenport?"

"I am. Very happy. Last time I saw him I wasn't sure if he was willing to be our agent, especially with Hector de Vile breathing down his neck. But today? He seems to have made up his mind to be his own man. I didn't mention de Vile, and neither did he, so I presume he's sorted something out."

"Funny you should say that. The same thing has happened with our sugar business."

She frowned. "That awful night that Bully died, that disagreement we had . . . I swear Bully was frightened of something that night. Something to do with taking my sugar. I know it sounds weird. But I'm certain he was under pressure not to handle it. And now Will has no problem with it."

She shrugged. "I don't know what's going on, but he's said he'll be our agent, so I'm not asking any more questions." She changed tack again. "Speaking of Bully, have you heard anything more about the investigation?"

"Not a thing."

She hesitated. "I hope your latest round with that French journalist has silenced him forever."

Aristide's chest lurched. "He hasn't been back?"

"No, thankfully. I hope he never does."

"I think you're safe. The governor read him the Riot Act. Told him he was the one responsible for Belle's death. That his misleading reports had done irreparable damage to several lives. And that he will make sure the *Alta* editor knows all about it."

He set down his cup with a final clink. "You'll be seeing an account setting the record straight in the *Alta* any day now. That's one thing I can be grateful for out of this mess. We have an ally in Governor Hunt. He credits me with saving his life."

He shrugged. "Honestly, I'm no hero,
but I couldn't have done anything else.
I wish it had worked out differently.
Maybe at last we're making some
progress. At last."

Twenty-seven

"How did you know when it's the right man to marry, Misty?"

Ever since her encounter with Aristide Laurent this afternoon, Lani's head had whirled with the craziest notions. She didn't understand it.

Leilani Manolo, the girl who was so used to being one of the boys that her head had never been turned by any one of them, and now she couldn't stop thinking about a man.

And such an unsuitable one. A romancer who'd already accounted for two women in the very short time she'd known him. One of whom had killed herself, and the other he'd apparently dumped on his way to Will Davenport's door. They were only talking because Vino d'Oro had chosen someone other than Meadows to represent them.

She was sorry about the French woman who'd killed herself, but she was a tad ashamed at the hot triumph she hugged to herself over Candy. What a nasty tongue that woman had. What was it they used to say at the mission school? *Out of the overflow of the heart the mouth speaks.*

Yeah. She bet Candy had a really black heart.

Misty's fork was poised in front of her mouth, one eyebrow raised in her characteristic ironic query. "Marry, Leilani?" She put a mocking emphasis on the word *marry*.

"Good gracious, girl, you've only been in San Francisco a week. Don't tell me you're pining for some swain back in Honolulu already?"

Lani's cheeks were burning. "Of course not, Misty. I was just wondering. How did you know Cyrus was the right one for you?"

"Well, it wasn't because he made my heart go pitter-patter."

Misty's voice had a sharpness Lani hadn't noticed before.

Then her expression softened. "Oh Lani, what can I say? There is such a big difference between love and marriage. You'll discover that when you're older. I wouldn't worry your head about it now."

"How? How is there a difference? Tell me. I want to know."

Misty raised her glass of pineapple juice and hesitated. "What has brought on these questions, Lani? It's so unlike you. You haven't had your head turned by some fellow, have you? You know I don't like you going out without having someone with you. You haven't been accosted, have you?"

"Accosted?" Lani laughed merrily. Was having a coffee with Aristide Laurent being accosted?

"That fellow who saw you home today, that Mr. Laurent. You haven't got any silly ideas about him, have you?"

Lani felt so hot she was sure Misty would sense her discomfort.

"Of course not. As I told you, we happened to be at Bully's office at the same time and he offered to see me home. Nothing more to it than that."

"That's good, then," Misty said darkly, seeming suddenly in a grumpy mood. "Because he's most certainly not the marrying kind. Believe me. I know men. And a young heiress like you shouldn't be going anywhere near a man like him."

"A young heiress?" Lani was confused.

"You've got a heritage to protect. It's time you came to understand that. The time for frolicking in the surf with the boys is over. And Aristide Laurent is a frolic in the surf. Nothing more. Not a keeper like Cyrus."

A frolic in the surf. Not a keeper like Cyrus.

Long after they'd finished their supper and retired for the night, Lani lay in the dark turning over the day's conversations. First with Aristide, then with Misty.

Misty was right. Deep down, she knew that. Aristide was a charmer, and maybe nothing more. Consider his record in the last week. She'd be wise to get out of the surf as fast as they did at home when they spotted a black shadow in the foam.

So why did she want to stay in the water and risk the next ride?

And what did Misty know anyway? If Mamie's report was correct, she had maybe risked everything on a wild impulse.

And was Cyrus really the keeper Misty thought he was? As a foggy gray sleep finally rolled in, Lani's last thought was that Misty hadn't answered her question. *How do you know who is the right man to marry?*

Twenty-eight

It had been Sir John's idea to call together as many of San Francisco's newspapermen as he could and mount a publicity offensive to convert readers to their cause.

The circle of correspondents gathered around the octagonal picnic table near the top of Pavilion Hill in Woodward Gardens showed that Aristide Laurent's notoriety, coupled with d'Oro's challenge to the wine establishment, was a hot story, particularly with the prestigious Golden Gate competition looming.

Sir John's hasty invitations to come and hear what he had to say had drawn an impressive response. There was the beefy wine columnist from the *Chronicle*, his red cheeks advertising excessive consumption of the sponsor's product. The *Chronicle* was one of the leading papers in Newspaper Row, the newsprint cluster at the intersection of Market and Kearney Streets, where three of the city's top rags had their offices.

Another of the Big Three, the *Morning Call*, was represented by the tall, skinny Chamber of Commerce reporter, complete with monocle and thin, wispy beard. Completing the trifecta, the aging deputy editor from the *Examiner* had scrambled to the heights, grumbling about the climb as he arrived.

Along with representatives from the *Evening Bulletin* and the *Evening Post*, they listened with keen attention to

Aristide's account of the tragedy in Sacramento.

"The governor says you saved his life," said the man from the *Examiner.* "How do you react to that?"

"I did what I hope any civic-minded citizen would do," said Aristide in a measured tone. "I regret that it resulted in a young woman's death."

"Will you be going to her funeral?" This from the anti-Lincoln, pro-slavery *Examiner* man.

"Sir John has contributed generously to the expenses but no one from Vino d'Oro will be attending. Mademoiselle Gaston had no connection with our enterprise and our attendance would be highly inappropriate."

It helped enormously that Governor Hunt had already gone on the record saying that as a member of the board running the Golden Gate Wine Symposium on behalf of the San Francisco Chamber of Commerce, he opposed making entry to the wine competition dependent on membership of the Buena Vista Cooperative. He voted against the move, and as he had the deciding vote, it was defeated.

Aristide was not passing up on his opportunity of a platform to expound his wider concerns.

"Gentlemen, I want to make it clear this has much wider implications than a historic wrong and a young woman on the verge of insanity running amok. There are serious repercussions for the wine industry beyond the personal tragedy.

"What's happening in our new industry here in California has been happening in France for nearly a century, and it's proving detrimental for wine."

He went on to explain how wines from regions of high repute, like Burgundy and Bordeaux, were identified as much by the agent as by the producer. The practice had started in Burgundy of wines carrying the négociant's name being blended by the agent from juice from different growers.

In Bordeaux, producers would sell to more than one agent, and each merchant would manipulate the wine according to the preferences of his clients, sometimes mixed with juice or wine from Spain or the Rhône.

"Much of the wine in Bordeaux is the work of agents, rather than winemakers," Aristide explained. "If we want to establish a name for California wines internationally, we need to allow our winemakers to be the ones to direct the process, to get a consistent product year on year. Anything else is not in the interests of anyone except the agents. It's not good for discerning wine drinkers, or for winemakers."

"But enough talk. Allow us to open some wine and offer you a sample of our Zinfandel. See for yourselves what you think."

As if on cue waitresses from the Gardens' restaurant on a nearby terrace appeared with trays of glasses and bottles of wine. The newspapermen settled back into satisfied sipping, making quiet observations between themselves: "Hint of oak there . . . Touch of blush coming through . . . Good finish," until a derisive howl shattered the peaceful contentment.

"You're sure it's safe to drink that

rotgut? You're not worried about getting poisoned?"

Ramsden Meadows loomed over the gathering, gimlet eyes glaring, jaw set in a hard line.

"He's already killed the equivalent of a bowling team. I wouldn't give him a second chance."

The tipple forgotten, the newspapermen picked up their pens.

"Do you know something we don't, Meadows?" called one.

"The governor's satisfied there's been no foul play on Laurent's part," said another. "Do you disagree?"

Within minutes, the good press offensive was in ruins.

"Go get Ned. Hurry! Go now!" Aristide pointed to the restaurant doorway, where a bouncer with a boxer's build stood, feet spaced, hands clasped behind his back, on the watch for any discord.

The waitress dashed across and tugged at the man's sleeve. "Sir, you're needed here."

"Escort this man off the premises, please, Ned," Aristide said. "He's disturbing our meeting."

As if playing with a toy soldier, Ned clamped massive hands onto Ramsden Meadows and held his arms firmly behind his back. "Come with me, sir. You're interrupting a private party."

"You haven't heard the last of me, Laurent," Meadows snarled. "Not by a long shot!"

He scowled at the gathered party. "Men like Aristide Laurent don't belong in the wine industry. And I intend to make it my mission to keep him out."

Twenty-nine

"What do you mean the governor won't do it? You were supposed to have this all sorted. No hitches."

Senator Hector de Vile paced the length of his Russ Hotel suite and swung back to glare at Ramsden Meadows. "This is getting out of hand. The man has got to be stopped."

De Vile resumed his armchair in the sumptuous sitting room.

"When he began this caper he was nothing more than a gadfly. An inconvenient nuisance. Now he's becoming a rallying point for a full-scale winemaker revolt, with his stories of how the setup in France only benefits the negociants and warning them we don't want the same arrangements here. Thanks to your bumbling, it's got completely out of hand."

Ramsden Meadows' Adam's apple bobbed in his throat, as if the man was containing his response, before launching into a hot stream of invective.

"On the contrary, Senator. I followed your instructions down to the last detail."

Ramsden's forehead was shining, his breath rasping between sentences, as if he'd climbed back up Pavilion Hill.

"*Stir up Duchamp.* That's what you said. Well, I did stir him up. I threatened and cajoled to make him see the benefits of coming in on our side.

"*Pay him to cause trouble*, you said. I did that too, with money from *your* pocket." He paused, as if hinting some extra significance adhered to that fact.

The blood in de Vile's veins turned sluggish. Was the man threatening him? Suggesting his part in this could still be exposed?

But Meadows wasn't finished. As he gained momentum his voice took on a mocking note.

"*Malign the vintner to his boss*, you said. *Tittle-tattle about the doctored wine deaths*. Well, I did that too."

He raked his silvery mane with one hand, as if searching for more points to make.

"Why, I even hinted to Russell that Aristide was planning to marry Candy and defect back to Meadows' Estate. As if that will happen now. Never in a million years. I've wrecked my daughter's chances there—and all to satisfy you. I should have known better."

De Vile decided he'd heard enough.

"I don't care about your daughter's love life, Ramsden. I'm sure there're swains a-plenty lined up in that particular queue.

"What I'm concerned about is the way this has escalated from a simple case of smearing one individual's reputation to a debate about the whole industry. If we're not careful, a lot of the vintners we've persuaded to join the Co-op will start backing out. And we can't have that."

He turned frosty eyes on Ramsden Meadows, who was staring into a brandy glass he nursed in both hands. He didn't appear to have heard what de Vile had said.

"I knew he'd never join us. Nor marry Candy either, once he'd tasted that doctored wine."

His eyes went to de Vile's stony face. He still wasn't picking up the cue that the senator was furious.

"That was all your idea too. To serve him the blended wine. He's too smart not to have noticed, but also too smart to let on he'd noticed."

"Shut up, Meadows. You're getting maudlin. I want to know what you intend to do about it."

"Do? There's nothing we can do. The governor has ensured he can enter his wines in the competition. We have to hope he doesn't win, that's all."

"Leave it to 'hope'? Meadows, you disappoint me. I don't believe in 'hope.' I only believe in the certainty of power.

"And we can't have Aristide Laurent and Vino d'Oro winning the Golden Gate. He'll make us a laughingstock. The man who's publicly stood up to us winning the state's premier wine competition? Getting his wines featured in the top restaurants from Washington to Paris? It would confirm everything he's been saying. That winemakers make better wine in their cellars than agents do blending in their basements. That he can do better alone than everyone else can in a cooperative.

"No, Meadows, it won't do. Do you understand me? We've got to ensure Aristide Laurent doesn't win that contest. Buy those judges. Poison the devils if we have to. I don't care how you do it. But there's no 'hoping' about it. That French bigmouth can't be allowed to win."

He outlined a new set of instructions to Meadows, who appeared to accept them without protest. And then, cane swinging to a sudden jauntiness in his step, he went to make a private call on someone who could guarantee that Meadows would never be in the position to betray him. Or even hint at it. Ever again.

Thirty

"Ramsden Meadows will deliver some of the d'Oro vintage to you for the Golden Gate in the next day or two. I'd be grateful if you follow his instructions on what is to be done with it. Do you understand?"

Young Will Davenport didn't wither under de Vile's imperious stare. Indeed, the senator discerned that the steely gray of his eyes was matched by steel in his backbone, as he absorbed his gaze head on, eye to eye, unflinching. Davenport could certainly teach his only son and heir Alex a thing or two about maintaining a poker face during important negotiations.

Davenport clasped his hands on the desk in front of him, as if contemplating de Vile's statement.

"I quite understand the instructions, Senator. I'd have to be stupid not to."

He moved his hands to the edge of the desk and tipped back on the back legs of the chair, as if the talk made him restless. His eyes did not leave de Vile's face.

"However, I am mystified as to the purpose of this shipment. And indeed, why Meadows is involved at all. I understood there'd been a rupture there. A very recent one, I concede. But I had the impression it was a break not likely to be soon mended."

De Vile had begun to unwrap a cigar as the younger man was talking. "Want one?"

"Don't touch the foul things."

De Vile made an elaborate show of lighting the stogie and sending a blue puff to the ceiling at his first exhale.

He made a wide smoky arc with his arm. "As to the situation with the Frenchman . . ." He gave the boy a tight smile. "Shows your intelligence is not as good as mine is, doesn't it?" He glanced down and flicked cigar ash into a wastepaper bin under the desk.

"I guess he couldn't resist Miss Candy's charms. A prodigal roué like him? It's a quick route to wealth, isn't it? Stands to reason."

"What does? You've lost me." Davenport's face was cool, impenetrable.

"Well, he's not inheriting anything at d'Oro, even if he stays until he's ninety."

De Vile got the strange impression

that the remark hit a sore point with the agent, who moved awkwardly in his chair, like a man who'd noticed he was sitting on a tack.

"You think he's after an inheritance?"

Davenport's mouth hitched at one corner in a lopsided, flashing grin hard to interpret. Either dry amusement, or irritation. De Vile couldn't say which, it went as quickly as it appeared. Again, he had an uneasy sense there was something else going on here, something pushing at the back of his brain for recognition. Where had he seen a grin like that before?

Will Davenport was peering at him through his wire-rims, awaiting an answer.

De Vile took another pull on his cigar. "He'd be a fool to turn it down. Marrying the Meadows girl, I mean. One day she will inherit everything. There's no one else."

Davenport glanced away with an air of dismissal. "I'd say time will tell on that, Senator. I'm only concerned with what you want me to do for you today."

"Follow Ramsden's instructions and there'll be a very nice bonus in it for you. Quite apart from the new business I'm planning to divert your way."

"Oh? With the tight arrangement you had with Bully I'd have thought Pike Consulting would be getting the cream of your consignments anyway. Is that not so?" He gave a thin smile.

"You're not Bully Pike, Mr. Davenport. I understand that. But I'm keen to build a strong business relationship with you. I'd suggest you'd be cutting off your nose to spite your face in refusing me."

"Now, now," Davenport laughed. Laughed in his face. De Vile bristled. "Who said anything about refusing your advances, Senator? As if we would be so foolish. No, no. We're very happy to cooperate."

The smile he gave him was as tepid as all the others he'd cracked during this meeting.

De Vile was left with an unfamiliar sense of doubt. Was Will Davenport on board, or merely testing the wind?

Which was a damned nuisance. With Meadows fumbling the ball he needed a backup, and he wasn't certain Will Davenport was it, no matter what he said.

Thirty-one

Leilani had never seen Misty anything but self-assured and unflappable. She'd grown up hearing stories of a young Misty maintaining her black-swan serenity while drunken swains threatened to duel for her favors.

The same Misty stood before her in her husband's office sobbing her heart out in great, lung-sucking squalls. Mingled tears and saliva flowed like a burst dam she had no will or ability to control.

It was a quiet Friday afternoon in the May household. Cyrus and Kaleo were out and Misty and Leilani had been enjoying a lazy time together, their first real chance to chill out since Bully's funeral. They'd donned the comfortable flowing Hawaiian home dress, the muumuu, for a cozy stay-at-home day.

Misty was writing letters, and Leilani offered to make them both mamaki tea—a Hawaiian nettle concoction Misty kept in the pantry for old times' sake. It was housekeeper Mrs. Roderiquez's afternoon off, and Lani was in the kitchen preparing the tray when an eerie keening sound shattered the drowsy domestic peace. She'd rushed to Cyrus's den, unsure of what she'd find.

She gaped, for what she saw struck her as far worse than she'd expected.

"Misty May! What's wrong? Are you in pain?"

She had visions of Misty in a hospital bed. Was it heart pain? Or appendicitis? What on earth could come on her so suddenly? She's been serene and happy ten minutes ago.

Then she saw it. Bully's *nei niho palaoa*, dangling from Misty's elegant long fingers. There was no mistaking the historic heirloom. It hung from its woven circlet, the curved whale's tooth hook a rare symbol of the ocean god Kanaloa and Bully's ali'i nobility.

"What . . . What is that?"

Lani gasped like a landed fish, her mouth opening and closing over nonsense. And the tooth hung off Misty's hand. She knew what she was seeing.

"How did it get here?"

Misty shook her head, mute.

The hand holding the treasure trembled.

Lani crossed the room and circled an arm around Misty's back. "Come and sit, Ant-ee." She used the pidgin honorific. "You've had a big shock. Come and rest."

Misty swayed in the middle of the room, resisting Lani's efforts to lead her to the sofa.

"Come on now. You'll collapse if you don't sit down."

Her second appeal aroused Misty from her shock. With Lani's support she tottered to the settee and allowed Lani to guide her into the plush cushions.

"And now I'll go and get the tea. You stay there. I won't be a moment."

She turned to leave the room and the front doorbell chimed.

The hand holding the necklace flew to Misty's mouth, shaking violently.

"It's all right, Ant-ee. It's not Cyrus. He has his own key. I'll get rid of whoever it is."

She went to the front door, her heart pounding, hoping against hope she was correct, and it wasn't Cyrus on the doorstep.

She opened the door gingerly and peered out.

Aristide Laurent stood there looking, if anything, more attractive than he'd appeared yesterday despite his arm still being hoisted to half-mast in a sling.

He had on a loose-fitting, sporty pea-jacket in a tweed with flat, brown, velvet lapels that left plenty of room for his free arm to move—and also highlighted his sparkling eyes.

He made a slight bow when he saw her, the formality of the gesture lightened by the pleased smile that played across his face, which was pinker than usual. He was happy to see her. She could see it in his eyes, in his flushed complexion.

She opened the door wider. "Mr. Laurent, I'm afraid this isn't the best time for a social call. My aunt is indisposed and I am in the middle of getting her tea."

She hovered, the door open but barely wide enough for Laurent to enter. He stepped forward and took hold of the doorframe.

His eyes went instantly to her face. "Is everything all right? You look upset."

"No. No, it isn't all right."

She swung around, checking that Misty was still in the sitting room, unsure of what to do next.

"I'm not planning on staying long, Miss Manolo. I wanted to invite you to an event. An occasion that's very important to me. Can you give me a few minutes to explain? It won't take long and it's urgent."

She dithered for a few more seconds, and then stepped back to allow him entry.

"Come in. But do understand, we've got a personal crisis here. I want you to wait in the kitchen while I take Misty her tea. Then I can join you back here briefly."

When she returned to Cyrus's den the necklace was nowhere to be seen. Misty was settled back into the sofa, her eyes closed, as if asleep.

Lani set the tray down and put out Misty's cup ready to pour. "Misty, where did you find that thing? And what have you done with it?"

The older woman's eyes opened with a dazed glaze as she reached for her cup. "What thing?"

Lani stared in disbelief. "Misty, you know very well what I am talking about. Bully's tooth. Where is it?"

Misty braced her shoulders. "We're not mentioning this again, Leilani Lilolilo. I'm sure Cyrus will have an explanation. And until we hear it, it's best kept between us."

Her lips trembled. Her characteristic smooth fall of hair hung around her face in tangled knots.

Lani spoke gently, as you would to a child. "Misty, we can't keep it a secret. You know we can't."

She heard the thud of the front door shutting. No! Not Cyrus! Not at this most inopportune of all moments.

"Hey ho. Where are you?"

Her uncle's cheerful baritone echoed down the hall. Lani's feet were fixed. She couldn't move or take her eyes from Misty's face. She couldn't mount an intervention.

Cyrus exclaimed in surprise as he came upon Aristide in the kitchen. "Laurent! What are you doing here? And where are the women?"

She heard Aristide's quiet mumble in response and then Cyrus was in the den doorway, his eyes blazing. "What the devil are you doing in here? Haven't I made it clear this is my private den?"

He glared past Lani to Misty, who shrank further into the sofa, frailer and more unsure than Lani had ever seen her.

"Misty, what are you doing in here? I told you to stay out."

He took three big steps across the room and placed his hands under her elbows, lifting her up from the cushions.

She cried out, and stiffened against

his rough handling. "Leave me alone!" She gasped out the words, wrenched herself from his grip. "Take your hands off me."

Leilani sensed Aristide's presence at her back, but she could not take her eyes off the struggle unfolding before her.

She took a small step toward the pair, but Aristide caught her arm and restrained her.

His warm breath sent a shiver through her. "Leave them," he said quietly into her ear. "Don't come between a man and his wife. It's dangerous."

She turned her surprised eyes on him then, for a few seconds drawn into his dark, spellbinding depths.

With effort she turned back to Cyrus and Misty. The room was filled with an ominous silence. The ceiling seemed several inches lower than minutes ago, giving the room a heavy, threatening atmosphere.

Then she saw it. Misty had stuffed the whale's tooth under the folds of her tangerine muumuu.

When Cyrus hauled her to her feet, the emblem lay exposed for all to see on the sofa's rose fabric.

The consul stood transfixed, his face the same red as the sofa velvet.

Then he grabbed Misty by the shoulders and shook her violently. "What have you done, woman? Where did you find that?"

She reared back from him, seeming to belatedly draw upon the icy reserves from deep within.

"Where did I find it?" She spat the words into her husband's face.

"The question we want answered, Cyrus, is why was it hidden in your writing desk?"

Thirty-two

Cyrus dropped his hands from his wife's shoulders. He drew in a rasping, startled breath, and stared at the relic, seemingly insensible to anything but the accusing cream curve of the ancient tooth.

Then the first flickering of a luminous rage brightened his cheeks before suffusing his whole face. Pure molten rage. Aristide tapped Lani on the shoulder with his good hand and mouthed to her: "Don't move."

Then he was across the room to the fireplace, grabbing the brass poker that hung from fire irons on the hearth, wrenching it free. In two big strides he was at Cyrus's back. Cyrus was a good three or four inches taller than his willowy wife, and weighed twice what she did.

He was standing in front of her, clenching and unclenching his fists, staring. Then a rumbling started deep in his throat. He reached for Misty's slim neck and grabbed her around the throat, thumbs pressing on her vulnerable larynx.

"If it wasn't for *you*, you slut . . ." The words died away, the sentence left hanging.

He was holding Misty's neck so tightly that Aristide could see vivid red thumb marks on her porcelain skin.

She'll be dead in the next minute if no one stops him.

Aristide raised the poker high over his head with his good right hand and slammed it down on the flat plane of Cyrus's shoulder with every ounce of one-handed strength he could muster.

The big man howled, and let go. Misty slumped to the floor gasping and dribbling, clutching her neck with both hands.

For a minute Cyrus appeared paralyzed, caught by shock, and then he whirled on Aristide.

"No! No, Cyrus." Lani darted between the two men, waving her hands before Cyrus's face as if waking a sleepwalker. "We've got to help Misty."

She put her hand in the middle of Cyrus's chest. "Cyrus. Misty needs help."

He grabbed the front of Lani's bright flowing muumuu in a tight fist. The bunched fabric of the Hawaiian dress tore as he threw her aside. "Get out of my way! Get out!"

Lani dropped to her knees and crawled to where Misty lay collapsed on the Oriental rug, a wretched human blob.

She caught Aristide's warning and nodded. *Get her out of here.*

She hitched her arms under Misty's armpits and backed out, dragging her toward the kitchen, giving the men a wide berth. The older woman was passive and floppy, a dead weight in Lani's arms. Unconscious, it appeared.

Aristide switched his attention back to Cyrus, and spoke loudly, in a sergeant major's voice of authority. "Mr. May. Consul, sir. You don't want to do this. Sir, please. Get a hold of yourself. Calm down. You don't want to do this."

All while still backing away, wielding

the poker like a fencing foil.

The soft drag of Misty's heels on the parquet floor sounded down the hall and then the click of the front-door latch told him that Lani had got Misty out to the street.

Cyrus seemed aware of it too. He halted his advance across the room. The wildness in his eyes quietened. Rather like a madman coming around after a fit of insanity, Aristide imagined.

He collapsed onto a nearby armchair like a popped balloon, pressing his hands into his eyes.

He was shaking his head from side to side and whispering a short phrase to himself, like a religious chant.

"What have I done? Oh God, Misty, what have I done?"

Thirty-three

"She can't stay here. We'll take her to the Sisters of Mercy."

Aristide waited for Lani to answer. To say something. Anything.

But she was focusing all her attention on her aunt, gently stroking her cheek and making quiet comforting noises. "We're here, Misty. You'll be fine."

She was holding Misty half-upright on a wrought-iron bench in the garden. The older woman sagged against her.

"Do you think she needs to be in hospital?" Lani's voice was anxious, tentative.

The Irish Sisters ran one of the more accessible hospitals in the city—the old

County and City Hospital on the corner
of Stockton and Francisco Streets,
where they'd recently taken full control
and renamed it St. Mary's Hospital,
after running it on behalf of the city for
more than a decade. The order was
respected by all classes for their
compassionate, selfless nursing through
a recent smallpox epidemic, but
protecting vulnerable women was one of
their particular missions.

Aristide pumped his response with a
confidence he didn't feel. "She certainly
needs a doctor to check out if there's
any serious damage. After that? I don't
know. But we can't leave her here. Not
when Cyrus is like he is. Goodness
knows what could happen."

As if in response to his words, Misty
opened her eyes.

"Why . . ." Her eyes were bewildered.

"Why . . ." Her head flopped to one side. She rallied and straightened it. "What happened? Why am I here?"

Lani stroked her consolingly. "You had a disagreement, Aunt. With Cyrus. Don't you remember?"

She rubbed her eyes. "It's a muddle," she said haltingly.

Lani tried to fill in the picture. "Ab-ab-ab-" Her hand went to her throat, as if to calm her stutter. "About B-B-Bully's whale tooth."

Misty gazed at her blankly, the china-white of her eyes blood red in the afternoon light. Then she pulled herself up to a full sitting position, her senses returning.

Mirroring Lani's gesture of a minute before, she brought her hand up to her throat. She winced as she touched flesh. "My voice is scratchy," she wheezed.

"My throat is sore."

Aristide spoke. "Misty, we need to get you to a doctor, maybe a hospital, to get that throat checked out. Cyrus squeezed you hard."

Lani's hand gripped her abdomen, as if the shock of Cyrus's attack had set off stomach pain.

The girl had been so strong throughout this ordeal, Aristide thought. Without her quick action he could never have stopped Cyrus and got Misty out alone, not with his arm in a sling. He thrilled at her resilience, her stoic calm.

"Are you all right, Lani? Is your stomach sore?"

She pulled her hand away, disowning the gesture. "I'm fine. Just fine. Misty is the one who needs attention."

When the gray-headed doctor who'd been called by the neighbors arrived, he was in no doubt. Misty needed at least one night in hospital under observation to ensure she wasn't suffering from complications of strangulation.

"In the worst case there's possible danger of seizure or stroke-like symptoms from having your blood supply cut off even for a short time. I'm confident this won't happen, but I'd rather be safe than sorry. The Sisters will make you very comfortable."

Much later, with Misty in a hospital bed under mild sedation, Lani and Aristide sat one to either side of her, watching her chest lift and fall in a peaceful rhythm.

Lani yawned. "I'm so dog-tired I can't stir myself to get up and go home." She pulled a face. "Quite apart from the fact that I don't want to share a house with Cyrus at present."

Aristide shook his head.

"Not on your life, Lani. We haven't had a chance to talk about it, but we've got to start doing that right now. Does this mean Cyrus killed Bully? Is there any other reasonable explanation for how he came to have the heirloom in his study? Seemingly hidden. Isn't that a statement of guilt, right there?"

She rubbed watery, pink-rimmed eyes. Even with her crème-de-caramel complexion tinged gray with exhaustion, her dark hair mussed and out of place, his heart lifted with a happy zing whenever his eyes rested on her.

"I'm getting you a room at my hotel," he said. "Until we have a better idea of what's going on, it's not safe for you to be there."

She gave him a weak smile. "You

don't have to be responsible for me, Aristide. But I do agree. I can't stay at Misty's. I'm pretty sure the nuns have an annex for this kind of emergency. I'll ask the nurse when she comes by next."

They sat in companionable silence, and then Lani said quietly, "What do you think?"

She stared across bright white sheets. "I mean about Cyrus. Consider this little scenario. He gets rid of the *hei tiki*. Misty backs him up. Says that the last time she saw it, it was around Bully's neck. How would us insisting we'd seen it in their house go down with a sheriff, considering neither of us is considered a model citizen?"

He gave a deep sigh, thinking hard. *She's right, isn't she?*

"Do you think he did it?" Lani

continued. "Killed Bully, I mean. Maybe he discovered about the affair."

Aristide's head jerked up. "Affair? What affair?"

She squeezed her eyes tightly shut, as if wanting the picture before them to go away.

"Oh, that's right. I haven't had a chance to tell you."

She pushed her long locks back off her face, as if clearing the decks for a long story.

He gazed into her intense sad eyes and wanted to lose himself in them.

She seemed to share the tender mood, gazing back with a vulnerability that answered his own.

They sat, suspended in the moment.

He reached across and tucked a lock that had fallen across her cheek behind her ear.

A simple gesture, but he'd rarely sensed one so intimate.

"Go on," he whispered, his heart in his throat, her eyes sparkling back at him.

She traced the movement his hand had taken, securing the lock, and broke eye contact. When she looked back, she was her pragmatic self again, all business.

"Mamie Bilouxie, that seamstress whose common-law husband Sam works at the Occidental—you know her, Teddy's mother—says she's seen Misty out and about with Bully, going off on private drives and other stuff the wife of the Hawaiian consul ordinarily shouldn't be doing. Not without good reason. Of course, she was working for Bully, so maybe she had good reason. But Mamie had an odd feeling about it. She suspected they may have been conducting *une liaison passionnée*. She was worried I might get dragged into it."

Aristide stroked his short dark beard.

"I wonder if, without knowing it, we just did. Get dragged into it, I mean. What did you think?" Lani smoothed the immaculate ironed sheet in front of her.

"A lot to take in," said Aristide. "Even in her forties Misty is a desirable woman. I don't know what to think."

Lani's face was loving as she gazed at the sleeping woman.

"I don't think I realized until tonight that she was your aunt," said Aristide.

Lani shrugged. "My mother's half-sister. Same mother, different father. I think she was very sad when my mother died. Bully and the Mays have been friends since way back—their whole lives. Does that make it more or less likely they'd engage in what we're suggesting?" She pursed her lips.

Aristide found it hard to concentrate on what she was saying when she did that. And so unaware of her own beauty.

"I couldn't ask Misty directly." She grinned and raised an ironic eyebrow. "And when I asked the Countess, she was evasive."

Aristide twitched in his chair, alert to something other than Lani's desirability.

"The Countess? Who in heaven's name is the Countess, and what does she have to do with it?"

Lani explained. When she finished they sat in another contemplative silence.

Eventually Aristide stirred. "So she knew your mother? And de Vile. And the

Mays. Not much room for secrets, is there?"

Lani shrugged again. "Honolulu is a pretty small place, even now. Twenty years ago, even more so. But who knows?"

She tapped the side of her head with her index finger, made a big silent "O" with her lips. "That reminds me. Talking about secrets, it seems like a week since you came to the house this afternoon, but you said you wanted to ask me somewhere. What was that all about?"

So he told her.

About the final night of judging for the Golden Gate award, about his crazy, soul-deep hunger to win and prove once and for all that he was not like his father. And his desire to have her at his side to enjoy the victory.

"Come as my companion. I'd love to have you there, whether I win or not. You are the person I'd like by my side in a storm—as you've proven today—or, even better, to celebrate its passing."

He gave her a wry grin. "I guess, if nothing else, tonight has showed that we make a great team, Mademoiselle Manolo."

Thirty-four

"I owe my life to you, girl, and I'll never be able to thank you enough."

The purple bruising on Misty May's neck was more pronounced today, and Lani suspected it would darken and look much worse in coming days.

Despite this, she giggled, close to light-headed with relief as she sat at Misty's hospital bedside the day after the attack.

"I'm glad you're glad. It would be dreadful to go to such lengths and then find the person didn't want to live."

Misty fiddled with the top bedsheet. Lani leaned over and patted her arm. "You never know. You mightn't have wanted to be saved!"

She attempted a weak laugh but Misty did not join in.

"Oh, sorry. Bad taste, I know. But it wasn't all me. I hate to think where you'd be now if Mr. Laurent hadn't hit Cyrus with that poker. That was a heck of a thump for a one-armed man."

The red flecking in the whites of Misty's eyes—a typical consequence of violence to the throat, the doctor said— was fading, and although Misty was more subdued than usual, she seemed to be recovering well.

"Let's talk about Mr. Laurent for a moment, Leilani. Why was he there? It was my good fortune, I'm not complaining. But I am curious. Why was he calling on our household? Was he on business? Or was he coming a-courting?"

She tilted her chin at a teasing angle and smiled.

Lani knew she was blushing. She was such a novice at this stuff. Here she was, nearly twenty-four, and she'd never had a serious beau. Never bothered too much with her appearance or what man was paying her attention. Her entire focus in life had been their family—disjointed though it was to non-Hawaiian eyes—and the estate she had known for a long time she would take over when Archie went to be with his Maker. She'd been trained for it, and she'd responded by reacting more like a young man than a young woman.

For a fleeting moment she asked herself why Archie had always taken her aside rather than Kaleo when he was discussing family business, but she'd had her answer in seconds.

Because Kaleo is plain bored by it, while you are enthralled.

Archie had seen that by the time they were ten years old.

And that was all fine and good. Except now, when she'd met a man she wanted to think highly of her, she was at a loss on how to impress him

She plumped up the pillow behind Misty's neck. The doctor had given her aunt permission to leave her bed and sit in a chair when she felt ready for it, but he still wanted her supported and coddled at all times. Lani sat down again. Took a deep breath. Decided to use the strategy of distraction rather than answer Misty's questions.

"Misty, what happened yesterday? What do you make of it all? Everything happened so fast, and it was all so confusing. Can you explain it for me?"

Her aunt nursed the coffee cup she was holding in both hands and regarded her with a steady gaze. "I wish I knew, Leilani. I really do."

There were tints of high pink on her iceberg cheekbones. Lani wished she believed her.

She changed tack. "I know I keep coming back to this, but Bully wasn't his usual self either, that last night we were together."

She appealed to Misty with questioning eyes. "Do you know what was wrong? You probably know more about his business than anyone."

Misty shook her head a fraction too quickly. "I was the office manager, Lani. I have no special knowledge."

"Then why do you think Cyrus went crazy? And how did he get Bully's tooth? I can't help thinking there's a connection."

"I don't know. I just know I can't go back there. I'm glad Will's found someone else for the job." She licked her lips. "And you've got to stop talking like that, Leilani. When he gets a chance, Cyrus will explain."

Lani took her aunt's hands in hers and regarded her with warm affection.

"Really, Misty? Then why didn't he do that—explain, I mean—instead of nearly throttling you to death? What kind of explanation are you expecting?"

Misty pulled back, disengaging her hands. "Don't get smart with me, young lady."

Lani was catapulted back to her early teens, when she'd sweated under the restraints Misty had placed on her "for her own good" without giving decent reasons.

She shook her head. "I'm not thirteen any more, Misty." She signaled the end of the discussion by getting up and moving to a side table which bore a tray with a water pitcher and glasses on it.

"Fancy some water?"

At Misty's nod she poured two glasses.

"To answer your earlier question, Mr. Laurent came to the house because he wanted to invite me to the Golden Gate Wine Symposium dinner next Saturday." She gazed back at Misty, a tilt of triumph in the curves of her lips.

"Is that so?" Misty said. "And what else?"

"What do you mean, 'What else?' Isn't that enough?"

"What are you proposing to wear?"

Lani shrugged. "I'm not sure. What *should* I wear?"

"And why is he asking you?"

Lani shrugged again. "How should I know? Because he enjoys my company? Does it have to be any more complicated than that?"

She was aware her face was getting flushed again.

What is it with this thing? Whenever his name comes up I get hot and bothered.

She tried to wind back on her embarrassment. "I don't know anything about men, Misty. You're the expert on that topic. We both know that."

She was annoyed that her voice had taken on a whiny note.

"I need your help with this one."

They stared at one another across the chair's space between them, neither speaking.

Lani broke the silence with a heaving

sigh. "You know how I asked you, a few days ago, how you knew Cyrus was the right one? You never gave me an answer. And I really want to know."

There it is again. The plaintive note.

Misty's face filled with a depth of sadness Lani had last seen at Bully's funeral.

"I never answered, Lani, because I've spent a lot of time pondering exactly that question. And I fear that now, I'll never know the answer."

She licked her lips. A light blue bruise was marbling through the translucent skin at her mouth's corner. "Or I will get an answer I don't want."

The mask she had worn all her life—in Lani's presence, at least—shattered.

And underneath the commanding profile, the teasing, confident eyes, the husk of a once-vibrant woman lay revealed. A woman broken and bewildered at the shore she'd washed up on.

To reach this point in life, and be so unsure of love's worth. . .

They didn't need to talk about it any more.

They both knew something had broken that couldn't be repaired.

Lani lay her head in Misty's lap, and her aunt caressed her shoulders, her arms, her back, soothing, loving, stroking, consoling her as she wept. As if Misty, white-faced and dry-eyed, was not the one whose world had shattered into a thousand pieces.

Thirty-five

"Sir John. Laurent."

The Washington senator raised his hat and bowed.

"Eager to get started, are we?"

Around them the limited number of participants and judges invited to attend the preliminary judging for the Golden Gate Symposium gathered in small knots of nervous chatter while hotel staff went about their business, setting up the judging dais, lining up multiple tasting glasses, smoothing the top table's stiff, starched tablecloth, all under Sam Morley's watchful eye.

Sam was in charge of the functional part of the night, making sure the judges had everything they needed. Governor Hunt, as honorary chair of the Symposium, and a range of state functionaries were responsible for the event's official business.

Hector de Vile waved a sheet of paper in front of John Russell.

"Seen this? Strictly confidential. A run sheet for the night, with names of anyone you'd want to know — judge's credentials, which winemakers made the short list, the whole thing."

If he'd been trying to keep the note of triumph out of his voice, he hadn't succeeded.

Sir John raised an eyebrow, the perfect picture of indifference. He wasn't going to bite.

"Really? A security breach before we've even got started? I do hope that's not an indication of things to come."

De Vile barked in laughter. "Not at all! As senator I am obviously a neutral party to tonight's proceedings. All I want is for the best wine to win, and for California to shine bright."

"Of course." Sir John's response was as crisp as the driest Riesling.

"Now, now, don't be like that. Take a look."

He placed the paper on the table before them. After a moment's hesitation, Sir John picked it up, his eyes gliding down the pages with sharp attention.

He handed it on to Aristide. "Nothing too surprising there, de Vile. Exactly as we would have expected."

De Vile had been standing over them, but now slipped into a chair on the other side of the table.

"And you're still confident you've got

a good chance?" His eyes raked Aristide's face before turning to focus on Sir John.

"We've got as good a chance as the next chap, better than most," Russell replied, his voice still cool, disengaged.

"Want to put some money on it?"

"You should know me by now, de Vile, I only bet on things I can control."

"And you're saying you can't control this? With your oh-so-talented vintner, French-trained? Winemaking's been in the family for generations, hasn't it, Mr. Laurent? Not willing to take a little flutter on it? Give your man a vote of confidence?"

His eyes narrowed threateningly.

"One thousand dollars on it, Russell. One thousand dollars says you can't do it. Won't do it. You won't even make the final for Saturday night, let alone win the whole shooting box. Because your star vintner here is no better at making wine than he is at staying loyal to those who trust him.

"And we all know his track record there. Casualty list growing by the day."

Thirty-six

The gauntlet had been thrown and Russell had no choice but to respond. The slur of Hector de Vile's innuendo was too nasty to ignore.

A thousand dollars on a d'Oro wine at least making the first cut tonight—the preliminary tasting which would form the basis for the final selection for Saturday night.

And a gentleman's handshake on it—no matter who won, the money would be donated to the Alycia Stockton Trust. That was the only way Russell would ever agree to it.

A deep unease gnawed at Aristide's gut. De Vile was too cocky. He knew the man was a professional conman togged up in tails. Nevertheless, even for a robber baron he was too certain of a win.

And so Aristide found himself in the hotel's back rooms, alive with staff moving hither and thither servicing the night's preparations, seeking out Will Davenport.

As a man experienced in receiving and dispatching goods, and with an office on the premises, Davenport had been enlisted by the Golden Gate organizing committee as the reception point for the presentation of the wines and their distribution to the judges.

Aristide had already ensured he had personally supervised the delivery of the d'Oro consignment to Will, accompanied by strict instructions to keep it in a locked safe. But the niggling memory of the doctored wine at the last Meadows dinner, together with de Vile's exaggerated bonhomie, made him anxious.

What if de Vile has sent someone with an alternative shipment of tainted wine? What if Will has been duped, or worse, bribed into accepting it as a replacement?

The arm he'd removed from his sling as a concession to his appearance tonight ached as his eyes searched for Will's slight figure among the black-suited attendants and buzzing backstage staff.

He caught sight of Sam Morley, the genial, broad-shouldered Englishman Leilani referred to as the Big Kahuna. He gathered that was a Hawaiian term for "big boss." He put out his arm to catch Sam's attention and was reminded by the jabbing pain that he still wasn't back to full health.

"Sam!" he called over the low buzz of men at work. "Is Will around? Do you know where he is?"

Sam pulled up and faced him. "Mr. Davenport? Haven't seen him in the last few minutes. Can I help?"

"I was wanting to double-check on our wines." He let his arms drop to his sides. "Can't be too careful."

Surprise, and then a guarded look passed across Sam's bright countenance, like clouds momentarily obscuring the sun.

"Funny you should say that, Mr. Laurent. Mr. Meadows brought some wine out back, wanted Mr. Will. Said it was a late delivery for tonight. I took hold of it and told him I would see it got to the right place."

The space between his bushy dark eyebrows creased into parallel deep lines.

"I took it to Mr. Davenport, but he wanted none of it. Said if it hadn't come direct from you, it wasn't approved merchandise. So I left it out back to dispose of later. Haven't had time to do much else with it."

Even as he spoke a man came up seeking instructions for what to do about the placement of water carafes. Aristide watched, his heart hitched up to an aberrant beat, foot tapping nervously.

"These bottles, Sam. Did they have our labels on them?"

"Oh yes, Mr. Laurent. I can show you."

They proceeded to the kitchens, where four bottles of wine stood on a scullery shelf.

Sam gestured proudly. "Here they are, Mr. Laurent. Just as I said." His brows creased with worry. "Except I could have sworn there were half a dozen of them. There's only four there."

He swung around, as if looking for a wine thief. "I can't blame them. There's an unwritten rule that stuff we leave in the scullery is surplus to requirements. We often distribute it to staff if we've no further use for it."

He bowed in apology. "Sorry, sir. I might be able to track it down after the function is over, but really, I have to get back to work now. Do you want to take these extra bottles back?"

Aristide hesitated. "Maybe one of them, Sam. Just to test if they've been messed with. You can keep the rest. Let the staff have them. We don't mind."

He returned to his seat alongside Sir

John, the extra bottle in his right hand. When he got to the table he asked his merchant boss for his fountain pen, and marked a big cross across the simple label to designate the wine as faulty. He didn't want it getting confused with any of their premium vintage—he was certain it was spoiled.

His unruly heart maintained its galloping pace.

Was he justified in being excited that Sam and Will had blocked an attempt to befoul d'Oro's entry?

Or did his intuition know something his brain had not yet recognized—that de Vile had good cause for his confidence about winning a thousand greenbacks?

Thirty-seven

"There's an old saying, I'm sure you will have heard it, 'If bread be the staff of life, wine is life itself.'"

Governor Henry Hunt left a practiced pause, anticipating his audience, and the gathering seated before him responded with chuckles and muttered Amens.

The crowd was much smaller than it would be on a Saturday night, when tickets at $50 a head had been sold so the audience could also share in a full dinner as well as the wines being tested. But as Sir John Russell gazed around the assembled audience he saw most—if not all—of the shakers and movers of the local wine scene lounging in their black evening jackets at white-clothed tables, drinking in Hunt's paean to the Bacchus of Napa, San Joaquin and Sonoma.

And Sacramento too. I hope Laurent is correct in his notion that we've held off the adulterers. Wine adulterers, that is.

Hunt pursed his lips. "I knew I'd find agreement for that sentiment here tonight, at the preliminary judging of the much-vaunted Golden Gate Symposium Best Wines award.

"It's my role as your Democrat governor to welcome you here tonight and to offer special thanks to the people who have made this august event possible, in particular our Republican Senator Hector de Vile. Never say I'm partisan in my praise. And to our judges who've come from the farthest corners of the world to devote their educated palates to tasting and rating our wines.

"I will be introducing these highly qualified gentlemen—from Paris, New York and our very own native terroir—to you very soon, but I want to first devote some time to acknowledging the singular role the senator has played in ensuring that this very important event takes place."

Russell studied the men lined up on the judges' dais, about to be served California's finest wines from individual glasses with no sign of branding in sight. A true blind tasting.

The judges' identities had been a badly kept secret. Supposedly they were kept quiet to protect them from any attempts to lobby them, although if the blind tasting was run according to the rules there should be no place for pressure being brought to bear.

Russell's eye ran along the dais. The future of Vino d'Oro rested on the subtlety of nose and palate, and the integrity, of these men.

The Broissart brothers, Julliard and Pierre, cellar masters and owners of a celebrated Paris restaurant, Trois Frères Provençaux. Like many of the best restaurateurs, they'd started out as winemakers and expanded the food they offered to complement the wines which were the main part of their business.

The cellar master from New York's legendary fine dining house Delmonico's was there. Delmonico's had converted New Yorkers from British to French cuisine. Russell hoped that might give their wines an edge.

And then there were the locals, men he knew well. Local vintners and organizers, men destined to become wine commissioners someday, if they weren't already. Blowers from Sacramento, Isaac De Turk from Sonoma, George West from San Joaquin. Despite the industry's tarnished reputation, these were all men he trusted.

Unlike de Vile. I know him too well to ever trust him for a semi-second.

Still occupying the lectern, Governor Hunt had the crowd's rapt attention.

"We have with us here tonight the premier winemakers, negociants, wine merchants, restauranteurs and commentators on the national wine scene, and we all agree our industry desperately needs the boost and recognition that an event like this can bring.

"We all know that a good volume of the wine sold in California as 'French' is produced here. We are all aware this is a nationwide problem. And as the senator knows better than any of us, it is an even bigger problem on the East Coast, in the finest restaurants in New York and Washington.

"As one local critic has commented: 'So-called California wine drunk on the Eastern Coast is as a general thing manufactured in a three-story brick vineyard on a back street not far from where it is offered for sale, and in the majority of cases contains everything but grape juice.'

"And we have only ourselves to blame for that. As that same commentator observed: 'The snobbish American habit of demanding overseas wine is the reason for wholesale deception by otherwise reputable California firms. It's small consolation that the fact that the fraud is not detected speaks well for the quality of the wine itself.'"

Hunt paused and smiled across at de Vile, who occupied a seat at the top table.

"Senator de Vile has shown the way in marshalling our local growers and winemakers into a united front under the banner of the Buena Vista Cooperative, and he has played a key role in launching this seminal event to win the acclaim for our locally produced vintage it so richly deserves.

"Some of the finest San Francisco restaurants are guilty of pouring California wine into bottles with French labels—a sign both of the undeservedly inferior reputation of California wine, and also of the reluctance of our nation to consider wine a domestic agricultural product.

"The senator is making a grand effort to change that view. Tonight we select the preliminary winners, to go through to the final contest on Saturday. The Grand Prize winners—the wines which are selected as the finest in their category by our judges here—will be offered places on the wine lists of top eating houses in Paris and out East.

"Senator de Vile is committed not only to recognizing California as a great winemaking state, but also to see her standing at the foremost in the production of fine wines."

The crowd as one rose to their feet and applauded, Sir John Russell and Aristide Laurent reluctantly joining in so as not to attract notice.

As they sat down Russell muttered into Aristide's ear, "Well, that's one side of the story. I sincerely hope we are not about to discover the other side."

Thirty-eight

Aristide knew he would relive this moment for years to come.

The breath-sucking instant when Vino d'Oro was announced as one of the finalists in the Golden Gate Symposium Wine Awards. Selected by the august judges as one of eight wineries whose vintage had been deemed worthy to continue on to the final round in a few days, poised to win the Saturday Gala event.

His heart leapt to his throat. His eyes met Russell's dark glittering orbs, as they both jumped to their feet, clapping and cheering with the rest of the crowd, propelled by a sense of elation he'd never before experienced.

He flashed Russell an exuberant grin. "Your thousand bucks is safe. I wouldn't want that on my conscience."

They cackled with laughter.

Everyone in the banquet room was on their feet, giving a standing ovation to the judges, the winemakers, to de Vile as the architect of the event. For a few moments those present basked in the celebration of their own success.

Then Aristide's eyes were drawn like a magnet seeking iron filings to Hector de Vile's table, where the king of commerce sat like an emperor, flanked by his loyal flunkies, Candy and Ramsden Meadows. He'd observed them as they'd flattered and fawned their way through the evening, their smugness needling him.

But not now. De Vile's face was a

thunderous slate, his eyebrows set in a hard line, while father and daughter were a deathly white, their jaws dropped.

They hadn't expected this. He was so sickeningly confident about his bet because he was sure they'd fixed us.

Aristide's elation was replaced by nausea that gripped his vitals like a vice.

What had they done now? And he did have anything to fear from what might be coming? The answer came much sooner than he'd expected.

Thirty-nine

"Why would they want to kill anyone? It doesn't make sense."

In the futile hope it might help him understand Leilani Manolo's early-dawn news more clearly, Aristide wiped his hand across his eyes for the second time in five minutes.

He'd barely fallen asleep after a night of carousing before he and John Russell were awakened by an urgent banging on their hotel suite.

They scrambled out of bed to find the Manolo twins in the hall, Leilani's face drained of color, a fine fretwork of fatigue lines shadowing her eyes. Her brother Kaleo towered, his indomitable impassive self, at her side.

"Sir John," Lani began, her voice cracking.

Russell motioned her with a calm hand to stop. "Not in the hallway. I take it this isn't a social call."

He shot her a worried frown before waving her into the room. "Sit down and tell us. What disaster now?"

Leilani glanced at the seat he'd gestured her to. "I can't . . . I can't sit, Sir John. I'm too worked up."

She gazed up to him with beseeching eyes, wringing her hands as she did.

"I've . . ." She flicked her eyes briefly to Kaleo, who shadowed her every step. "We've got terrible news. I'm very sorry."

She glanced to Aristide and her face contorted.

"People are getting sick. Maybe will

even die. And your wine is being blamed."

"What?" Sir John gave a loud, angry bark. "What are you talking about?"

Aristide was frozen to the carpeted floor, his body temperature dropping like mercury.

He echoed Russell's sharp query. "How is that possible? Do you mean one of the judges is sick?"

"Not the judges, no. This is much worse."

"Worse? How can it be worse?"

Sir John intervened. "You really do need to sit down, Miss Manolo, and tell us the full story. From the start. I'll get some coffee sent up to keep us awake."

Long before the maid arrived with a carafe of hot coffee the story tumbled out. How Lani had been urgently summoned to Mamie Bilouxie's home in the middle of the night.

"Mamie has taken sick. Awful sick. And she was calling for me," Lani explained. "Sam sent her son Teddy to get me."

She gazed at Sir John, her eyes brimming. "She is in hospital. I don't know if she will make it. But the thing is, she's not the only one. There's a whole lot of them, folks from the kitchen and serving staff, who got into some of your wine after all the work was over. And they're all sick with the same symptoms."

"No!" The cathartic cry came from deep within Aristide. "This is that wine Ramsden Meadows brought in. The wine Sam told me about. Must be." He glanced over to the sideboard, where the single bottle Sam had given him stood.

Russell's eagle eyes followed his.

"But why?" Aristide continued. "If it had been served up to the judges, which I presumed was what they'd intended when Sam told me about it, then the panel would be sprawled about dead or dying. And apart from anything else, that would sabotage de Vile's great event. So why would they do it?"

"Beats me, Aristide." John Russell's words were dry, clipped. "But I intend to find out."

He was onto his third coffee when Aristide was struck by the stray thought: wouldn't Felix Duchamp enjoy this?

Second poisoning at hands of French wine master.

French vintner adds another dozen to his death list.

As he rose from his chair he could

barely lift one foot in front of the other. His legs were like the chunks of oak he'd watched fairground axemen chop into.

He parted the curtains and peered out into the street, where the gas lamps burned, fending off the darkness.

There'd be no easy way of protecting d'Oro from this latest disaster.

I am not like my father.

Like a repeating refrain, the words bubbled up from deep within him.

But he knew it didn't matter. His name would be blackened anyway.

All before the first lonely notes of the dawn chorus announced a day that only a few short hours before seemed filled with new promise.

Forty

"So what the hell happened? Were you planning to kill all our esteemed judges or what?"

Senator Hector de Vile glared from Ramsden to Candy Meadows, while father and daughter stood speechless before him.

"Well? Say something. Explain what's going on here, because it appears someone left me out of the plan."

De Vile ran his thumb along the center of his forehead, trying to iron out the throbbing while marshalling his thoughts. It was too early in the morning to be cleaning up someone else's mess. His head ached from a drink or two too many last night. And now he had to deal with these clowns.

The future of the illustrious Symposium was under threat because these fools had left tainted wine around for useless freeloaders to guzzle. Who could care less? The refuse of society blinded or paralyzed drinking doctored wine? It wasn't all that uncommon, especially in the badlands where they made moonshine. Out there, no one took any notice.

But this wasn't moonshine in Appalachia. This was the Golden Gate Symposium. And it occurred at the very same time the eminent panel was tasting the fine-wine selection.

In a city of more than a dozen newspapers, wine newsletters and news sheets, this scandal would attract national attention. And California wine—

and, by association, Hector de Vile—
would be a laughingstock.

After the governor's laudatory speech
last night—what had he said? "Senator
de Vile is committed not only to
recognizing California as a great
winemaking state, but also to see her
standing at the foremost in the
production of fine wines."

He shuddered. He'd be the butt of
jokes in every yellow news sheet in the
land. And he was a few months out
from re-election.

He lumbered over to the whiskey
decanter and sloshed some of the
golden liquid into a glass. Too early for
booze, but today was the exception that
proved the rule. It was never too early
for whiskey.

He turned his attention back to the
Meadows couple leaning into each

other, as if punch-drunk, in the entryway to his Russ House suite. The daughter was swaying on her feet, as if about to collapse. Her father had his arm around her, propping her up.

"Sit down, for God's sake. I don't want her fainting on me."

They sank into the ample sofa with such visible relief he wondered if they would ever rise from it again.

"I told you I wanted those wines fixed so they wouldn't rate. I didn't plan on you endangering lives."

His words hissed with venom. Low enough not to be heard by anyone outside the room but vehement enough to communicate his displeasure.

"What in God's name were you doing? What went wrong?"

Ramsden shot Candy a wild look and she answered in kind. The girl was terrified and, de Vile thought, if he wasn't mistaken, was also guilty.

Ramsden replied in a blustering baritone, "Senator, we did nothing that would lead to people getting sick, I can assure you. Someone must have tampered with the wine after I delivered it. That is the only explanation I can think of. We never intended to harm anyone."

His voice was brazen, but the eyes above the strong mouth made de Vile think of a stallion surprised by a rattlesnake.

Ransom drew a protective arm around his daughter. "Candy had nothing to do with this. I was the one who took care of it. And I didn't put anything in that brew that could explain these events."

A lie. De Vile had a sixth sense for them.

"How exactly did you carry out this 'delivery' anyway? We've got to get to the bottom of this. Did you deliver it to Will Davenport as instructed?"

Meadows' tightly held lips faltered. He looked to the floor, unable to meet de Vile's eye.

"I couldn't find Davenport. He was busy with the judges. I gave it to that head man, Sam someone, the one who runs the kitchens. He said he'd pass it on to Davenport when he was free."

"And do we know if that ever occurred?"

Ramsden Meadows was silent. His jowls hung over his neat white collar. His face had turned a sickly gray, his cheeks collapsed in slack anxiety.

"I cannot say for sure," he said in a voice that was a lot quieter and less certain than the bluster of a few minutes ago.

"Then you'd better start making things right. Straight away. Call on your old mate Felix Duchamp with a story of 'Now he's done it again.' I don't care how many lies you tell. But if any of this mess comes anywhere near me, I can guarantee one thing. You'll wish that you and your daughter weren't alive to see it."

Forty-one

The senator's face was grave as the captain of police read a prepared statement to the small crowd gathered in the Symposium meeting room—the members of the organizing committee, some of the local judges, law enforcement, Sir John Russell and himself and a few other local winemakers including the Meadows father and daughter.

Aristide's chest pinched for his old boss despite the fury that raged within.

They always seem to have a finger in the pie.

Both Ramsden and Candy had the vacant eyes of civilians caught under cannon fire, and Aristide knew what that was like. Ramsden seemed to have aged ten years, from the dapper, energetic organizer with a ready smile to an old man with hollow eyes and haggard cheeks.

Word had spread like wildfire that the wine had been brought into the Occidental's kitchens by the Meadows. The worker grapevine would not be denied. Aristide's lungs burned with a fierce gratitude at how fast the rumor had spread and been accepted.

If his hopes and dreams could survive this disaster, he needed all the help he could get from the hotel rumor mill.

Senator Hector de Vile, operating in his capacity of honorary coordinator, had quickly stepped in to dampen down the storm. He'd urgently convened this meeting to address the question of where to now? Could the Symposium be rescued? And how would they explain the awful events to a sensation-hungry public?

The captain of police, James Burns, had been the first officer invited to make a report, and the burly, bearded Irishman was giving a summary of the consequences.

Six people affected, two in a critical condition in hospital. People who drank the wine first developed headaches, then vomiting, abdominal pain and vertigo. Over a longer period, they became breathless and their vision was impaired. Those who survived may be permanently affected, he said, even blinded.

All those who took sick had the distinctive sweet, pungent smell of wood alcohol on their breath, and although no further tests had yet been done, he believed time would reveal that the wine contained methanol, a dangerous byproduct frequently found in moonshine whiskey.

"We're fairly confident of the chemistry. We don't understand how it got there."

He glanced at de Vile, as if he'd said his piece and was passing the baton back.

De Vile turned to Ramsden Meadows. "Mr. Meadows, you're an experienced winemaker and wine blender. In your opinion, would methanol be found naturally during the winemaking fermentation process?"

Meadows blinked slowly, as if surprised to be asked, absorbing the question.

"No, Senator. Very unlikely—in fact impossible—for it to have been generated from natural processes. It must have been added to the barrel or bottle manually at some stage."

"I see. So, there can't be anything accidental about this. It was done deliberately."

Meadows shuffled uneasily. "I can't say anything more than it would not normally be found in naturally fermented wine, Senator."

Several others in the circle grunted their assent. "Quite right, Meadows."

De Vile turned back to the captain. "How far have you got with your inquiries, Chief? Have you any idea yet how the poison got there, and who put it there?"

"Far too early to say, Senator. We are only halfway through our questioning of various parties."

De Vile brought a gavel down on the tabletop, like an auctioneer closing a sale.

"In that case I believe we have no option but to withdraw Vino d'Oro entries from the Golden Gate contest. We can hardly expect the judges to go on tasting wines from this estate when they've poisoned half a dozen people with the self-same drop. Thank our lucky stars it never found its way to the judges' table, that's all I can say."

As a murmuring broke out John Russell stood. "Senator, as the principal of Vino d'Oro, may I make a request to address the gathering? I believe it's a matter of natural justice."

De Vile fixed him with a calculated stare, while around him the murmurs rose to a babble.

"Give him a chance, Senator . . . Nasty business . . . It could be any of us targeted by these villains."

De Vile capitulated, raising his hands. "I've no desire to be unreasonable, Russell," he said.

"Even if keeping them out makes you ten grand?" a ruddy-faced man jibed. "We all heard about the bet you two took."

The benign ease on de Vile's face hardened. "To Hades with the bet. We've got a serious matter on our hands here—saving the reputation of our whole industry."

John Russell stood with the command of a man used to taking the lead and cast his eye around the gathering, taking in the black-suited committee men—the merchants and managers—as well as the more casually jacketed audience, including Felix Duchamp, Aristide noted, who lounged along the back wall.

"For better or worse, there will not be a man in this room tonight who has not heard the name Aristide Laurent. If you hadn't heard it before a week ago, you certainly would have by now. His notoriety has preceded him, thanks largely to the efforts of Mr. Felix Duchamp from *Alta California.*"

He gave a theatrical nod to Duchamp.

"Good evening to you, Duchamp. I hope your report of these proceedings is more accurate than the first account was."

Some in the crowd twisted to view Duchamp, whose face reddened at the attention.

Funny, Aristide mused, how those who enjoyed putting others under a spotlight didn't appear so comfortable when it was them being exposed.

"We've already settled the question of an ancient wrong done to Mr. Laurent by his father. The truth of it has recently been accepted by Governor Hunt, who found that my winemaker had nothing to do with the calamity his father perpetuated and then attributed to his son. Yes, it is tragic that deaths resulted from his father's bad practice. But that is a past matter, and settled. Is that not correct, Governor?"

He pivoted toward Hunt, who was primly poised in one of the empty elevated chairs on the judge's dais.

The governor assented without hesitation. "I am fully satisfied that Mr. Laurent had no culpability in that matter."

Russell's shoulders relaxed. "So that brings us to this latest tragedy. Before we confront that, I think it would be fair to say that Mr. Laurent has also earned notoriety of a different kind since he landed on our California shores, as a man who is opposed—*strongly* opposed—to adulteration of any kind in the natural winemaking process. He has voiced those opinions to anyone willing to listen—and to some who weren't."

The sense of tension building in the room momentarily eased with an exhaling of soft laughter.

Russell milked the fellowship of men together, a camaraderie you could smell in the muted male scent of moth-balled suits, lingering tobacco and sweat. Men leaned back in their chairs, relaxed into tribal agreement. Jaws softened, heads nodded. Aristide's spirits lifted at the display.

The man's a genius. He should be the politician.

"And it has not made him popular in some quarters."

Russell turned to de Vile. "Indeed, I think the senator's own Buena Vista Cooperative has on occasion been exasperated, outraged even, by Laurent's views.

"You understand what I am getting at here. How likely is it that a man who had built his career on producing the purest wines he can, would deliberately adulterate one of his marque wines with deadly poison and leave it around for anyone to drink?"

His piercing dark eyes suddenly took on an even blacker hue. "And what on God's earth would he gain from it? What possible motivation could he have for such an act? Particularly given the family history."

Again he scanned the room, his eagle

gaze penetrating anyone brave enough to challenge him.

"So that leaves us with a conundrum. Who had both access and motive to tamper with them, to bring harm to their maker? Those are the questions I think everyone here . . ." He flicked a glance to the corner where Ramsden and Candy Meadows sat, perched near de Vile, ready to take flight at any moment. "Almost everyone here wants answered. Who did it?"

The last words prompted an audible stirring. Someone at the back whistled approval.

Sir John turned to the captain. "Who did it, Captain Burns? Do you know?"

Burns stroked his rough ginger beard. "Not yet, Russell. But I will."

The San Francisco Police Force had risen from unpromising Gold Rush beginnings, when they were seen as no more than as a band of ex-bandits and extortionists, feared as much as the criminals they were supposed to catch. Things had improved since those bad old days, but Russell wasn't sure by how much. As recently as five years ago the famed newspaperman Mark Twain had publicly claimed that the Police Chief Martin Burke was corrupt. Russell hoped Burns was a better man.

He turned back to the governor. "What about you, Governor Hunt? Do you know who did it?"

Hunt shook his head. "I know who *didn't* do it. And that is Aristide Laurent."

De Vile jumped to his feet, his face red and sweating. "Now look here, Russell. Let's cut the theatrics. Have you got something new to tell us or not?"

"I most certainly have, Senator. And I'm calling some witnesses to prove it."

"Witnesses? This isn't a court. We're not here to try anyone—or, for that matter, to present evidence or solve crimes. We're simply deciding on what's happening to the Symposium. And there's no question, as far as I'm concerned.

"Vino d'Oro must withdraw while this investigation continues. If you won't withdraw, I'm afraid the committee will take a vote to rescind your place as a finalist. We can't have a company that's been responsible for such a disaster representing our state."

Russell responded with a grim smile. "If our company was responsible, Senator, I entirely agree. But I am confident I can entirely clear our name, and I believe these men consider I deserve the chance to do that."

An approving hum rose to the domed ceiling.

"I take that as a yes."

Russell peered around de Vile's shoulder to the Meadows. Ramsden was darting his head around him, as if searching for the culprit. And Candy . . . She sat in stark terror, white-knuckled hands clenched in her lap, eyes squeezed tightly shut, as though she'd seen a ghost and was hoping that when she opened them it would have gone away.

Aristide knew then that she'd been in on this. That if she hadn't played an active role, she certainly was aware of what her father was doing.

The mild euphoria he'd enjoyed at the way Russell's speech had swayed the crowd was smothered by a roiling nausea that started deep in his stomach and threatened to overwhelm him.

He slapped his hand to his mouth and turned to the door.

He hadn't quite reached it when he heard the boom of Russell's insistent rounded vowels, echoes of his Hong Kong birth and English education, never fully flattened by his years in California.

"I'd like to start at the beginning by inviting Mr. Sam Morley to join us. Mr. Morley will set the scene for us. And after that, I believe Ramsden Meadows has something important to contribute."

Aristide swiveled, unable to miss this even if he was close to puking.

Ramsden's face was defiant and sweating. "Me? I've got nothing to say."

He jerked his white face to de Vile, as if expecting his support.

"Out of order, Sir John. You've got to

do better than pitch a few wild balls."
De Vile puffed out his chest. "Until
we're satisfied there are good grounds,
you can't pluck a man out of a crowd
and subject him to the third degree."

Russell studied the pair, the
Washington boss man and his lackey. As
he took their measure, he seemed to
relax, as if he'd read signs in them that
were not visible to anyone else.

He turned back to face the room,
rubbing his hands in anticipation. "When
men have something germane and
timely to bring to seeing justice done,
Senator, I think I can."

He cracked his knuckles, right hand
against left, as if preparing for a fight.

"Listen hard, gentlemen. I believe
you'll find the next few minutes highly
educational."

Forty-two

Russell suspected Aristide might have been on his way to the men's room but he didn't want to lose his momentum. He swung toward the door.

"Mr. Laurent, could you please fetch Mr. Morley for us? From the management office? And send someone for Mr. Will Davenport too. They both have valuable information to contribute."

The room relaxed in the same way as a court does when in recess, with pent-up anticipation that the best action is still to come. Men stood around and chatted quietly as they waited, eyes glittering with excitement. De Vile sauntered over to Russell, affecting a total lack of concern with the turn of events. Only his hostile eyes betrayed his true feelings.

"This better be good, Russell," he said. A tic flickered and pulsed beneath his right eye. "Or you're for the skids. A thousand bucks will be the least of your problems."

"Thanks for the advice, Senator." Russell brushed his hand down his suit coat, as if removing lint. "Now let me give you some as well. As we used to say when I was a boy growing up, 'If you don't want people to know what you are doing, then don't do it. Confucius says.'"

De Vile's confident grin was undimmed. "Nice try, Russell, but you don't scare me."

The unfriendly banter was interrupted

by Aristide's return with Sam Morley, followed closely by the Manolo twins and Will Davenport.

The room hushed and turned as one to assess the new arrivals.

As his vintner walked across the floor toward him, Russell had a few moments to consider the group. These two men—Morley and Davenport—would make or break his bid to absolve Vino d'Oro of any involvement in this tragedy. Morley's shoulders were hunched, his face desolate, and Davenport was right on his heels, an intelligent energy radiating from behind his wire-rimmed spectacles.

As for the Hawaiians, Russell was unsure why they were here. The brother was an impressive specimen, with a powerful frame and serious dark eyes above sculpted cheekbones. The distinct

scar that curved through one brow gave
him an added frisson of danger. He was
raw strength and refinement, all in one
face. A man not to be underestimated.

As for the sister, she was equally
eye-catching. She wore a fashionable
pink dress with a black wrap across her
shoulders, but the feminine color
conveyed no hint of ditzy prettiness.
She was a serious beauty, with the
same chiseled cheekbones as her twin,
and a determined gravity in gait and
gesture which spoke of maturity well
beyond her years.

He saw by the way she quietly
conferred with Sam, and then turned
into Aristide's anxious gaze with an
inquiring raised brow, that she already
had full command of the situation, and
of his man. In one small gesture he saw
all he needed to.

Aristide's outstretched arm, reaching fleetingly to touch her forearm, a gesture of care and concern, as if satisfying himself she was safe. And then as hastily withdrawn.

So that's the way it is. He guessed he was likely to be seeing a lot more of this young woman, whether he liked it or not.

The next minute Will Davenport stood in front of him, while the others held back, like herded sheep reluctant to enter the fold. They reminded him of the timid animals he'd seen on his walking tour holidays while at school in England.

The young agent presented an assured hand. "Will Davenport, Sir John. Currently filling in for Bully at Pike Consulting—though no one can fill those empty shoes."

He flashed a self-deprecating smile. His grasp was reassuringly firm, his hand warm and dry.

"I feel terrible about this mess. It happened on my watch, and it shouldn't have." He glanced back at the rest of the party, removing his glasses as he did. He had indented pressure marks across the curve of his nose, but it didn't detract from the face that was handsome without spectacles.

"I'm afraid we've got some very ill people, and it will be hours or days before we know if they will recover. Two in hospital, including Sam Morley's fiancée Mamie. She might not make it, Sir John, so he's very upset."

Davenport's voice was low and urgent. John Russell noticed Aristide was arranging chairs for Sam and the Manolos.

"He's really in no state to talk to a crowd like this. He's here to bear witness to what happened. If it's all right with you, we'll leave most of the talking to me and Miss Manolo. She knows Mamie well and has spoken with her since she fell ill. In fact, she's just come from the hospital with Sam."

Davenport's gray eyes were steady and compassionate. Russell liked him instantly.

"Happy to take your advice on this, Davenport. You obviously know a lot more about it than I do." He stepped forward to face the room. "Let's not waste any more time, shall we? Let's get started."

He used the governor's gavel to quieten the crowd and explained the situation, introduced the little group which had recently entered, and then made way for Will Davenport and Sam Morley and the woman. The brother, Russell noted, remained seated, steadily watching his sister, as if on guard duty. A man of few words perhaps, but one who missed nothing of the goings-on around him.

Will Davenport began with a mea culpa of sorts, explaining that he was the man in charge of getting the wine to the judges, and outlining the great care he and the d'Oro men had taken in ensuring their wine was held secure.

"I regret to say Mr. Laurent has previously found his wines to be tampered with by others, so he was particularly cautious. He gave me very strict instructions to keep his wines under lock and key, which I did. The wines he submitted were the wines the judges tested, no question about it.

"As for the rogue batch, that is a very different story, I regret to say. Mr. Morley will give us a brief explanation of how these wines came to be here, and if there are further questions Miss Manolo may be able to answer on his behalf. She has talked at length with Sam's fiancée, who is one of the victims."

Sam stepped up reluctantly and explained the succession of events: How Ramsden Meadows had come backstage claiming to have a late entry for d'Oro, how he hadn't been able to locate Will Davenport and so he'd left the half a dozen bottles with Sam.

How when Sam mentioned the wines to Will, he said there must be some misunderstanding, that the d'Oro wines were already submitted. How in the back room rush he'd left the consignment in the scullery for his attention later. And how, as was sometimes the case, workers at the end of their shift, thinking the wine to be "surplus to requirements," had purloined the bottles to have a quiet after-work drink together.

Sam's delivery was labored and hesitant. As soon as he'd said his piece he slipped back to his seat.

Russell stepped up. "So, Mr. Davenport, you are satisfied the wine that caused harm was delivered here by Mr. Meadows? There is no other explanation for how it got here?"

"That is correct, Sir John. No other possibility."

Senator de Vile waved his arms, objecting. "Now come on, chaps. How do we know the wine that these sorry folks drank was the same batch? It could have come from anywhere. All we know is the wine Mr. Meadows is said to have delivered is the wine you say they drank. But how do we know that?"

Will nodded in Leilani's direction. "I think Miss Manolo can answer that. Could you tell us what Sam's wife Mamie, told you, Miss Manolo?"

Leilani Manolo rose to her feet. Tall and willowy, she was several inches shorter than her brother but had the same athletic strength about her.

Her voice was lower than Russell would have expected from a young woman, and it carried an authority not usual in her age or sex.

"Mamie spoke with Sam near to the end of the evening. He was to join them in the after-work celebration but got delayed—thank goodness. She was very clear that they'd taken the wine from the shelf Sam had indicated to her."

She drew her black wrap more closely around her shoulders, seeming to grow in her command as she continued. "Mamie and the others who were poisoned, they are decent hard-working people. They don't deserve for something like this to happen. And I believe there is a way we can test if the poisoned wine came from the batch Mr. Meadows delivered."

The room grew pin-drop quiet. No one shuffled or sniffed. Every eye was fixed on the woman standing next to Will Davenport.

"Sam told me that when Mr. Laurent went out back to check that everything was all right, he told him about the extra delivery. He gave Mr. Laurent a bottle of the wine from the batch Mr. Meadows delivered to take away. So he could have it checked if he wished to do so. Just as an extra precaution."

She glanced at Russell, then Aristide.

"If you test the wine in that bottle, you would you be able to tell if it's the same batch as the toxic one. And wouldn't that settle the question?"

The raised eyebrow, the wicked smile that curved the corners of her desirable mouth, told anyone who cared to notice that she already fully understood the answer—and its potentially disastrous implications.

Forty-three

Hector de Vile stood transfixed by what was unfolding before him. The swift course of events. The rock-solid testimony it seemed impossible to bring into question. But most of all, that woman. That wicked smile.

For a moment he forgot he was in a meeting room at the Occidental Hotel in San Francisco in 1870. The reality of the November ballot box, of San Francisco in July, faded.

The sure knowledge that—unless he grabbed back the initiative—this scandal would ditch his re-election chances dissolved away, swamped in old memories.

He was back in a balmy Honolulu night more than twenty years ago, in the company of a beautiful woman. The velvety touch of her skin, the floral scent of the multi-blossomed leis that hung around their necks as they stood hand in hand in front of a ferny altar. He relived the moment. The smell of the mossy foliage, the bloom of her skin, her rounded belly. The promise of new beginnings, and of a full life ahead of them.

The electric tingle that ran up his spine that day was exactly the same as the magnetic prickle that crawled from the base of his body to the top of his head now, making it impossible to think of anything else.

Who was this chit of a girl who had mesmerized a roomful of mature men, not just with her beauty, but with her regal presence and intelligence? Who else had come up with such a simple solution to the poisoned wine problem, a solution which spelled calamity for him if allowed to proceed?

He stared at her, as if seeing a ghost.

"Senator! Senator de Vile!"

Through the haze of his memories he heard his name. John Russell was calling to him. He pinched between his eyes punishingly, told himself to keep his nerve. This girl was nothing like the woman he couldn't forget. Her hair was a lighter brown, her face was broader, her expression much more serious. She was a Hawaiian female. That was the only similarity.

And he couldn't think any more about that now. He had some very serious business to complete.

Aristide realized that Leilani had been addressing him, and as she did, his exchange with Sam that night came into sharp focus. He hadn't just taken the bottle. He marked the label with a big black cross so he'd never mistake it for anything else but a reject. And he still had it, here at his feet.

He held up the bottle Sam had given him for all to see. Showed everyone the cross he had scrawled across it to alert himself to the fact that it was suspect.

Quiet comments swelled from the floor, then quietened again as Sam Morley confirmed he had given Laurent the bottle, then Sir John confirmed that Aristide had used his pen to mark it in his presence.

He marveled again that it was Leilani who had grasped the significance of the extra bottle, when he'd forgotten its very existence. He'd only been reminded of it when they retraced just now every step in the unfolding tragedy.

Sam took the bottle from Aristide and sniffed around the cork. "It's definitely from the same lot," he said with a catch in his breath that might have been interpreted as a sob if he was a woman. "It's got the same funny smell as the others."

The smell. The sweet pungent odor of wood alcohol. Aristide remembered it from his father's cellars. He bent over, repressing the bile that rose in his throat. When his attention was back on the proceedings, Russell had once more assumed the initiative.

"So now, I believe, is the appropriate time to ask Mr. Meadows some questions. We've established without any shadow of doubt that he brought this suspect wine into the hotel. It's time he told us where he got it from and why he brought it here? Are we all agreed?"

Men stamped their approval and thundered in agreement. Ramsden Meadows clutched at his throat, his deathly pale face guttered in dark lines. Candy clung to his elbow, her fingers white with tension, unwilling to let go.

Ramsden bent to her ear and whispered, and she shook her head in vehement disagreement. Then he gently released her clenched fingers, one by one, stood up and moved toward Russell with the shuffling gait of an old man.

Russell remained calm. "Ramsden, you're known and respected in this place. It's hard to believe you would deliberately poison people. But it seems clear that you did bring in this suspect wine. Can you explain to us what happened here?"

His voice was kind rather than accusing, genuinely seeking answers.

Meadows shifted from one foot to the other, licking his lips, glancing with feverish eyes from de Vile to Candy and back again, as if considering his response.

He took a deep breath, and when they came, his words were rasping, tripping into one another.

"I didn't know there was anything wrong with the wine."

He stared around the room with unseeing eyes.

"Well, nothing seriously wrong. You've got to believe me. I did not know."

Out of the corner of his eye Aristide saw Candy bury her face in her hands.

"But you *did* bring it here. Why?"

Yet again Meadows flicked his

attention to de Vile, who stood a few feet away to his left.

"I was asked to give it to Will Davenport. I was told it was needed for the judging. That's all."

"And who told you that?"

"I . . . I can't say. Privileged information, Sir John. No. I can't say."

Yet again his eyes jittered past the senator, without coming to rest.

He hardly needed to use words. His eyes told the story.

Russell's voice was even more searching, considerate. "And yet you swear you didn't add the poison."

Russell held up the black-green glass bottle with the slashed black-and-white label, a figurative skull and crossbones.

Ramsden shook his head violently. "I did not. I would never have brought it here if I thought it would make people ill."

De Vile stepped forward, interjecting himself into the space between Russell and Meadows.

"Rather an inconsistent tale, isn't it, Meadows? You admit you brought it here, but you didn't know it was poisoned? So where did you find it? Did the poisoner break into your cellars when you were asleep?"

The senator's tone was menacing as he loomed over the trembling wine merchant, a schoolyard bully in full flight. Ramsden Meadows' eyes widened in shock, as if he'd had a sudden realization of what was about to happen, but he did not speak. Instead his eyes searched out Candy's stricken face and he gave her the gentlest, most loving of smiles.

Understand what I am about to do.

"If you really believed that bottle was

harmless, you'd be willing to drink the contents to prove it, wouldn't you?" De Vile was a relentless bloodhound.

"As I've said, Senator de Vile, I don't know how it got contaminated."

Ramsden seemed to be regaining his strength. His voice was the clearest, the most determined, it had been since the questioning began.

The Washington potentate raised his voice by several decibels.

"It's like this, Mr. Meadows. We all know how close you and your daughter were to Aristide Laurent. Why, he was practically like a son to you, wasn't he? He brought you his wine for your approval. You had d'Oro vintage in your cellars.

"It's not hard to see that when he went off to join Sir John Russell, when it was plain he wasn't going to marry your beautiful daughter, you got angry. Very angry. And you wanted revenge for the way he'd rejected your advances, and her. He wasn't choosing you as d'Oro's agent, was he, Meadows?"

He shook his head in silent reproof.

"So you sought revenge. And you didn't care who you hurt to get it."

Meadows stood tall, shoulders back, staring into de Vile's venomous countenance, no longer the shrinking violet.

"No. It wasn't like that, as well you know, Senator. Not at all." He put a heavy emphasis on the title.

De Vile suddenly dropped the volume to a dangerous hiss.

"If you really believe that wine did not get poisoned while it was sitting in your cellars, you should prove it. Drink it!"

Candy jumped to her feet, hand to her lips, a strangled cry issuing from between clenched teeth. "No! No!"

And in that moment Aristide knew, with a soul-deep certainty, who was responsible for the poisoned wine.

And why Ramsden Meadows would accept the challenge to drink himself to a certain death, rather than let his daughter face the consequences.

Forty-four

The marked bottle sat on the floor at Aristide's feet, where he'd placed it when Russell had handed it back to him.

Hector de Vile planted himself inches from Russell's face, hands stiff by his sides.

"The bottle, Russell. Pass. Him. The bottle."

A gust of air blew through the room, lifting hair off dozens of temples as men expelled long, shocked breaths, exhaling in concert. Aristide's own temples were clammy. The temperature in the stuffy space had increased by several degrees over the last five minutes, he was sure.

The men at the back of the room, who hadn't heard de Vile's low challenge, were standing on tiptoe to see over the heads of the men in front. Mumbling word fragments reached Aristide's ears.

"What's going on?"

"Drink it, you say?

"No. Never!" The last said with an edge of utter disbelief.

"He wouldn't be that crazy."

But it seemed Ramsden Meadows *was* that crazy.

He stepped closer to John Russell, his hands clasped tightly in front of him.

De Vile had one hand stretched out, ready to receive the bottle.

Aristide kept it firmly clasped between his feet.

Sir John remonstrated, "Really, Hector, you're taking this too far. As you yourself said only fifteen minutes ago, we should leave the proper authorities to complete their investigation. We can wait to know the whole story until then."

A silent communication passed between de Vile and Meadows.

"I don't think we need to do that if Ramsden is ready to meet the test," the senator said, each word fastidiously articulated.

De Vile regarded Ramsden with a viper's eyes. "Are you ready, Ramsden?"

Ramsden's lips curled with disdain. He ignored de Vile, as if he was not worth acknowledging, and moved his eyes to Russell.

"The senator has issued the challenge, and I'm ready to accept it," he said. "He is right. It's a matter of honor."

Sir John shook his head. "I don't understand what's going on here, Ramsden. But I am willing to believe in your innocence. You were not aware the poison was in the wine."

He raised his voice and addressed the room. "How many are satisfied we need to know more of this?"

A low rumble of voices answered, more questioning than decisive. The men were confused and perplexed by the unfolding drama.

"The senator seems to be saying that Ramsden Meadows laced the d'Oro wine with poison to take revenge on Mr. Laurent here."

Russell let his words hang in the air, then shook his head.

"It doesn't make sense for Ramsden to do this. And I for one do not want to stand by and push an innocent man into a crass act of self-harm."

He gestured to Aristide. "Hold up that bottle so everyone can see, Laurent."

Aristide obeyed. Men shifted uneasily in their boots. Russell tapped the cork.

"Poison is generally not used for crimes of passion—if this is what de Vile is saying this was. A crime of passion? No. Poison is a tool of stealth, often used when the other side is unaware that there is a war being fought in the first place. And if war has been declared, we at Vino d'Oro are certainly not aware of it.

"What was it that General Carl von Clausewitz wrote about the art of war? It is an act of violence intended to compel our opponent to fulfill our will."

He surveyed the room. Aristide saw how he sought out the key players— Hunt, Burns, the wine judges, the scrabble of journalists at the back of the room—before continuing.

"So ask yourselves, what war is being fought here, and who is it against? Against my wine company? A war to destroy Aristide's reputation? What act is being compelled? A war to force us to withdraw from the contest? You can see it's a very clumsy and ineffectual attempt, if that's what was intended."

De Vile cut in with a voice like a buzz saw. "Cut the philosophy, Russell. Give me the bottle."

Russell blinked but otherwise ignored him.

"And I'd be asking, why is the senator so enthusiastic about pushing the point? Does Mr. Meadows know something the senator doesn't want revealed?"

De Vile's face flashed beetroot red. "Don't be ridiculous. A worm like this? A murderer? What on earth would I have to do with him?"

Russell turned to Ramsden Meadows.

"What would he have to do with you, Ramsden? Care to tell us?"

Meadows shook his head with a wan smile and put out his hand to take the wine bottle.

"Come on, son. Pass it to me."

The gouged lines that ran down his cheeks softened with tenderness, and his gray eyes sparkled with unshed tears. He regarded Aristide for a few silent moments, his lashes batting away the moisture.

"No hard feelings," he said, so softly only he and Russell could hear.

He stretched out his arm for the bottle.

Aristide watched the tableau unfolding in the stuffy crowded room and he burned hotter by the minute.

From his line of questioning he was certain that Russell was thinking as he was.

There was some hidden business being conducted here in plain sight, some underground negotiation involving de Vile and the Meadows that no one else here was party to.

He had worked for this man for several years, eaten at his table like a member of the family more times than he could count. They'd had their disagreements, yes. And Ramsden's business practice didn't match his own standards. But neither he nor Candy were killers. He would stake his life on it.

And Ramsden was willing to die right

here, right now, to protect Candy.

Aristide held the bottle by its neck and took a few steps toward Ramsden, arm extended, as if preparing to pass it to him.

He sniffed at the cork, and waved it under Ramsden's nose.

"Smell that."

Ramsden's smile dimmed, his face paled.

"You know what it is, don't you?"

Ramsden nodded.

"Then why on earth would you be prepared to drink it?"

The words exploded out of him.

He checked out the men at the back of the room. Yes, Duchamp was still there, absorbing every second of this, he was sure.

He raised the bottle up to his shoulder height with a stiff forearm and smashed it with force over the back of a wooden chair.

Red wine sprayed onto his shirt sleeve. The back of his hand prickled, peppered with tiny shards of green glass.

His ears were ringing with the shriek of breaking glass and then all was quiet as the blood-red liquid dripped through his fingers. The pungent smell of methanol was even stronger now the container was shattered.

"You're no Socrates, Ramsden. I'm not letting you do it."

He dropped the jagged neck on top of the wet mess of shattered green glass at his feet and glanced up at Russell, anxious about what he might see in his face, but he needn't have worried. His boss was gazing at him with an appreciative light in his eyes.

"Good work, Aristide," he said softly. And then the Hong Kong knight of the realm assumed authority like a familiar mantle and addressed the room.

"Show's over for tonight, folks. Let's all go home and get some sleep. We'll leave the constable and Sam's workers to do what they are best at. Cleaning up."

Forty-five

"This is a dreadful business, dreadful. It will take a lot to overcome the stain."

De Vile hovered at Governor Hunt's shoulder as the meeting dispersed, wondering if it was the right time to introduce the idea of disqualifying Vino d'Oro from the Golden Gate contest until the poisoning scandal had been solved to the satisfaction of Captain Burns.

He observed the friendly way in which Hunt shook John Russell's hand and guessed he wouldn't make much headway with such a proposal now. Russell had very adeptly wriggled off the hook, like the shark he was.

The governor turned with a placid expression. "I think you are worrying unnecessarily, Senator. Sir John seems to have tied up a lot of loose ends. Now we'll leave it to Captain Burns to handle the rest."

His brow puckered. "I admit it's very strange. How it all came about, I mean." His mouth widened in a big yawn which he hastily covered with two hands.

"But we'll not learn anything more tonight. I'm off to get some sleep and I suggest you do the same."

Sleep!

It was the last thing on de Vile's mind as he climbed the stairs to his second-floor room and pondered how everything had got so out of control.

He burned with frustration as he

recalled the restrained shoulder claps the French winemaker and his patron had exchanged, as people milled around congratulating Sir John Russell for the way he'd handled things and for getting into the Symposium finals.

He remembered the way the Manolo girl had turned to Sam Morley and Will Davenport with a beaming smile, before her candid joy dissolved into something else as that Laurent fellow approached. She'd attempted to hide it, but he'd got adept at reading his Hawaiian princess's moods.

Under Miss Manolo's detached grace he'd seen the rosy glow of attraction climb up her cheeks as she spoke to Laurent. And he hadn't missed the answering spark in the vintner's eye. She was uncannily like Abigail, the woman he'd come to know so well, and he couldn't deny it.

It must be a coincidence. And I can't afford to get distracted now.

He directed his thoughts back to Ramsden Meadows. That arch-botcher was supposed to replace the d'Oro entry with bad wine to eliminate them from the finals, but he'd never suggested they should poison anyone. He rubbed his hand over the top of his head in frustration.

You couldn't rely on anyone these days. Will Davenport was a disappointment too. He'd given the impression he was willing to play his part, but in the event he was nowhere to be found. It was too soon to say if that was deliberate or just bad luck for Meadows.

Thank goodness the dolt had failed, or they'd have dead and dying judges on their hands. That would have been a catastrophe neither he nor the city would recover from.

As it was, a few knaves getting sick—really, it was no big deal.

But Ramsden Meadows knew something he wasn't telling, or he'd never have fallen for the "Drink it and die" ploy. If he was a betting man de Vile would wager it had something to do with the daughter. And he was a betting man. He remembered the thousand bucks he owed Russell and groaned.

He had to admit it, Russell had won this round, but he would make damn sure it was the last one he did.

First he had to find a way to sideline the d'Oro wines. He couldn't countenance them winning the Golden Gate prize.

Then he had to kneecap the Frog.

And from what he'd seen, maybe the easiest way to ruin him was to go for the woman. Women seemed to be the man's weak point, and he had no doubt this new one was dangerous. She'd already shown that. And if she was in there pushing for Laurent, she was a double nuisance.

He put the key into the door of his Russ House suite and gave a grateful sigh as he stepped into the enveloping comfort of his surroundings. As was the routine, the hotel had placed a fresh flower arrangement on the hall stand, and the perfume of mixed stocks and lilies filled the air.

The evening staff had been in and plumped the pillows, stocked the silver drinks tray with his favorite whiskey along with his cigar case. They were as attentive as a good wife would be, and much less demanding. The stiffness in his shoulders eased as he pulled off his boots, put his stockinged feet up on the ottoman, and poured himself a nightcap.

He'd lost round one, but the war was far from over.

Tomorrow, he'd see if Cyrus had any idea where that Manolo woman came from. And if Cyrus couldn't—or wouldn't—help, he'd go to his last resort. He'd flush out the Countess.

Now that would be something. How many years was it since he'd last seen Elizabeth Wenderhoven?

He knew exactly how many, because it had also been the last night he'd seen Abigail alive.

Her perfect face, as smooth and unblemished as a wax image, unusually pale against the white sheets, but peaceful and composed.

He drew a deep breath. He wandered over to the flowers, checked if there was any maile there, because he could smell that familiar fragrance all over again. Common sense told him there wouldn't—couldn't—be. Maile was a Hawaiian native, its distinctive scent recognizable anywhere on the islands. But not here. Still he remembered the maile and green-fern fragrance of her skin. Heard the faint hiss of her febrile erratic breaths. That was the only sign that his wife was seriously ill. Her rapid, shallow breathing.

And then Elizabeth Wenderhoven had come to him. Archie hadn't even had the decency to tell him himself. He'd sent Abigail's best friend to tell him his wife was dead. He hadn't wanted to see the woman ever again. Never wanted to relive that night, because she'd been there, at Abigail's bedside, holding her hand in her final dying moments, when he'd been shut out.

Needs must, though, when the devil drives.

If anyone knew anything useful about Miss Manolo's origins, it would be the Rich Widow. He'd have to push this sentimental hogwash to one side, and get on with the business in front of him.

A shiver ran up his spine and the fragrance of the lilies suddenly seemed too much a reminder of death.

That had always been his way.

No point in letting tender feelings stop you from doing what was necessary.

He'd learned that the hard way, and it was too late to change now.

Forty-six

Cyrus's normally smooth salt-and-pepper hair was in tangled disarray. His fleshy face drooped, as if he'd had a palsy attack. The slope of his shoulders underlined the final aberration. Cyrus, usually a very modest drinker, was banged up to the eyes.

Hector de Vile removed his hat, deposited his cane in the umbrella holder in the hallway and fixed his shuffling old friend with a sharp eye.

"Been on the batter, have you, Cyrus? Is something wrong? It's very rarely we see you in your cups."

He glanced around. The house was cold and empty, different from its usual warm hospitality.

"And where's Misty? It's awfully quiet in here."

Cyrus regarded him with baleful eyes, shrugged and set off for the drawing room without a word.

De Vile followed.

"If you want some whiskey there's a glass over there." The words were slurred, their sense clarified by a clumsy gesture toward the occasional table where a silver tray and decanter sat.

"Your guests aren't staying any longer?"

Cyrus blinked. "Guests?"

"The Hawaiians, Cyrus. What was their name? The Manolos? Not here any longer?"

Cyrus's mouth was slack, his eyes uncomprehending.

Irritation prickled up de Vile's neck.

"You know who I mean."

Was Cyrus really this blued, or was it a convenient act?

"The twins who've been everywhere about town. Talking to Bully, too."

Was it his imagination, or did Cyrus flinch at the mention of Bully's name?

"You didn't say where Misty is. Maybe I can get more sense out of her."

Cyrus shook his head until the bedraggled hair fell over his eyes. He brushed it aside testily. "Not here. None of them are."

"Who are they anyway?"

Cyrus pulled a cigar out of the case he carried in his breast pocket and lit it.

"I'm curious. Do we know their family? Where do they come from?"

Despite the blank roll of his eyes, de Vile caught a gleam of comprehension crossing Cyrus's face. "No one important," he said.

"She reminds me of Abigail. It's weird. I haven't thought of her in years," de Vile lied.

Cyrus had his eyes fixed on a spot on the carpet. He didn't respond.

"Something about the way she moves. She's got a lot of poise for a girl. I mean, she's barely a woman. Abigail was the same."

Cyrus shook his head. "Nothing to do with Abigail, as far as I know."

De Vile eyed his old friend like a hawk.

"She said something weird to me about Bully too." He took a deep satisfying pull on his cigar and blew the smoke to the ceiling in a slow continuous stream.

"'Big, muscular, bruiser Bully.' That was it, that's what she said. 'Big, muscular, bruiser Bully.'

"Told me he was frightened. And then an hour later he was dead."

Cyrus shook his head.

"What?" said de Vile.

"Sounds like a lot of rubbish to me. Typical girl rubbish. Bully wasn't afraid of anything."

There it is. Cyrus still lying. And why is that?

Forty-seven

Visiting Ramsden and Candy Meadows was the first thing on the very long list of things he didn't want to do, but Aristide found himself standing in front of their imposing paneled Californian oak front door waiting for his knock to be answered.

He had the urge to run away like a mischievous schoolboy when he heard footsteps approaching, but he clenched his jaw and held on.

"You!" Ramsden blocked the entryway, holding the door open only a quarter wide. "Haven't we seen enough of each other to last a lifetime?" His voice was raspy and irritated.

So much for "No hard feelings."

Aristide took an involuntary step back.

"I've got unanswered questions, Ramsden, and in the circumstances I think you and your daughter owe me— and the townspeople—some answers."

The older man hesitated and then stepped back into the parquet-floored hallway to let him enter.

As Aristide stepped into the familiar aroma of home cooking, Candy appeared in the hallway.

"Owe you?" she barked. "We owe you precisely nothing. You've been leeching off us for years. My father nurtured you, introduced you to people who mattered, including your knight of the realm."

She advanced slowly toward him. The mariner eyes that had once reminded him of a balmy Mediterranean summer were now Arctic ice.

"And that's not even getting into the personal humiliation. Leading me on, letting the whole town think you were a hot suitor—and then dumping me, with no explanation."

Her face screwed up in disgust. "You think you're irresistible, applying your oh-so-seductive French charm. But you're not. You're a lying louse. You made a fool out of me and the world knows it."

Her eyes flickered toward her father, who was standing hard on Aristide's shoulder. "Now get out. I never want to see you again. Ever."

She'd come right up to him so flecks of spittle spattered his face from the vehemence of her words. Her eyes were no longer ice. They were blazing pools of fury. Her hands clenched. "You deserve every bad thing you get!"

He raised his hand slowly to his face to wipe away the traces of her.

"That may be," he said. "But those people lying in hospital fighting for their lives, they don't." He moved his hand from his cheek to a smidgen below her collarbone and with one finger gently pushed her backwards until they stood an arm's length apart.

"Your father might be willing to cover up for you, even die for you. But I'm not. I want to know why you poisoned that wine."

His last few words were low in volume, and steel-edged. Any sense of sympathy for her was drowned in a tsunami of anger. Even now she wasn't ready to admit culpability. She was still high on her precious self-justification.

He leaned in to her from where he stood, firmly planted, like a pine bending in a storm wind.

"Because I know it was you who poisoned those people, Candy. Everyone else might be playing the game of pretending it's still a mystery."

The poor little rich girl, surely it couldn't be her fault . . .

"Not me. I know what you're capable of. And I want answers, dammit. Not just for me. For the people who still might die because you didn't get what you wanted."

She reeled back, hands abruptly raised to her face, and howled like a desert dog.

Ramsden rushed to her side, couched her in his arms, whispering, "There, there, baby. It'll be all right."

Not for the first time Aristide

wondered at their claustrophobic intimacy. There was room for only one man or woman in their lives—Ramsden for Candy and Candy for Ramsden. Through the tumult of all the other emotions he saw it with a piercing clarity. She was a grown woman, being excused the inexcusable as if she were a child.

Then Ramsden spoke. "It was all a mistake, Aristide. A terrible mistake. And for that I am eternally sorry."

Candy's voice was whip sharp. "I'm not."

Ramsden buried her face in his shoulder. "Shush, girlie. You've said enough."

"Tell me what happened." Aristide's voice was implacable.

Candy lifted her head from her father's shoulder.

"You'll never know." She spat the words at him. "Your girlfriend is about to make quite a splash, though. I hope she enjoys it."

She was still smirking at some secret knowledge when her father took her by the shoulders and propelled her to the door.

When Ramsden turned back into the room his face was a blotchy gray, scored in deep lines and shadows.

"What is she talking about? My 'girlfriend'? What's all that about?"

Aristide tasted burning in his mouth. He was staring at Ramsden, willing him to answer, but the man avoided eye contact and shrugged.

"You'll find out soon enough."

"No. No, that's not good enough, Ramsden. Tell me. What's Candy done now?"

Ramsden shook his head and stepped away, as if disengaging from the conversation. "We won't be making any statements to the chief of police, Captain Burns, Aristide. And if you repeat anything of what I am about to tell you, I'll deny it all. Understood?"

Aristide's shoulders ached with the tension of holding on.

Ramsden had laced his fingers together as if he were conducting some winery tour. "De Vile wanted us to adulterate your entry to ensure you didn't make the final lineup."

He tapped his fingers together nervously, as if unable to repress the lies any longer. "Candy was breaking her neck to do it. You've no idea how much she hates you, Aristide."

Ramsden shrugged. "I didn't like the idea, but De Vile is a hard man to say no to and she was determined."

He expelled a lungful of air, and it took him so long to breathe back in, that for a second Aristide feared he would pass out on the parquet floor.

"She got the wrong pot. Instead of sulfur she put in wood alcohol. They were both in liquid form and she didn't know the difference."

He gave a weak shrug, as if acknowledging it was a pathetic excuse.

"She got the pots mixed up. That's all. Our labeling was off and she didn't understand they smell different. It was a terrible mistake, but no one intended for anyone to die."

Aristide shook his head in disbelief. "And you were willing to die to cover up for her?"

The old man stood in stubborn silence, his jaw set.

Aristide started to turn away, signaling he was leaving. "You're lucky Sir John's such a stickler for due process. He would never satisfy de Vile's lust for blood. I'd keep looking over my shoulder, though, if I was you. The senator's got a long memory."

He turned for the door but Ramsden lunged toward him, as if to prevent him leaving.

"Laurent, before you go. Has there been any word from the hospital?"

As if on cue, the hinges on the hallway door squeaked and Ramsden's cook peered into the subdued space.

"Mr. Meadows, sir, someone's come with a message for you."

Mrs. Mellsopp held a slip of paper in her trembling right hand. She stepped forward with her arm outstretched, as if the message the note carried was infectious.

Ramsden snatched the paper. As he read it, the last puff of fight leaked out of him.

"Mamie Bilouxie has died. And one of the night watchmen might not be far behind her."

He dismissed Mrs. Mellsopp and turned his stricken face to Aristide.

"You can forget everything I've told you. I won't be repeating any of it, to anyone."

He glanced over his shoulder, as if acknowledging Candy's absence.

"She never meant any harm to anyone except you. And as far as I'm concerned, that's where it ends."

Forty-eight

Aristide went in search of Duchamp immediately after leaving the Meadows' house, intent on setting him straight on any lies Candy might have fed him, but the man proved impossible to track down. Aristide returned to his Cosmopolitan Hotel room, nursing his sore feet from pounding the pavement, still worrying about Ramsden's comments in the Meadows drawing room.

He was like a dog with a bone, deciding on his best course of action.

Perhaps Candy was making false threats, in a desperate need to set him off-balance. He'd never thought her capable of murder either, but her reckless actions had disproven his belief, and Ramsden had confirmed it, though he'd made it clear he would deny all knowledge if challenged on it.

No doubt, either, that Ramsden would do everything he could to protect her from the consequences of her actions. They would have that cellar cleaned out by now, any trace of the adulterants removed. It was a secret they would conceal for the rest of their lives—he was sure of that if nothing else.

Next week, next month, they would sneak away on a European tour, and by the time they came back Mamie Bilouxie would be forgotten by everyone except Sam and Teddy. *Me and Lani too*, he added silently.

The Hawaiian princess had shown she

had a tender gift for friendship, and a keen eye for things others missed. He was incredibly lucky that she did. He might be sitting in a jail cell himself if she hadn't been so quick-thinking.

His fingers and toes felt icy as he rolled into bed on the second night after the first judging, even though the temperature in the room was mild. He slept only fitfully, and woke to bright daylight as exhausted as when he fell onto the mattress hours before. His brain was cotton wool, and a dull ache pulsed over his eyes. He scratched his head and swung his feet to the floor. Maybe a good dousing with cold water would wake him.

The slot in the door staff used for newspapers and letters clacked, and the morning dailies landed on the carpet with a cushioned, plopping sound.

He scooped them up, switched on the bedside lamp, punched the pillows into a back rest, pulled the blankets up over his knees, and settled down to read.

The *Alta California* gave a considered version of the Golden Gate disaster, quoting the governor reassuring people there was no public threat. The *Chronicle* went with the industry angle, talking to growers and judges and speculating on how much damage the poisoning would do to the state's reputation.

Senator de Vile calmed fears of a calculated attack on local winemakers and deemed the event a "very unfortunate episode caused by a deranged person or persons. The police are onto it and expect to make arrests within days," he assured readers.

Really?

Aristide checked the clock. The hour hand was creeping toward eight a.m. Room service was up and running. He could get some coffee to wake himself up. But first . . .He turned his attention to the yellow news sheets, the publications that thrived on shock-and-horror stories.

The wine poisoning was right up their lurid alley. What version of the truth were they running with?

The *Scarlet Runner* was the most notorious. He grew hotter as he rifled through the pile and unearthed it.

Golden Gate Wine Murders. The mysterious woman at the heart of not one, but two of our city's most recent notorious murders. A special report from wine correspondent Felix Duchamp.

Aristide's heart hammered in his chest.

The dramatic tale burbled on. How the beautiful but sinister Hawaiian was implicated in Bully Pike's stabbing, and now, remarkably, was also involved in the latest wine-poisoning case. She appeared to know more than anyone else about it. She had a close (very close, it was intimated) relationship with Aristide Laurent, Vino d'Oro's vintner, but she didn't take kindly to his longstanding love affair with prominent wine merchant Ramsden Meadows' daughter Candy.

Could it be a revenge attack? An attempt to get herself noticed? Perhaps a clumsy bid to cast blame on the Meadows Estate for something she'd done herself. Duchamp dwelt at length on the drama of Ramsden Meadows being willing to drink poisoned wine, speculating on why he would be so reckless.

An anonymous source "close to events on the night" described Miss Manolo as a "black tarantula. Very dangerous. You never know where she's been or where she's going."

Aristide forgot about coffee. He stopped noticing his pounding headache. As he threw on his day clothes and pulled on his boots, it was all he could to suppress a rising nausea.

Leilani Manolo was being branded as a deadly nightshade, a Black Widow, a woman no sensible person wanted to associate with, let alone accept as a business partner. Duchamp's account launched an out-and-out attack on her reputation, and it was all Aristide's fault. They couldn't reach him, so they were going after her.

Leilani's unfaltering kindness and loyalty, first to Mamie, and then to him, were her undoing. Her finest qualities had dumped her in this cesspool.

He had to warn her.

Forty-nine

"Beautiful, isn't she? Remind you of anyone?"

A man's voice, his breath hot on her neck, as he bowed low and whispered into her ear from behind.

Elizabeth Wenderhoven flinched at the intrusion, lost as she was in the proceedings in the front of the church.

She didn't need to turn to see who it was so rudely interrupting her reverie.

She knew the voice, and the smell. No one else she knew carried with them the same aura of wealth, refined leather, and fine tobacco.

Hector de Vile leaned into her private space in a back pew in the Cathedral of

St. Mary of the Immaculate Conception, the Roman Catholic cathedral on California Street in Chinatown, and the twenty years since she'd seen him last dissolved like mist under a hot Bay sun.

Down the nave at the high altar, a Requiem Mass for Mamie Bilouxie was under way, bathed in the ethereal glow of votive candles lighting shrines on the walls of the old stone and brick building.

She shifted across one seat space, tapped the empty pew cushion beside her and whispered, "For goodness' sake, Hector. Some decorum please." He slipped in beside her.

He was speaking of Leilani Manolo, that was obvious. He'd appeared at the moment when Leilani—who, along with Sam Morley, was one of the lead mourners—bowed and crossed herself before the simple oak coffin and slipped into a front pew alongside Sam.

Elizabeth put a warning index finger to her lips. "Later," she mouthed. She turned her attention back to the priest's commencement prayers and secretly hoped that "later" would never come.

She knew of the senator's latest dealings. She read the newspapers, had followed reports of his gaining a Senate seat two years ago, acquired without election by appointment of the governor when the previous incumbent died in office.

She knew he faced re-election in a few months, the first time the general public was voting for him as their preferred candidate.

And from the years she'd known him in Honolulu, she recognized immediately that he hadn't changed. He had simply grown into the man who was already nascent all those years ago, a man who considered himself born to rule the world.

The last time she'd seen him was etched forever in her memory. The night she'd been instructed by Archie to go and break the news that Abigail was dead. And alongside her, two bundles of joy, his twins, two little lives extinguished like their mother's, by measles.

And she'd known it to be a lie.

The feud between the two men, de Vile and his father-in-law Archie, was a titanic struggle from the first. They were cut from the same cloth: both ruthless, both determined to win. But Archie had started out as a man of God, and stuck to his Old Testament principles, a former missionary, ruthless in his intent, justified by his own righteous code. De Vile, an amoral and relentless sea captain, was willing to do anything to get his own way.

Archie's extensive East Coast business connections, made before he took on the brown serge of the Mission, convinced him that the merchant captain married Abigail to satisfy his dynastic ambitions. With her dead, he couldn't tolerate a tug-of-war over their children. In the freshness of grief, he was merciless.

"Tell him they're all dead and be rid of him."

She cast a covert glance de Vile's way. He'd always been strikingly handsome. The full flush of youth had faded, that was only to be expected, but his tamed vigor was complemented by his increased power and presence. With his chin-length, immaculately cut silver hair, lightly tanned complexion, porcelain-white straight teeth and eyes that changed color with his mood, from stormy gray to a sparkling sun-shower blue, de Vile dominated any opposition.

For a wanton second she thought of Abigail, and wondered . . . if she was still alive and Archie hadn't intervened, would she and de Vile still be together? She couldn't see it. Lani's mother was too much of a free spirit to settle for domesticity. But say she was here, with Leilani sitting next to her?

Hector already suspected skullduggery—his opening remark hinted at it. If they were seated here together, Abigail and Leilani, Hector would recognize the unavoidable truth of their relationship in an instant.

And she dreaded the moment when the penny dropped.

Fifty

The anticipated "later" occurred the next day, as Elizabeth knew it had to. If Hector de Vile set his mind to something, he was not easily deflected. She had pleaded fatigue after the funeral, but agreed to meet him in the City of Paris department store's popular café, rather than in her home. She wanted to maintain strong emotional barricades against de Vile's interrogation.

For more than twenty years she had dreaded the prospect of this day arriving, and finally, here it was.

She glanced around at the modish merchants' wives and lawyers' daughters, chattering like tropical birds over their afternoon engagements. The tinkle of bone-china coffee cups punctuated the high notes of female voices. She breathed in a delicious blend of chocolate, coffee and cinnamon and the tension between her shoulder blades eased. This was a good place to have the showdown that had been coming for so long.

She took comfort from the bass undertone of the rising chorus. There were enough men present—husbands, grandfathers, businessmen—to deter de Vile from making a scene. As he threaded his way to her table, no one bothered about a reclusive socialite and a politician sharing a brief coffee. She was safe. She could count on the potentially gossipy audience to keep de Vile on his best behavior.

One or two of his acquaintances dipped heads in acknowledgement as he passed, but she was satisfied she'd done the right thing when they turned back to their own conversations, finding the senator's arrival unworthy of comment.

She fixed her face with a "charmed, I'm sure" expression and smiled up at him as beguilingly as she could manage. "Hector," she cooed. "It's been a long time."

He raked her with his hooded eyes as he extended his hand in greeting and slid into the seat opposite. "Do you want me to cite the hours, days, minutes?"

She gave a tinkling laugh. She understood he was turning their long estrangement into a joke, but they both knew he could calculate the exact time if required. Hector did nothing in half measures, and Abigail and Hawaii had obsessed him.

The ritual of ordering coffee completed, de Vile wasted no more time on niceties.

"What's going on, Ellie? I've had a niggling suspicion for years they locked me out, and now I'm certain of it."

Ellie.

No one had called her Ellie since the 1840s. That young woman, with her certainties of life and love, had vanished long ago.

"Locked out?" She allowed her brow to crease into querying lines. She widened her eyes. "I don't think I know what you're getting at, Hector."

"Oh, spare me the bewildered ingénue, Ellie. You could carry that off to perfection when you were twenty.

But not now that you're . . . whatever age you wish to be."

He gave her a wry, gentlemanly smile.

"Let's drop the pretense that's reigned all these years. That girl, Leilani Manolo. I can't get her out of my mind. And Bully's murder? I can't shake the conviction they're related. Though I can't for the life of me see how."

He held his talk as the waitress arrived with their drinks.

Elizabeth said nothing.

He took his first sip, nodded approval, and fixed her with stormy eyes over the rim of the cup.

"You may not know all of it, Ellie, but I'm sure you know more than you're saying. Have said. To anyone."

He set the cup back down with a clunk, as if challenging her to a duel.

"*En garde* to you too, Hector."

She smiled to conceal the flickering anxiety in her belly.

He had the grace to smile back, but sat mute, watching, waiting.

She recognized it as one of his power plays, big silences that nervous people filled with incriminating confessions. But this secret was not hers to share.

"I truly don't know who or what was behind Bully's death," she said slowly, moderating every word with care. "I have no reason to link it to Miss Manolo. As for the Hawaiian princess, I'm told she is the daughter of Matthew Lilolilo Manolo. I've seen no evidence to cast doubt on it."

De Vile gave her a grim disbelieving smile. "You always were a fox. Even at twenty-two. Completely wasted on Charles, and on the good works you've made your life's work."

Her chest jabbed at the mention of her husband's name, but she suppressed any sign that de Vile had struck home.

He allowed a silence to fall between them, laden with unspoken thoughts. Then he echoed her last words. *"I've seen no evidence.* I wasn't asking for evidence, Ellie. I was asking if you had any ideas."

"Don't call me that. Don't call me Ellie. She died a long time ago." Her pitch was sharper, more intense than she'd intended. He'd see through her now.

"Oh, sorry. Beg pardon, Countess." He grinned, without a hint of repentance. "Charles did have faint links to an Austrian title, but I didn't know it mattered to you."

Now she was fully riled up. No one had got under her skin like this for two decades.

"All I am saying, Hector, is that I have no reason to disbelieve Miss Manolo's description of her family connections."

"So she's been here." His voice was sharp, insistent, and Elizabeth's head came up with a jolt. "To see you, I mean. Why?"

She took her time, swallowing hard.

"She was upset about Bully. She said she and her brother knew him when they were young. And she was upset she was present when it all happened. She thought I might know something about Bully's affairs, might know who or why they killed him."

"And what gave her that idea?"

De Vile's sense had quickened, like a

bloodhound picking up a scent. She could see it in the way his eyes glittered, hard and focused.

"She got the idea from Mamie. The woman we buried yesterday."

De Vile couldn't keep the surprise out of his voice. "What on earth does she have to do with it? She wasn't much more than a doxie, was she?"

Elizabeth clasped her hands in front of her and gazed back at the senator's undisguised disdain. "You really are intolerable, Hector. You know that?"

She flexed her fingers inside her soft kid gloves.

"Mamie Bilouxie was a sensible dressmaker with a heart of gold. She might have floundered in uncharted waters when left widowed with a small child without support. But those days are long gone. She was a respected member of the Tenderloin. And she saw comings and goings others might not notice."

"And what's that got to do with the Manolo girl? Surely she's not lurking about in the Tenderloin?"

Elizabeth shook her head, suddenly worn out with this conversation. A dull ache penetrated between her eyes. She put her hand to her forehead and rubbed it.

"Miss Manolo is one of those people who notices things others don't. She befriended Mamie's son on one of her first visits to downtown."

She dropped her hands to the table, checked her empty cup, signaled for the waitress. Met de Vile's determined eyes.

"Mamie was making her San Francisco dresses. She'd commissioned them in the blink of an eye, I guess because she saw Mamie needed the work. And Mamie was there the night Bully died. On Montgomery Street. Hellish experiences tend to create bonds."

"You don't have to tell me that."

De Vile's voice was low. Grief-laden, even. Or was that her fanciful imagination?

She scrutinized him. Shoulders broad and erect. The perfectly tailored dress coat with leather trim. The proud, handsome visage. But his aggression had evaporated.

"Hector, you're asking me about things that were never mine to tell. You understand that?"

"Damn your principles, Ellie." He put an ironic emphasis on her "forbidden" name. "I always thought they'd be your undoing."

He picked up his hat, reached for his cane.

"It's taking rather longer than I anticipated. I'll give you that." He gave her a ghost of a smile. "And did you tell Miss Manolo the same lies and obfuscations you've told me?"

The pain she saw in the fatigue lines around his mouth contradicted his jaunty tone.

"Perhaps I'm not the principled person you think I am, Hector," she said. "It's hard to not let someone down in these complicated family situations, whether you're planning to or not."

He rose from his chair with the careful hesitancy of a man with a sore hip.

"I will get to the bottom of this, you know," he said. "I hope no more heads roll before I do."

Fifty-one

Lani's face was pale as she peered up from the crumpled news sheet. The flimsy tissue shook in her hands, and she dropped it to the table as if she'd been contaminated by its contents. She balled her fists.

"That's so horrible. How can they write such things?"

Her brow furrowed in confusion. "Why would they do that?"

"They're trying to damage me by getting at you," Aristide said.

Aristide ached with his inability to do what he longed to. Reach out, gather her into his arms, soothe and caress her. Tell her everything would be all right.

Instead he sat ramrod-straight across the table from her in the Occidental's public dining room. Even though the hour was early, the place buzzed with travelers arriving or departing and breakfasting before or after. No one particularly noticed them, but he knew it wasn't the place to gather a woman into his arms.

More importantly, Leilani wouldn't like it.

Her head jerked up, and her eyes widened in shock.

Today she had on another fresh and free walking dress, this one in a red-and-white candy stripe, nipped in at her slender waist and short enough to give a glimpse of red ankle boots. He wondered idly if it was one of the frocks Mamie had made for her.

She repeated his phrase, as if

digesting every word. "Getting at you, by getting at me? Do explain. From where I sit it feels like a straight-out personal attack on me. They're accusing me of killing Bully and poisoning the wine because I'm jealous of Candy."

She flushed. "I mean, as if . . . There's nothing . . . There's never been…" She tossed her head in frustration. "Never mind. How is this getting at you exactly?"

He took a deep breath. Where to start? He could see she was embarrassed to be forced to even confront the issues.

"When I was at the Meadows' house yesterday, Candy made some very wild statements."

He paused, trying to remember her exact words.

Your girlfriend is about to make quite

a splash, though. I hope she enjoys it.

"Something about how you would make a splash and she hoped you enjoyed it."

She doesn't need to know the rest.

"A splash?"

"Yes. I took it to mean she'd planted something in the newspapers. I suspect it was the Meadows who put Duchamp up to those awful earlier stories about me."

She nodded. "But why would she want to this now? Hasn't she got enough on her plate?"

"She's not in her right mind, Leilani. She's lashing out to hurt me, discredit me. She knows I care about you, and she can get at me by getting at you."

He hesitated. "The thing is, she has succeeded, at least for a short time. I think it would be best if we don't see each other for a while, to protect you from any more scandal."

Lani had been reaching for her coffee cup as he was speaking, and at the last sentence her hand froze on the handle. She hesitated, and then continued with the movement of the cup to her lips.

"*Protect* me. Is that what this is about?"

She raised her eyebrows over the suspended cup. "This is all so weird, Aristide." She blushed. "I mean, there is nothing going on here. We are just friends. Anyone would think we're, you know. Whatever they call it, seeing each other."

Two spots of bright pink had formed at the apex of her gorgeous, straight cheekbones.

Her innocence struck him. There was no artifice about her. Wiliness, perhaps.

She wasn't naive. But nothing false. She was direct, sincere, and completely at sea.

She would never have dreamed of the dangers of being caught in the undertow of a practiced paramour like Candy Meadows. That's what made her so precious, and he liked her all the more for it.

"Candy really had her claws into me, Leilani, and she doesn't want to let go."

"And do you want her to let you go?"

Want. Her tone was light, disinterested, but her dark eyes bored into his.

"Never have I wanted anything more," he said. He was hitting the ball straight back to her, as direct and earnest as she was, and he'd never meant anything in the fullness of his soul so much, ever, in his life.

There was a long silence between them. "I tried to go after Duchamp. I was concerned about what she said. I wanted to head off any trouble she might have caused. But I couldn't find him. He wasn't in any of his usual haunts. I failed you on that. Badly. I'm sorry."

"I didn't even do anything . . ." There was a plaintive note to her voice. "I mean, I talked to Mamie." Her eyes filled with tears at the name, and she swiped one side of her face with an impatient cuff.

"I talked to Sam. That's all I did. Nothing to justify this attention."

She glanced up at him, her eyes suddenly mischievous. "I didn't notice any tarantulas climbing about when I was doing it."

Her laughter pealed like silver bells,

and he joined in her delight. "When you talk, exciting things happen," Aristide said. "Pity about the tarantulas."

They grinned, and then both went somber again.

"If you think it's best we don't see one another, of course I'll agree," Lani said.

"But it seems we're letting her win. And that's not right. Not right at all."

Fifty-two

He'd said they couldn't see each other to protect her. But as Leilani sat in her empty hotel room and tossed up between biting her fingernails or ordering a whiskey—and she'd never drunk whiskey—another bigger, darker thought wormed its way into her head.

What if his explanation for why they shouldn't see each other was an excuse to distance himself from her?

Maybe he was sensitive about the exposure of his name being associated with hers in such a public, scurrilous way. Especially straight after he'd been tarred with the Lothario brush for courting and then dropping the

Meadows heiress.

Her face heated up as she pondered the possibility.

I'm an embarrassment. He thinks being associated with me will hurt his chances in the competition, and he doesn't know any other way to get rid of me.

She shot out of her chair and paced her hotel room. She hated being here, separated from Misty and Kaleo and Cyrus. Away from the only family she had, because of that terrible scene the other night.

All of them were right. Even those horrible *Scarlet Runner* people were right. Ever since she came to San Francisco, she'd attracted trouble. It started with Bully and it hadn't let up since.

She saw in her mind's eye an image,

a lock of dark hair. The errant lock flopped over Aristide's sparkling dark eyes. Even at breakfast this morning, when he was at his most serious, his hair misbehaved. Her stomach did that breath-stopping, funny flip it did so often when he caught her unawares. Even when he was trying to be serious, his miscreant hair refused to observe convention.

She changed from her house shoes back into the red walking boots, grabbed her gloves and cape. She couldn't stay locked up in this room a minute more. She didn't know where she was headed, but she needed fresh air and exercise.

At her door she hesitated and swung back into the room. She snatched the crumpled *Scarlet Runner* newspaper from the bed. Smoothed out the crinkled newsprint to make it easier to read. And then slipped it into her bag. She might need it.

Two hours later she'd climbed to the Woodward Gardens lookout. She surveyed the city below her to east and west. She wandered through the five flower and plant houses, elegant crystal palaces filled with the beauty and fragrance of the rarest exotics. She barely registered anything she saw, she was so lost in thought. In her mind she was turning over everything that had happened—especially today's bombshell—in a pretend conversation with Kaleo. An imaginary Kaleo. He was off doing she knew not what.

"So why did we come here, Kaleo? Why? You might ask. We came here to find a good agent for our sugar. That was it, wasn't it? To feed the folks at home. To sort out the mess that Archie left behind. That was something we didn't see coming."

She walked on in silence. She'd progressed as far as The Hennery, where all types of fine fowl were penned on display, along with ostriches next door.

A niggling little voice sounded in the back of her head. "And then what happened, Kaleo? Even before Bully died. Bully got frightened. I told you. Bully, the man who was never frightened.

"I'm not mistaken. I keep coming back to it. Our big bold Bully was scared of something.

"And I can't shake the thought that it had something to do with Archie. He as good as told me it was."

She stopped in her tracks. "Misty would know. She *must* know. She knows everything there is to know about Cyrus and Bully."

She whirled around, to head back down the hill to catch the streetcar to the hospital. Aristide was quite right. She had no business getting muddled up in his life. She had plenty to sort out in her own. She'd come here to settle the sugar exports, and that, and that alone, was what she must focus on.

How she had allowed herself to get so badly distracted by a feckless Frenchman, she couldn't say.

Fifty-three

Misty was out of bed, dressed in a light day frock and sitting in a cane garden chair enjoying the afternoon sun in a paved area off the ground floor ward. A silk scarf muffled her throat, but Lani could see faint bruising on her jawline and presumed that under the silk her throat would be a mass of purple.

The older woman couldn't conceal her delight at Lani's arrival. Her eyes lit up with a mocking glint, and she extended her hand like an Eastern maharani receiving a tribute. Her long, slender fingers were cream-polished and buffed a perfectly manicured light pink, as if to compensate for her unadorned, brutalized face.

"Lani! How wonderful of you to come." Her voice, deep and languorous, sounded like the old Misty.

Lani leaned over her and kissed the top of her head. Her silver-blonde hair smelled of fresh soap and lemon. "They've been caring for you all right, I hope?"

"Wonderfully. But they say I can go home today. Cyrus will be along soon."

Lani's insides jabbed. "Really? Is that a good idea?"

"What? Me going home? Where else would I go?"

"After what happened, I'd think anywhere but home."

Lani pulled over a nearby wrought-iron stool and perched alongside the matriarch.

"We both know what happened, even if you haven't wanted to talk about it.

Who's to say it won't happen again?"

Misty took hold of her forearm and gave it an urgent squeeze. "Now, Lani, you've got to forget all about that unfortunate incident. Cyrus is very sorry. He'll never do anything like that again. He's promised."

"And what about Bully's *lei niho*? The whale's tooth? Is that nothing too?"

"Oh, that was all such a terrible mixup. Cyrus says Bully left it to him. In his will."

Lani felt as if she'd been skewered in the chest. "He what?"

"He bequeathed it to him. He can't have been wearing it the night he was killed. Bully says it was delivered to the house with a note from his executor saying it was Bully's last wish that Cyrus have it. Isn't that a lovely thought?"

Lani stared into Misty's face,

searching for a hint of bluff, of subterfuge, but earnest wishfulness was all she saw. Misty wanted to believe this hogwash of a story because it was easier than facing the truth.

"Are you sure?" Lani glanced away and frowned. "Bully always wore it. He was never parted from it. He had it on at that last dinner, I'm sure. You know how important it was to him. Tracing his ancestry right back to the days of the four gods of sky and creation, war and peace, fertility, rain and the ocean."

Misty's expression was stony, unyielding.

Lani charged on, relentless. "Kaleo was the one who pointed it out. Bully's neck carried abrasions consistent with someone removing it with force. They'd probably have needed a knife to cut the hair."

Misty shook her head emphatically. "His murderer must have grabbed at his neck in the struggle. Those marks had nothing to do with the *lei niho*."

She fluttered her perfect nails in front of her face. "Anyway, this is getting boring, Leilani. And you know how I hate boring. What's been happening in your life?" Her tone was sardonic, derisive.

Lani remembered the newspaper and drew it from her bag. "I've made a splash in the *Scarlet Runner*. That's what someone called it. A most unwelcome splash."

The pages rustled as she passed them to Misty. "Best start at the beginning and read on. Everything will be horribly clear."

Lani waited in patient silence as Misty read down the columns of fine print.

When she finished she raised a querulous eyebrow. "Why on earth would they do this?"

"Aristide Laurent says it's the Meadows crowd behind it. Candy in particular. He says they're using me to get at him. Because they hate him. After everything that's happened."

She was hollowed out and empty, drained after earlier being so charged with indignation. Glumness hovered like a black cloud.

"Though I can't see it, really. Why should she care? Maybe he's using it as an excuse to drop me."

Misty's mouth fell open. "Whoa. Stop right there. This mare is running far too fast for me. Back up please—"

Heedless, Lani galloped on. After having nearly half a day to get herself primed, she was ready to crash the starting gates. "Misty, you know I'd never kill Bully, don't you? That I'd never do a thing like that."

She was wailing now. "So why is this muck sticking? Now they're trying to make out I had something to do with the poisoned wine, when all I did was talk to Mamie *after* she'd drunk it. And then I reminded Aristide that Sam had given him one of the original bottles. That's all."

The pitch of her voice was rising higher, the words tumbling out faster. "So why are they picking on me?"

Misty placed her hands one either side of Lani's hand to calm her. "Because they can. Because you're an easy target."

"What do you mean?"

Misty's brow puckered in concentration. "Well, you haven't got someone powerful who is obviously on your side."

"Someone like Cyrus, or Sir John, or the senator, you mean?"

Misty nodded. "Yes. Someone like that. Someone who might threaten to sue them. To go after them. To make life uncomfortable for them."

Lani thought of the last time she'd hoped Cyrus might speak up for her, when that offensive Duchamp fellow had come calling. He'd left her high and dry that time, and it wasn't likely to be any different next time.

"Cyrus wasn't too interested in helping last time," she said tentatively. "You couldn't . . . You wouldn't have a word with him, would you?"

Misty pulled back sharply. "Me?"

"Yes. You know as much about this as anyone. Probably more. Are you sure you don't remember something that might help crack this? Something about Archie? About why Bully was frightened?"

Misty's mouth tightened. Her eyes coalesced into gimlet points of hard resolve. The open, engaged woman of a few minutes ago had battened down the hatches.

"Really, Lani. You always did have a vivid imagination. I can't imagine Bully being frightened of anything, and certainly not of an old man who is dead and buried."

The stabbing pain in Lani's chest propelled her hand up to clutch at her ribcage. To hear the beloved old patriarch, her grandfather in name if not in blood, dismissed so callously . . .

"Misty, you don't understand. Archie did something that created a feud that's still spilling blood. Bully gave me that impression, anyway."

"All your imagination, Leilani. A lot of crazy nonsense."

Lani sighed and stood. She would not get anywhere here.

But that didn't mean she was giving up.

Fifty-four

How did I know Cyrus was the one?

It seemed a lifetime since Leilani had asked her that question, although it was only a few days ago. Misty turned it over in her mind as she lay in her hospital bed. She searched for the man she'd married in the Cyrus who came to take her home.

Her Cyrus was easygoing, straightforward, kind, so different from her own languid sensuality. He never got riled by the male attention she attracted, nor did he object if she wanted a quiet evening at home in her own company. He had crinkle lines at the corners of his eyes from his affable exchanges with old women and young children.

The Cyrus who arrived at the hospital to bring her home was nothing like that man. Her stomach flipped with a hollow thud as she studied him covertly in the hansom ride on the way back to Folsom Street. Deep pain-curves shadowed the corners of his mouth. Dark hollows ringed his eyes, which darted fretfully.

He'd irritably dismissed a newspaper boy who approached hoping to make a sale, his face red with displeasure. The man who'd been a byword for genial openness seemed to be on guard, putting up the bulwarks against anyone who approached them.

Worst of all, the gaze which used to rest adoringly on her now skittered away whenever their eyes met. When had Cyrus become this man she did not know? Was it a recent change? Or had it been happening for months or years and she'd stopped noticing?

Heat crept up her cheeks as the full extent of her myopia registered.

The man she was sitting next to had nearly strangled her less than a week ago, and she'd accepted his desperate pleas for forgiveness, his proclamations of undying love and lifelong repentance, because she wanted to turn back the clock. So badly wanted to turn it back.

She was terrified she'd just made one more terrible mistake.

She thought back to the conversation she'd had this afternoon with Leilani, and her insides clenched.

How do I know Cyrus is the one?

If I ever did know the answer to that

question, Leilani, I have long since forgotten it.

"If that's all you need me for tonight, sir, ma'am, I'll be off home now."

Mrs. Roderiquez stood in the entryway, wiping her hands on her apron, surveying the dining-room table with its serving dishes of vegetables, the cooling beef roast, the rhubarb cream dessert laid out on the sideboard.

"You've done us proud, Marianna. We can clean up when we're through here. You go home. You've had a long day."

Misty's eyes flickered toward Cyrus, her lashes quivering with uncertainty. "Is that all right with you, dear?"

He gave an exaggerated sigh to mask his annoyance.

This fake, unfaithful version of his strong-minded wife infuriated him. He loathed the marbled, blue bruising showing through her porcelain complexion. The diffident way she deferred to him, as if ducking, fending off another violent attack. The way she refused to admit to her affair. Most of all, he hated her ability to prompt his guilt.

She's the one who's guilty, dammit.

Most of all he hated that she was the one who had brought all this about—her, not him—and yet neither of them could bring themselves to acknowledge it. They were cowards, both of them.

"Whatever you want, my love."

The words sounded facile, even to him. They would never get back on safe ground. The lies they had both told made it impossible.

"When did you last see Bully alive, Cyrus?"

Her lips curved in that peculiar smile of hers, the one that hooked up one side of her finely sculpted mouth. Her voice low and sexy.

The irritation of a few moments ago dropped away as abruptly as it had risen.

"Why do you ask that?" His voice was knife-edged, cold.

She was gazing at him with a soft, dreamy expression. "We never talked about it. Not that I remember, anyway. I'm curious."

"Well, it wasn't the same place you last saw him, that's for sure."

Without wanting it, his mind's eye filled with the picture he'd never wanted to see. His best friend and his wife in bed together, her hair spread in abandoned glory across his pillows, the expensive linen sheets in a twisted mess only half-concealing their entwined bodies.

Had he really seen that, or simply imagined it a thousand times?

"What do you mean?" Voice sharp, she half-rose from her chair, her palms flat on the tablecloth, pushing back, her jaw jutting forward.

Then she seemed to reconsider and sank back down into her chair. Defeated.

"What do you mean by that?" A more moderated voice.

Like a dam which can no longer hold back against the spring thaw, Cyrus's inner bulwarks were collapsing, dissolving in a desperate flood of guilt and grief and loss.

"You know damn well what I mean. Do you think I'm stupid, Misty? Do you think I don't know you've been carrying on with my best friend? That you were seriously considering leaving me for him?"

She stared, her eyes wide in shock, but she didn't deny it.

The silence hung between them. And then it was as if she had cracked in turn.

"It wasn't like that."

"Then how was it?"

The words were like bullets.

His voice rose in angry desperation. "How was it?"

They heard the front door click.

"That must be Marianna going home," Misty said. "Would you like some more beef?"

Fifty-five

"It wasn't like that."

Hector de Vile stood stock still in the Mays' hallway and listened.

Silence.

"Then how was it?"

He made sure the door closed behind the departing housekeeper. Then he stood exactly where he was, silent and motionless as the Rockies, listening to the words floating down the hall.

He could imagine Cyrus shaking his head at the offer of more meat. "Misty . . ."

His voice pleaded a warning.

Then Misty's voice, hoarse and cracked. "Lani. She knows. She knows what you've done."

She sounded close to a breaking point. "I don't want to lose you too, Cyrus. I can't lose you."

De Vile heard the sound of a dining chair being pushed back in haste, a screech of wooden legs on oak floor.

"It's too late for that, Misty."

She continued as if he hadn't spoken.

"That Frenchman of hers. He knows, too. They saw the whale's tooth. It's only a matter of time before they prattle to someone like Jim Burns or Russell's nosy brother. He's hand-in-glove with the police department protecting his brother's interests."

"We can make sure that doesn't happen." Cyrus's gruff bass.

"How?"

"There are ways. That girl's flying too close to the sun."

Misty moaning, low. "No . . . You can't mean . . . Are you talking about Lani?"

"Of course I'm talking about Lani, you silly cow. Who else would I be talking about? We don't need that complication along with everything else."

"Be sensible, Cyrus. We don't want any more trouble, either. And she's still our baby girl."

"She's trouble, and that's all there is to it."

Another chair pushed back, and then light steps across the room. Misty getting her cigarette case from the drawer in the decanter tray table.

"She said Bully was upset about something on the night he died. Do you know what it was?"

"Apart from not having you in his

bed, you mean?"

"Don't get smart, Cyrus. It doesn't suit you."

De Vile heard the flare of a match, smelt the familiar aroma of sulfur and camphor.

Another long silence.

"What's wrong? Do you want one too?"

De Vile imagined Misty's beautiful wide mouth in a round O, puffing smoke rings.

"The thing is, Cyrus, you know what Hector says—it's always best to know the worst."

"He only says that because he doesn't know the worst."

"What's worse than killing a man, Cyrus? What's worse than killing your best friend?"

"Living a lie for more than twenty

years? Leading a man to believe his children are dead when they're alive and kicking? Bully has a lot to answer for."

"Are you saying that's why Bully was twitchy? Because Leilani and Kaleo turned up here?"

"What do *you* think, Misty?"

Leading a man to believe . . .?

De Vile's chest was on fire. His heart was slashed wide open. The pain! He was pierced through. He slumped forward, grabbing at his ribcage, falling to his knees on the hard floor with a soft thump. The heels of his leather boots scraped on the parquet floor.

Ever since his conversation with Elizabeth his suspicions had been growing, but nothing had prepared him for this. His world had narrowed to one reality. Crashed, semi-kneeling, crucified by chest pain.

Then Cyrus's loud voice broke through. "Who the blazes is that? Someone's out there."

De Vile was paralyzed. Unable to rise, he awaited inevitable discovery.

Cyrus emerged from the dining room, a black pistol held in two hands, aimed straight at de Vile's chest.

"Oh, it's you, Hector. Fancy that. Why didn't you say you wanted to join the party?"

Fifty-six

"His story about a bequest makes no sense. None at all."

The loud clock ticking in Will Davenport's office magnified the silence as Will and Sir John Russell sat poker-faced before Lani, giving no clue as to whether they believed what she was saying or not. They had kindly allowed her to crash the meeting they'd been completing.

I have to get them to understand. To take this seriously.

She shifted in her chair. From down the hall she could hear the muted sounds of conversation and laughter. Kaleo was talking to Will's receptionist Sarah.

He'd accompanied her on this visit to Pike Consulting, but she soon picked up he was more interested in chatting with Sarah than being part of this conversation. "You're the one who knows about it. You saw Cyrus attack Misty. I wasn't even there," he'd explained with a grin.

She was coming to the end of her appeal. She didn't want to bring up the subject of Misty's unfaithfulness. It was too sensitive, too private to be disclosed to these men who weren't family. Besides, she didn't have any proof it was true, and now that Mamie was dead, she didn't know who else to ask— except Misty, and she wasn't talking.

"How could Cyrus have got his hands on the whale's tooth unless he was with Bully on the night he died? Bully always wore it."

She pushed back into her chair, enjoying the sense of protection it gave her.

"If it was sent to him as he claims, then it was from someone shouldn't have had it. And if that's the case, why didn't Cyrus take it straight to the police?"

Russell raised an encouraging eyebrow.

She shook her head. "I'm not here to try and solve Bully's death. Truly I'm not. But that horrible story in the *Scarlet Runner*, insinuating I had something to do with it, all over again . . ."

She wiped the corner of her eye, as tears threatened to spill over.

"All I wanted to do was find a reliable importer for our sugar and meet up with our old Hawaii family. It's all gone horribly wrong."

She eyeballed Will, her brows raised. "You're still with us, aren't you? This latest slur hasn't influenced you to change your mind? Whatever was bothering Bully hasn't put you off?"

Sarah appeared in the doorway without warning, Kaleo hovering at her shoulder. "Want some coffee? I'm about to make some."

In the last half hour. Lani thought, this girl and her brother seemed to have thawed social barriers. They were at ease with one another—she could sense it in the way they stood together in the doorway. It was so unusual for Kaleo to notice a woman. He spent most of his time running away from women who noticed him.

"That would be lovely, thanks, Sarah. And that useless lump hiding behind you can do some talking in here for a change. I'm running out of voice."

Kaleo dodged around Sarah and dutifully stood beside her.

"Can you take a turn here?" Lani said. "Explain to these gentlemen about our complicated family."

Kaleo's face wore that stubborn expression he adopted whenever he was hauled in on something she thought was a great idea.

"Really, Leilani? I can't see the point of boring these people with our personal history. How is it relevant to what is happening right now? It won't get you off murder charges." He raised his scarred eyebrow with a mischievous glint.

A bolt of annoyance shot through her. Did he ever take anything seriously?

"Kaleo, there's something we're

missing. I feel it in my bones. Bully hinted at it. Something to do with Archie."

Her brother lowered himself into the last spare chair around the table. He aimed a reluctant smile at Sarah, who still hovered in the doorway.

"Conversation to be resumed," he said.

She gave an answering nod. "I'll leave you to it and get the coffee."

They shifted their chairs to give themselves space, wriggled to get their haunches more comfortable, and waited expectantly for Kaleo to begin.

"Our mother Apialaki—Abigail in English—Kamamalu Arnold had noble blood. She was the daughter of a high priest and a favorite cousin of the fourth king, Liholiho.

"Sadly, her mother—our

540

grandmother—died young as well, and Abigail was given to Archie Arnold, one of the court's American advisers, as an adopted daughter. They call it *haina* at home. I don't know if you're familiar with the Hawaiian tradition, but it was common to give the first-born child to the grandparents. It was the highest form of love and respect you could bestow on parents.

"Archie originally went to Hawaii as one of the first missionaries in the 1820s, and he and his wife Cornelia had no children of their own. The Hawaiian royal house wouldn't stand for that, so they gave them Abigail. That's how they did things in the old days."

Russell cleared his throat. "So your grandfather was Archibald Arnold, one of the king's advisers for, well, decades. I know the name."

Kaleo dipped his head in acknowledgment.

"Archie was a smart man. He'd worked in government and the law before he joined the Foreign Mission Board, and he was drafted in as an adviser when the Hawaiian royals realized they had to change some of the old ways to survive. The island was being overrun by whalers and gold diggers and goodness knows who else. Everyone was fighting for a piece of the pie.

"He went from missionary to government minister, but he never lost the righteous faith. He made it his business to keep us all on the straight and narrow. He had a bit of an uphill battle with our mother."

Sarah arrived with the coffee. While she was dispensing cups of the java,

Russell grinned at Kaleo. "I can quite imagine. From what I've heard they lived riotous lives before the missionaries quietened things down."

Kaleo laughed. "I believe so. Abigail was as wild as an Oahu surf break, if the stories told of her are true."

Russell nodded sympathetically. "So what happened? You've got me intrigued."

Kaleo rolled his shoulders, as if aware he'd stiffened up as he talked.

"A predictable story, I guess. She entertained more young admirers than Archie liked. Those were the days when Cyrus and Bully and Misty were all part of her group."

"And Elizabeth Wenderhoven," interjected Lani.

Kaleo stretched his legs. "Her too. Do you want to continue the story?"

Lani shook her head. "No. You're doing great."

"The next thing she's marrying one of the young men in her circle with a pedigree Archie and the king approved of. Matthew Lilolilo Manolo. They even produced some story that they'd been chosen for one another when they were children. The rest—as someone once said of Napoleon—is history."

"Not quite," said Lani. "You've forgotten the next bit. Us."

Kaleo gave an approving, gurgling laugh. "Never let me get away with anything, do you?"

He paused to drink some coffee. "Sadly for all of us, our mum died during a measles epidemic when we were less than a year old. Our father died not long after. Archie and Cornelia naturally took over. We've always regarded them as our true parents."

He sighed. "Cornelia died when we were about six years old and we got passed back to our mother's Kamamalu line—what was left of it. By then the Royal School the king and the missionaries set up was closed, but we were still raised to assume civic responsibilities. It was drummed into us. We've always known we're expected to make a contribution to our family, our community.

"And we inherited the land from our mother's side that's in sugar. It's all held in trust, but we've got significant plantations, mostly on Maui."

He wriggled in his chair, signaling the story was over.

"And what about the sugar?" prompted Russell. "You've mentioned you had problems with Bully. What was that about?"

Kaleo relaxed into his chair. "I think this is where Leilani should take over. She's the one who talked to Bully." He ran his fingers through his hair, sweeping it clear off his face, and his jaw eased.

"Still with us, Will?" Lani asked. "You're likely to know more than either Kaleo or me about this next bit. We don't want to lose you now."

He gave a reassuring flick of a grin. "I'm with you, Lani. Don't stop."

"Archie oversaw our mother's estate when we were younger. We relied on him to keep it all working smoothly, and it did. That was it, until six months ago, when he died."

Her chest tightened. She wasn't idiot enough to cry here, was she? She raised her eyes to canvass the men at the table. Kaleo was patting spilled coffee with a napkin, but Russell and Will gazed at her attentively.

Russell cleared his throat again. "I'm sorry to hear that, Leilani. I imagine that was a significant loss for you."

Lani swallowed hard. "It was. And he was hardly buried before things started falling apart. We'd dealt for years with a reputable sugar exporter on the island, Universal Sugar. They'd been our representatives forever. I suppose we weren't paying enough attention.

"Without us knowing, they were bought by a competitor, Diamond Sugar. Then we were told our long-term contract with Universal was void. We'd have to negotiate a new one. And the terms Diamond Sugar is offering aren't workable. We'd go out of business if we accepted them."

She brought her hands together and

squeezed her fingers, as if trying to defuse the anxious, high-wire energy building inside her. "I've talked with some of the other owners, and no one else has been offered the lousy deal we have."

She leaned over her linked hands and gave a big sigh. "I don't know if you keep up with sugar prices, Sir John, but it's a tough time for producers at the moment. The easy ride we had during the American War when Louisiana sugar was blocked by the North ended in '61, when the war ended. And despite our best efforts, we haven't got a free-trade agreement yet, so we're paying tariffs on everything we land here. If you add the squeeze Diamond is putting on us on top of all that, we'll go broke."

She glanced up and saw that Kaleo was watching her, an admiring warmth in his eyes.

"We've got people—villages of people—relying on us. We can't go home and say "'Sorry. We're leaving the sugar to rot in the ground.' We can't do it."

She twisted up her mouth into a grimace. "I've begun to wonder if it's a deliberate campaign to drive us out of business. To push us into selling up to one of our competitors. Like Diamond. I suspect they might want to become producers as well as exporters."

She shook her head in disbelief. "I know it sounds far-fetched, but honestly. Who knows how deep this goes?

"Thing is, that night I talked with Bully, he made some remark about how it was 'Archie's fault and he should have known better.'

"He made it sound like a vendetta

against Archie and we were caught in the crossfire."

She put her hand over her mouth and swallowed.

"Bully's excuse was he had an exclusive deal for Diamond Sugar clients, and if we weren't one of them he couldn't help."

She was about to ask Will if he was bound by the same restrictions when Russell interrupted.

"You mentioned Diamond Sugar, Leilani. Hector de Vile has a controlling interest there. Have you asked him about it?"

"The senator? Really? I didn't know that."

"Nor did I," said Will. "That's strange."

Lani's heart slowed right down. The thumping pulse reverberated in her ears. *Pump, pump, pump*.

She raised her eyes to Sir John. She knew he'd be watching her like a hawk, and he was.

She grimaced. "So what do you think, Sir John? How do we handle this? What's the next step, before our people starve?"

Fifty-seven

Cyrus was standing no more than six feet away, his mouth opening and closing, shaping words, but they were drowned out by the intense buzzing in Hector's head.

He put his hands to his ears and tipped his head from side to side as if he had water in his ears. The noise faded to a dull hiss, through which his friend's voice echoed.

Bully has a lot to answer for . . . Leading a man to believe his children are dead when they're alive and kicking.

He glanced down the hallway. Cyrus was still there, gun at the ready, a sardonic grin on his lips, as if waiting for him to speak.

"Sorry, Cyrus, what did you say?"

He wobbled to his feet, his legs unsteady, the space between his ears reverberating with distorted sound.

"I said, why didn't you say you wanted to join the party? The more the merrier!"

Cyrus waved him through with the gun, as if it was routine to greet a friend with a weapon in hand, but his icy eyes vetoed conversation.

Misty shrank back into the big cherry-red cushions of the velvet sofa, femme fatale no longer.

Cyrus gestured to the vacant spot on the sofa beside her. "Sit there."

Her hand crept across the soft fabric to touch his arm, but she neither looked at him nor spoke.

"Touching. So touching," Cyrus mocked. Her hand flew back to her lap, as if she'd fingered hot metal.

Hector cleared his throat. "What's with the gun, Cyrus?"

The consul glanced at the black object in his hand as if seeing it for the first time.

"Just being safe. You never know who you can trust these days," he said, his eyes roving to Misty.

"I don't know about that."

Cyrus dropped into one of the chairs at the table, but maintained his vigilance.

"But then, it seems there's a lot I didn't know."

Hector was overwhelmed with an intense fatigue, as if years of playing top dog had finally become too much. He pushed his back against the luxurious plumpness of the sofa cushion and a wave of dizziness briefly destabilized him. His body couldn't maintain its fortitude a minute longer.

He would probably die here, because Cyrus had clearly gone mad.

A jewel-like clarity overtook the brain fog.

A woman, running from him laughing, her dark eyes flashing, black hair streaming behind her, as she plunges into the waves, inviting him to give chase. He is charged again with the surge of challenge, the delight of his certainty that she wants to be caught, wants to surrender to his strong arms.

He smells the saline tang of the air, hears the gulls wheeling overhead, and when he searches for her, he is almost blinded by the bright sunlight glinting along the fall line of the foaming surf.

He is in his twenties again, captain of the *Independence,* one of the most successful of the merchant fleet visiting Lahaina, and he's filled with an exhilarating certainty only possible for a brilliant and ambitious young man with no doubt he will one day rule the world.

Offshore from the harbor, in the deep Pacific channel known as Lahaina Roads, up to a hundred vessels jostle, bow to stern, for safe anchorage, and many of the captains aboard those vessels would agree that he is the rising man.

And the woman teasing him with her rush into the surf, inviting him to the mutual pleasure of capture, she's the one who will help him make that happen. Apialaki Kamamalu Arnold, noble-born, a favorite of King Kamehameha III, a match for him in every sense, as wild and handsome as he. Sealing an alliance with this woman is the path to power and riches in the Paradise Kingdom. He is about to seal his future by marrying the most desirable and eligible of them all.

Hector opened his eyes with a jarring jolt.

Misty had shifted a barely perceptible distance closer to him, clearly fearing her husband. Cyrus was sitting where he was before, twirling the gun around his index finger.

"I hope you haven't got that thing loaded," Hector said. "I'd rather my life didn't end just yet."

Cyrus snickered.

Hector put his elbows on his knees and leaned forward in a man-to-man gesture of solidarity.

"I apologize. I don't mean to intrude. I arrived as your housekeeper was leaving and she let me in. And then, I didn't want to interrupt."

"You didn't want to interrupt." Cyrus's voice was jeering. "Come on, Hector. You always want to be the center of attention. Anywhere. Anytime. Now you've got your wish."

"Cyrus, Hector's done nothing except happen to be in the wrong place at the wrong time." Misty's voice had regained some of its usual strength. "Be reasonable."

Cyrus's eyes were blistering. "We've heard too much from you already."

Hector interjected into their bickering. "The funny thing is, I was coming here to ask you about those Hawaiians—the Manolo twins."

His eyes went from Cyrus to Misty and back again.

"No one—not Elizabeth

Wenderhoven, not you, none of the people I'd expect to know—is willing to talk about them."

He rocked back on the sofa, extended his arms in an expansive gesture along the backrest, claiming the space on both sides. "It's important to me, because that Frenchman Laurent is getting under my skin. And I've concluded the easiest way to get to Laurent is through the Manolo girl."

Misty finished one cigarette and lit another. Hector directed his attention back to Cyrus.

"Can I get a cigar out of my coat pocket, old mate? You won't shoot me if I reach for it? A cigar. That's all."

Cyrus waved the gun as an assent. "Get one for me too."

He handed a cigar to Cyrus, lit his and took a couple of puffs, shifted his weight yet again, and sank back into the pillows. "That's the reason I am here. Not to spy on you. Just to learn all I can about the girl and her brother."

He took his time, inhaling a big draw on the Cuban, then exhaling it in perfect little smoke rings.

He fixed his eyes on Misty, because she was the softest touch. "From what I heard out there, there's more to it than I imagined. After twenty-three years I've got a right to hear about it, don't you think? Because unless I'm going soft in the head, you've just said Leilani Manolo is my daughter."

The buzzing in his head started up again, though not as intensely. He couldn't trust his legs. He was glad he was sitting down.

"I ask myself, how can this be? Didn't I attend those babies' funeral? A funeral I will never forget, in the King's Palace at Maui, on the island of Moku'ula. Three coffins lined up, one full-size, two tiny, in the exact same place where I'd married their mother less than a year before."

He dropped his eyes to his hands. His knuckles were white. His heart was a hard, cold stone in his chest. When he raised his gaze back to Misty, her exquisite, ravaged face flowed with silent tears.

Fifty-eight

Lahaina, 1847

The greenery, the flowers, were the same. Once he had inhaled their scent in lightness and joy, but now in angry disbelief.

All of them. Gone.

He'd insisted on coming, even though Archie Arnold had made it clear he was unwelcome. The thunderous faces of Archie's missionary cronies when he entered the sacred hall made that plain. He was persona non grata here.

But as soon as he stepped inside the funeral chamber he knew why he'd come. He was taken back to his wedding day, celebrated here in the same green, forest freshness, the blending of oxygen and salt spray and earth with the fragrance of a dozen flowers—the glossy leaf-shine of the native maile, the fragrance of white-and-yellow ginger, the small, white pikake flowers with their big scent, and the bright red he'e berries, found year-round throughout the kingdom.

Moku'ula was a place familiar with mourning. Indeed, it was almost created for it. The sacred island, linked to the Lahaina seashore by a causeway, enclosed Mokuhinia, a large inland lake, said to be protected by a powerful spiritual guardian, the lizard goddess Kihawahine. Even more significantly, it was seen as a spiritual umbilicus for the nation, situated as it was roughly in the center of the island chain.

The king had interred his beloved sister here a decade ago, in a specially built stone mausoleum complete with pipe organ. Because of his refusal to be parted from his Nahi'ena'ena, Kamehameha III made Moku'ula his primary residence for eight years after her death so he could live alongside her, only agreeing to move to Honolulu when the capital relocated there.

Fleetingly, de Vile asked himself if the place might be cursed. Like the princess's before them, the coffins of his wife and children rested on a floral bier draped in scarlet velvet.

He was hollow inside, detached from the wailing that signified the honoring of departed loved ones. Strapping great men—the warriors of a previous generation—stood guard at each end of the funeral platform, armed with red, green and yellow feathered standards, the Kāhili which they raised and waved to a chorus of genealogical chants.

The people appreciated that the pomp on display reflected the king's fondness for Abigail, rather than her minor ali'i status, but it underlined Archie's unassailable position in the kingdom.

De Vile was Abigail's unlawful husband, and then only fleetingly. They had married in willfulness, without the assent of her family or the king, and the unapproved wedding brought him no status here.

Archie had seen him as an unrepentant gold digger. Hector had been associated with too many of the king's profligate companions, before His Royal Highness was corralled by the missionaries and turned to righteousness, at least in the eyes of the people.

Archie had accused him of using Abigail for his own empire-building ends. The very idea that he expected his wife to make her home wherever he made his—and most likely, when his sailing days were over, in the United States—was anathema to Archie. And, as it turned out, to Abigail also.

Within a few months, while he was away at sea, Archie and the king arranged an island-style dissolution—after all, they'd married island-style in the first place—and Abigail married someone else.

He made himself invisible, his back pressed against a wall, his face nursed in shadow, eyes roving the room for the new husband. Matthew Lilolilo Manolo. He spotted him prostrating himself before the bier, perfunctory in his movement, then moving off in a cohort of young men, intent on getting drunk.

As he observed, Archie emerged into the light of the oil lamps that lit the front of the room. With the sense of an old dog seeking out familiar prey, or because he'd been tipped off by one of his intimates, he lifted his hooded eyes and sniffed out Hector's scent. He wended his way through the mourning throng, slowly drawing closer.

"My condolences, de Vile." After more than twenty years in the kingdom, he still had the Boston Brahman's upper-crust accent.

"My condolences," he repeated, as if he couldn't think of anything to add. "But I told you. You don't belong here. You're doing yourself no good insisting on coming. If Kamehameha sees you, he'll get his monkey up. You'd best preserve the peace.'

De Vile didn't need a translation.

Here's the thing. This will stand badly for you if you ever need royal favor.

And goodness knew, most merchants only did their business in the islands with the king's tacit permission. De Vile swallowed pebbles. He eyeballed Archie for a few more seconds, then pushed away from the wall. The old man was right. He didn't belong here. The *Independence* was due to leave at dawn and there was still cargo to load. He stalked out without a backward glance, telling himself that this chapter might be over, but he still had plenty to prove.

Fifty-nine

"I was there," Hector said. "I saw them."

Misty nestled in the sofa corner, mopping her slowing tears with a white linen handkerchief that smelled of peppermint. She sniffed. "Things weren't what they seemed."

"Obviously." Hector turned to Cyrus. "How long have you known about this?"

Cyrus shrugged. "Since forever. But it was only ever whispered. Never openly discussed. Bully was the keeper of secrets, the confidante of the king. And they had the royal blessing, so no one dared speak of it."

"I can't believe it. You're telling me

Archie staged a funeral? Deliberately faked those two little coffins? The man is more of an arch-fiend than I ever imagined."

His mouth was so dry his words weren't forming properly.

"Cyrus, can I have some water? I'm parched here."

Misty rose. "I'll get it."

She hesitated, looked at Cyrus. "Can I get us some water?"

Cyrus put the gun down on the table and nodded. "Yeah. Course."

"I can't get my head around this," said Hector. "I really can't. I wouldn't have believed it."

Cyrus shrugged. "Abigail died. He couldn't fake that. They all got measles bad, Abigail and the babies. It was touch and go for all of them. The babies by some miracle pulled through. But that gave Archie the idea. If he led you to believe the kids were dead, you'd have no interest in hanging around. No grounds for any claim on them.

"Matthew wasn't interested in being a father. It wasn't his thing. Archie and Cornelia had been taking care of the children anyway, so it wasn't a big change. And when Cornelia died Ani took over. They were raised with their cousins."

Cyrus steepled his fingers. "The king remained involved his whole life. He was very fond of them both."

"And do they know any of this?"

He shook his head. "Nothing whatever. And I suggest that's how it should remain."

"Why do you say that?"

"Think about it, Hector. What if it came out that you've got a couple of

Island children you knew nothing about? Do you really need that a few months before an election? Isn't it adding unwanted complications?"

De Vile's chest rose and fell again.

Abigail's children. Once they'd been the focus of his ambitions. Of his desire to fulfill the terms of his father's will by presenting him with a lawful son. He shivered as he recalled the lengths he'd gone to, to meet his father's demands.

He rested his right hand on his stomach, and remembered the glow of pleasure he'd experienced resting his hand on Abigail's fruitfulness. She'd been a couple of months pregnant when they married.

But Archie was justified in his suspicions. Hector had seen his wife as a vessel for his ambition. If he'd any inkling Kaleo was alive, he'd have moved heaven and earth to lay claim to him. His father's will demanded it. Present him with a legitimate son before he was thirty, his father decreed, as a condition of claiming the lion's share of his estate as the oldest son.

Archie had stymied his first bid to provide that son, and Hector had hated him all these years because of it. But now he wondered if he'd underrated the old schemer. Had Archie somehow got wind of information he'd been certain was buried in the deepest of family vaults—the contents of his father's will?

He reached into his coat for another cigar.

"Want one?" He pressed a second on Cyrus. Concentrated on lighting both of them, savoring the first few puffs as Misty returned with a carafe, glasses and water for everyone.

"I suppose you're right, Cyrus," he
said through a cloud of pungent smoke.
"No point in turning over old stones.
Who knows what you'll find under
them?"

Sixty

Hector de Vile beamed and reminded himself of the old saying, "Revenge is a dish best eaten cold."

If only Archie could see me now!

"Can I suggest the sweetbreads to start, perhaps followed by the duck and venison?"

Leilani Manolo's eyes widened in surprise.

"I'm not sure I could eat that much." She glanced toward her brother with a dimpled smile. "But I suppose Kaleo can help out."

"Then we'll follow that with apple fritters with wine sauce and crème brulée."

Jack's on Sacramento Street was the place where politicians and businessmen entertained their clients or got together to exchange city gossip, the fashionable French menu one of its many drawcards. The dark walls, numerous gilt carvings and ornate wrought-iron banisters gave out a clear message: "You have arrived. You're one of us—a San Francisco success."

It had the aura of an exclusive men's club, so not surprisingly women could not eat here alone. It was the sort of place where a man took his secretary for lunch in a private room upstairs, and his wife for dinner in the downstairs dining room.

Hector de Vile raised his glass in a toast. "To the Manolo twins. So glad I have at last got the chance to know you. I might be able to help you."

He found it hard to keep the triumphant heat that filled him from flaring in his eyes.

If only Archie could see me now!

Leilani glanced at her silent brother, a flicker of uncertainty crossing her finely sculpted face. She was so like her mother!

Now that he knew of the relationship, he was amazed he hadn't seen it the first time he'd laid eyes on her. It was there in the confident smile, the erect, dancer's poise, the bold questions and wicked, flashing eyes.

"Senator, we very much appreciate this wonderful evening. To be taken out to Jack's! That's a special honor. But I am wondering why. You've an election coming. Haven't you things that are a lot more important than entertaining a couple of out-of-towners?"

"You do yourself a disservice, my dear," de Vile said. "I'm always interested in how our state is managing its business relationships—with locals and with visitors.

"As I think I've already mentioned, I spent some time in Hawaii in my youth. Even considered getting into sugar myself. As it happened life took me in other directions, but I have very fond memories of the Kingdom."

"And we've established before, you were good friends with Bully?"

"That's right. Why?"

"I'm curious. He was like an uncle to us when we were growing up. We'd hoped he'd be able to help with our sugar business, but he died before that was possible."

De Vile clamped down his jaw at the sharp stab her words provoked.

"Like an uncle, you say?" He forced a chuckle. "Hard to imagine. We only saw the dyed-in-the-wool bachelor here. I can't recall ever seeing him with a child."

"Oh no, at home he was great. He taught us to surf, didn't he, Kaleo? He was one of the few people Archie trusted to take us out."

"Is that right? And who, may I ask, is Archie?"

Leilani widened her eyes, feigning surprise.

"Our grandfather. Archie Arnold. I'm surprised you didn't know him if you were doing business in Honolulu. He was a bit of an old stick-in-the-mud but we owe him everything, don't we, Kaleo?"

She turned to her brother with an almost desperate appeal in her voice.

He gave her the most fleeting of winks and cleared his throat.

"We certainly do. Did you ever try surfing, Senator? Bully was a master at it."

De Vile toyed with his wineglass before raising it again.

The girl was an intelligent beauty, no doubt about it, but you'd be silly to overlook the silent Hawaiian Adonis who was her twin. A man of few words, certainly, but as shrewd as—well, as his father—and as perceptive as his sister.

"I did venture in a few times." He gave a self-mocking pout. "But I couldn't keep up with Bully. You're right. He was a master. How about you? Could you keep up with him?"

Kaleo grinned. "Nearly. Toward the end there, when I was getting bigger and he was getting older."

He glanced to his sister. "But Lani was nearly as good as I was." He winked at her again. "Nearly. But not quite."

She gave his arm a playful push. "The senator doesn't want to hear about our childhood games."

De Vile's temperature continued to rise. His chest tightened.

Oh, you don't know how wrong you are.

"And what about your parents? I hope you don't mind me asking, but what happened to them?"

Kaleo answered, "They both died when we were very young. We don't remember either of them. But we had a very good upbringing in the Hawaiian way. You know. Shared families. Hānai mothers."

He shrugged, as if the absence of

natural parents was of no consequence to him. "It worked fine for us."

The waiter brought the first round of dishes, and the conversation turned to the reasons for their visit, the calumny of Diamond Sugar, pricing them out of their contract following Archie's death.

"We inherited some productive sugar land from our family, but it's of no use if we can't sell the sugar at a decent price," said Leilani. "We have responsibilities to our people back home. We aren't planning to be here long."

She fiddled with the stem of her wineglass, an unusual sign of uncertainty.

"We had heard, Senator, that you had interests in Diamond Sugar. Is that correct?"

De Vile shrugged. "I don't advertise

my business interests. I find it's better not to. But I may have some influence there."

The conversation paused while the servers cleared their dirty dishes. The caramelized sugary aroma of duck à l'orange, the next course, reminded him it was a long time since he'd eaten lunch. The waiter topped up their glasses.

"What are you wanting?" De Vile deliberately made the enquiry sound lazy, casual. "For the sugar deal, I mean."

"Nothing unusual. A fair price and an undertaking to buy everything we produce, I guess."

Kaleo had taken up the cudgels again. De Vile liked this young man.

"I see. And what are you willing to do for it?" His voice had crisped up, hardened.

Their heads jerked up from their plates.

Leilani frowned. "Pardon me?"

"You heard me. What would you do to land this beneficial deal?"

She raised her hands, palms up in surrender. She glanced at Kaleo, stuttered a few half words, took a deep breath and began again.

"I'm not sure we have anything that would be of value, Senator." she said carefully. "Particularly to you."

Her mouth curled up in one corner, a quirky enquiry. "Clients of integrity? Raw product delivered to the highest standards without contamination?"

De Vile shook his head. "The first they probably wouldn't give a fig about. The second is a given."

Her eyes sharpened. "Then perhaps you'd like to tell us what *you* have in mind," she said, enunciating the words slowly and carefully.

The girl was a fast learner, de Vile thought.

"Oh, there's a lot of things. Lease back some of your land to Diamond, for them to grow cane?"

Lani stiffened.

Wow! Maybe the conspiracies I suggested to Will and Sir John weren't so far off the mark.

She drew down the corners of her mouth, indicating regret.

"Not something we're able to do, sorry. The land is all held in trust."

"I see. So how about this? Suppose you retracted what you said about that toxic wine the other night? Suggest doubt about Mamie Bilouxie and Sam Morley, what they said. I'm sure that French newspaperman would write something complimentary about you, if you did."

Leilani's eyes widened in shock.

"Something like you got confused. On reflection you were mistaken. You got carried away because of your upset over Mamie? Along those lines—"

"But why would I do that? It wouldn't be true. And it would cause trouble for Sir John and Mr. Laurent."

She stared at Kaleo, seeking help.

He obliged. He stroked down one side of his face, as if in deep contemplation. Then he nodded toward de Vile.

"That's what you want, isn't it, Senator? Trouble for Aristide Laurent? You can't stand him winning that competition. If you can discredit him and force him to withdraw, one of your approved flunkies will win instead.

"My guess is that's been the whole

point of us being here." He gestured around the table. "Getting us to play Judas."

Leilani pushed back her chair, half on her feet.

"Sit down," de Vile barked. "No one walks out on Hector de Vile and doesn't live to regret it."

She sank back into her chair.

"You have a straightforward choice, Miss Manolo." He glanced at Kaleo. "You too, young man. Play on my team and win. Or on the other side and lose. I'm certain of that. You'll lose. No sugar contract, and highly likely no Aristide Laurent, either. What's it to be?"

Leilani glanced toward her brother and a silent communication passed between them, a resolve back and forth that made de Vile think of soldiers arming for battle.

"We are most grateful for a fine meal, Senator," Leilani said. "Please accept our sincere thanks for the food and your interest in our business."

She brought the palms of her hands together and rested her chin on her clasped thumbs. Watched him like a hawk over her laced fingers. Then she pulled back her chin to give herself space to speak without distortion.

"We're not in the habit of betraying our friends for thirty pieces of silver—or a sugar contract," she said with a quiet decision.

"It's not the way we do things in the islands. Not the way Archie and Bully brought us up."

She gave him a clipped smile, as if she'd guessed how much pain the statement might inflict.

"They didn't live that way."

She signaled to the waiter for her coat with the assurance of someone who regularly dined at Jack's. "I'm sorry we can't oblige you. Nothing personal."

"You'll regret this, both of you. You'll be very sorry indeed. And don't come whining to me when you do."

"Be assured, Senator. We have no intention of asking anything of you. Ever. Whining or otherwise. Now, if you'll excuse us?"

The waiter was standing at her back. De Vile made a good show of standing, offering her a cordial departure, covering the wounds.

But inside, he smarted as though vinegar had been splashed on an open sore.

His daughter sure did know how to dress a man down. But he was still right. She would be sorry she had.

Sixty-one

Lani farewelled Kaleo and went back to the Occidental to run a long hot bath and soak off the grime clinging to her after her dinner with de Vile.

What a stealthy python of a man he was. Her cheeks were hot at the thought that he'd achieved high office with morals that stank to high heaven. The arrogance with which he'd suggested she lie to discredit Aristide settled heavily upon her. He'd resorted to blackmail before. Most likely it was his normal method of operating.

A shiver ran up her spine. She would ensure she was careful from now on, but really, what could he do to her? He would hardly gun her down in the street, and she'd done nothing wrong.

She luxuriated in the silky water, softened and perfumed by bath crystals the hotel provided. After a good long soak, she stepped out and wrapped herself in the hotel's fluffy white towels with the exact edge of crispness to tickle and pleasurably chafe her skin. She imagined a life where she could always enjoy such luxuries—and then thought of the folk at home who were depending on her.

Only a few weeks more. She would work it out and then she could go home. OK, she'd got on the wrong side of the senator, but Will Davenport seemed solid, unless de Vile had got to him somehow. And then there'd be nothing holding her here.

Her heart didn't do the happy little

bounce she'd expected at the thought.
If anything, her mood turned
melancholy.

She was contemplating cheering
herself up with hot chocolate from room
service when there was a loud rap on
her door.

She was wearing the terry toweling
bathrobe and slippers the Occidental
provided to all guests. Hardly the thing
for answering the door in. She tiptoed
over to the viewing glass and peeped
out.

A policeman in uniform stood on the
other side.

"Oh goodness. Just a minute."

She dashed to the bedroom, threw on
the Ming blue dress she'd worn to
dinner and rushed back to the door.

"Sorry to keep you waiting."

"Miss Manolo?"

The policeman was a stout, bald man with a walrus mustache and small, mud-colored eyes that were set too close together. She tamped down a rising sense of alarm and then chided herself.

What is wrong with you? The poor man can't help it if his appearance is disagreeable.

Then she noticed with a jolt that Cyrus was hanging back in the hotel corridor, like a bad smell on the officer's shoulder.

She gasped, "Oh no, Cyrus. It's not Kaleo? He's all right, isn't he?"

Kaleo had left her to return to the May house where he was still staying.

Cyrus flushed and shook his head. "Nothing to do with Kaleo."

The piggy-eyed policeman stepped forward. "Miss Manolo, I ask that you remain sequestered here with Mr. May while I search the premises."

"Sequestered? What are you playing at, Cyrus?"

She searched his face, but he ignored her, moving his weight from one foot to the other, his eyes scanning over her shoulder, taking in the room.

"Very nice. I can see why you prefer this to Folsom Street."

He gave her a sly grin. Such an odd thing for Cyrus to do. He was usually so benign. Open. Transparent. He had the pleased air of someone who knew something she didn't, and wasn't telling.

Next door she could hear the deputy banging about, opening and closing the wardrobe, pulling out drawers, switching on and off lamps

"What's going on?" she said. "You know why I'm here and it's got nothing to do with the quality of the sheets."

The retort came out with a tarter edge than she'd intended, but Cyrus was annoying her. The man seemed to think he could get away with murder. Literally.

Cyrus returned his attention to her. His eyes were hard and cold. That too was not like the Cyrus she knew. She was overwhelmed with pins and needles of alarm.

"You'll see soon enough."

She broke out in a cold sweat, the memory of the warm, soothing water dispelled in a moment.

These men had not come here on a random visit. They were setting her up.

The realization barely registered before the deputy emerged from her bedroom, Bully's *lei niho palaoa* dangling from his right hand.

He sucked his teeth, as if savoring the moment. "Is this it?" he asked Cyrus. "Is the item you saw among this woman's possessions?"

Cyrus nodded. "Yes, sir, it is."

The policeman turned back to Leilani and leaned in to her so she got another whiff of his bad breath. "Leilani Manolo, it is my duty as a sworn officer of the court to ask you some questions. I request that you answer them all truthfully." He paused and snuffled through his nose, as if the exertion of the search had been too taxing for him.

He held up the whale tooth. "How did you come by this item?"

"Officer, the last time I saw that item it was in the possession of this man here."

She pointed at Cyrus. "I recognize it. I have seen it often. But I have never,

never had it in my possession."

"Then how can you explain that I found it in your hotel room? Hidden under feminine items in your drawers?"

He sucked on his teeth again.

Lani eyeballed Cyrus once more. "I cannot explain it. I repeat, I have never had it in my possession."

Pig Face detached a pair of handcuffs from his belt. "Well, Miss Manolo, the facts clearly contradict that statement. I am arresting you for the murder of Bully Pike. Get your coat and put on some shoes. You'll be accompanying me to the Old City Hall where you'll remain in custody, held over for trial."

She could barely breathe. Her chest was tight and sore, the air rasping in her throat, but she held on to her grit. When she spoke it was a croak, but a determined croak.

"I'll give you something, Cyrus. De Vile sure is a fast worker."

A fleeting shame chased across his face, then he wheeled and stalked out.

Sixty-two

Lani had slept on a thin straw mattress, the hay stalks poking stiff and scratchy through a thin calico cover. A threadbare gray blanket barely covered her tightly curled body, so she was glad to have the extra warmth of her coat. She'd fallen into an exhausted sleep soon after the bald officer had deposited her there, saying he was off-duty and would question her in the morning. She woke an hour later to an itching line of bedbug bites that ran up her arm and over her shoulder.

The irritation made it impossible to get back to sleep, but it didn't really matter, because at about that time her new cellmates arrived, filling up the three-cell women's block with profanity and drunken belching.

The one on her right was a matted-haired loudmouth, a six-foot Amazon who wore thick makeup and the gaudy flounces of the bordello. When her profanities failed to raise anyone, she raked a tin cup back and forth across the bars to voice her displeasure.

On her left, two skinny, washed-out blondes, possibly sisters, had tumbled into the cell as if it was their second home, declaiming loudly that they "hadn't stolen no money from no drunken drifters."

Lani pinched her nostrils to escape the sharp acrid tang of urine from the overflowing slop buckets.

What will I do? How will I get out of here?

She was tempted to slump into a lather of fear and self-pity.

Everything had gone wrong since Bully's death.

She'd done everything she could to work things out, and she'd still made a muck of it.

She angrily dashed away a tear. She was experiencing a new low, and she had to get over it.

She roused herself, swung her legs to the cold floor, and pulled the blanket around herself like a shawl. Her Ming blue skirt was crumpled, the front speckled with tiny, rusty blood marks from the bed bug activity. She would burn everything she had on when she got out of here.

When I get out.

She buried her head in her hands.

What she wouldn't give to sink down,

up over her shoulders, into another of those sweet, steamy Occidental baths and then sleep. The soaking she'd been so rudely dragged away from last night was now a distant memory.

But before there could be any more baths, she had to work out how to get out of here.

The timbre of men's voices echoed down the corridor, floating into the dim cell space. The barred main door opened and the entry area was suddenly full of well-dressed men, the aroma of tobacco and cologne briefly supplanting that of human waste.

Voices, faces she knew. They were standing right in front of her, and she'd never been happier to see anyone. Sir John Russell, dark and grave. Beside him, his military brother Sebastian loomed, tall and commanding.

Shadowing them was a ginger-haired policeman she'd never seen before. He introduced himself as Officer Carnahan. He deferred to both of the Russell men, and avoided direct eye contact.

She wondered if they'd replaced Pig Face who'd locked her up because they suspected him of planting the necklace.

Then she recalled in a panicky rush that Sebastian Russell had been close to pushing for her arrest the night of Bully's murder. Did he consider they now held a conclusive piece of damning evidence? Case closed?

How likely was he to believe her naïve-sounding defense of dumb ignorance? Her heart banged in her chest, and as she scanned his face she worried that she detected deep skepticism in his eyes. She didn't blame him. Her explanation for how the *lei niho* got into her possession sounded weak to her too, though it was the truth.

Her eyes turned to the last of the quartet. Aristide Laurent, the womanizer who wanted her to keep her distance. His tanned face from long days in the vineyard was wan in the early morning light. Why had *he* bothered coming?

She tamped down the instant attraction tingling to the tips of her fingers, tried to ignore the magnetic pull of his sparkling eyes and mobile mouth.

He glanced at her fleetingly, then away again. A fluttering panic replaced anticipation, and then surging annoyance. She didn't want his pity or help. He'd made it clear he didn't want her around, and she was more than happy to oblige.

The group's arrival woke the snoring

Amazon, who hovered at her cell bars voicing choice invitations. When they ignored her, she followed up with a reprise of the deafening tin-cup symphony.

Sebastian spoke first, yelling above the din. "Miss Manolo! We need to talk."

She clutched at her cell bars and the blanket fell away from her shoulders. She crossed her arms over her chest, suddenly cold.

Sebastian gestured to the policeman, who reached for a key on his belt and unlocked the door to her cell. "Come with us. We'll find somewhere upstairs."

Sebastian organized coffee and bagels. Found her a bathroom where she could wash up, even gave her ointment for the bites. It was a lick and a promise, and she'd had to put her soiled clothes back on, but she combed them for insects before she did.

They assembled around a table in one of the offices in the police department, steaming mugs of coffee in front of them.

"Are you cold? Put your coat on if you are. We can't have you getting a chill."

She wondered if Sebastian Russell was this understanding with all his prisoners.

"Thank you. It's here if I need it."

"Tell me, Miss Manolo, where did you first see Bully Pike's whale-tooth pendant? Can you recall?"

She took a sip of the scalding black coffee and shuddered with pleasure as the hot liquid went down.

She shook her head. "I wouldn't be able to say exactly, Mr. Russell. Many years ago, when I was a child. He used to take me and my brother swimming, and he always wore it. Never took it off. He said it was part of who he was."

In her mind's eye she remembered riding his shoulders in the surf, her legs tucked under his armpits, his tanned back slick with salt spray, the soft caress of the twisted length of thick human hair the sacred object hung from pressing against the back of her thighs. She could taste the sea salt on her lips, shivered with the deep rumble of Bully's laugh rising up, it seemed to her, from the very sand on which he stood.

"Can you explain a little more about the significance of objects like it?"

"They are special. Considered sacred, even. We Hawaiians see—or used to see, anyway, before the missionaries came—whales as reincarnations of the ocean god Kanaloa. They were never hunted, but if they beached naturally our ancestors collected the teeth. Their rarity meant that only the highest-ranking men acquired them.

"To show they were for chiefs only, there was an old saying: 'Above, below, the upland, the lowland; the whale that washes ashore—all belong to the chief.'"

She had wrapped her hands around the coffee mug for comfort. She lifted it to her lips and another surge of reviving energy went down her throat.

She loved the old stories, these magic tales of her people, and she always got carried away in the telling of them. She glanced around the circle of men, unsure whether she had said too much.

John Russell raised his hand in an encouraging gesture. "Keep going, Leilani. It's fascinating stuff."

She gave a slight laugh. "I don't want to bore you."

"No danger of that. Please, carry on." Sebastian's face held the same grave, rapt expression as his brother's.

Lani took another sip and continued. "In old times both men and women of noble birth wore the *lei niho palaoa*, particularly on occasions like ceremonies or battles. The hair that they were strung from was important too, because they considered it a repository of power, linking the wearer right back to their ancestors and our ancestral gods in an unbroken chain."

She hesitated. "I don't believe Bully would ever have left it to Cyrus in his will, as Misty claimed. He would have said that was the *haole* way—the white man's way. He wouldn't have done it that way, even if he wanted Cyrus to have it. He'd have believed the ancestors would ensure it found its way to the man or woman it was intended for."

"Whoa!" Sebastian held up his hand. "Who said anything about a will?"

Lani glanced around in confusion. "Misty. She told me that Cyrus received the *lei niho palaoa* in the mail with a note saying it had been left to him in Bully's will."

She was talking faster, desperate to get all the twists and turns of the tale out in the open.

"Because she found it in his desk, you see. Last week."

She reluctantly glanced toward Aristide. "Mr. Laurent was there. He saw it."

Sebastian nodded assent. "Right now we're interested to hear what you saw."

"When Misty found it, Cyrus was so mad he assaulted her, nearly strangled her."

She repeated her refrain, desperate for confirmation. "Mr. Laurent saw that too."

Aristide nodded in Sebastian's direction, but remained mute.

"Let's focus on what you know, Miss Manolo. Start from the beginning."

She sighed. "Sorry, it seems so complicated."

She took a deep breath. "That night when Bully died, Kaleo noticed the lei had gone, and he suggested that whoever had it would probably know something about Bully's death, maybe even have been responsible for it. You were there, Mr. Russell, when we noticed it was missing."

Her throat was dry. She took another sip of coffee.

"Well, nearly a week later, on the Friday, I was making Misty a cup of coffee. She'd been writing letters in Cyrus's office. When I went in there, she was holding up the lei. She'd poked around in Cyrus's desk and found it in the back of a drawer. She was distraught, nearly hysterical. I'm sure she feared the worst—that it meant Cyrus had killed Bully.

"She was still very upset when Cyrus came home not long after. He was furious when he saw she had the tooth and attacked her. He'd have killed her if Aristide—Mr. Laurent—hadn't intervened."

She averted her eyes to Laurent. "Isn't that true, Mr. Laurent?"

Aristide nodded. "I've already told him. Why do you think I'm here?"

Leilani's cheeks stung as though

someone had slapped her, though it bewildered her why she deserved a rebuff.

"And then?" prompted Sebastian.

"Mr. Laurent and I took Misty to hospital because we didn't consider she was safe at home, and I moved into a hotel because I didn't feel safe either. But after she'd been in hospital a few days Misty had second thoughts.

"She didn't want to believe her husband was guilty of anything. I think she feared losing him. He came to visit her and made big noises about being sorry. That was when she said Bully had left it to him."

She stopped for more coffee. "Sorry. This is thirsty work."

"Mrs. Elizabeth Wenderhoven is Bully's executor. I haven't had a chance to ask her yet, but I bet there's no mention in the will of leaving it to Cyrus. It's complete flapdoodle."

Sebastian held up his hand again, index finger pointed skyward.

"I'll do that, Miss Manolo, don't you worry. I have one more question for you. How do you think the totem ended up in your hotel room last night?"

His sternness made her mouth taste sour.

"Truly, Mr. Russell, I have no proof. None. But I don't think it's any coincidence that only an hour or two before that, I had a showdown, shall we say, with Senator de Vile. He wanted me to do something for him I was unwilling to do."

She cast a glance in Aristide's direction, then hauled it back. "He made threats. Told me I would be very sorry for not being willing to help him out."

She gave a grim smile. "I know it sounds far-fetched, but I think he already had it set up with Cyrus. I don't want to be rude, but either Cyrus got into my room while I was out, or that police officer brought it with him.

"I wouldn't be de Vile's obedient monkey, so he arranged instant punishment. Last night I hinted to Cyrus that was the case and he appeared guilty to me. That's all I can say."

Sixty-three

"No! No! Don't let them take him!"

Misty clutched at her husband's arm, appealing to Hector de Vile. "They can't take him!"

Hector knocked back a second shot of whiskey and scowled.

They were back in the Mays' Folsom Street sitting room, but after the rout at the police station this morning, Cyrus was no longer holding an empty pistol on him.

De Vile was the man now in control, and Cyrus a fugitive wanted for murder. Or would be, once the cops realized he'd gone on the run.

For Cyrus was plainly guilty of Bully's

murder. De Vile hadn't been surprised to learn that the last time he'd been here and inadvertently eavesdropped on the damning conversation between the two of them. Misty hadn't been as discreet about her liaison with Bully as she thought she'd been—de Vile had already heard whispers of their goings-on before Bully's death.

She bore a big part of the blame for this mess, and she needed reminding of the fact.

"Burn my britches, Misty. Will you stop sniveling? If you'd kept to your own bed, Cyrus wouldn't be in this mess. Now you've got no choice but to run too. Vamoose."

Her jaw dropped open. "What?"

"Leave. You'll need to leave. South America? Europe? Who cares? You can't stay here unless you want to be a jail widow. Worse yet, the widow of a hanged man."

She put her head in her hands and wailed. "No! This can't be happening."

"You've been harboring a man you knew to be guilty of a capital crime. You might be charged yourself."

The hands dropped from her face immediately. She stared at him, growing paler by the minute.

Then she turned on Cyrus, ripping herself away from his sheltering arm, her mouth twisted in an angry snarl. "What have you done? You've destroyed our lives."

Like a deflated balloon, the fight went out of Cyrus. The amused light that had so often played in his eyes was extinguished.

"No, my dear, you did that. And sadly, you weren't even smart enough to realize it."

Her hand went to her face as if she'd been slapped.

Her attention returned to de Vile. "What happens now? Are you planning to turn him in?"

"Far from it," de Vile said. "I'll help you both get away."

He allowed a studied pause, and Misty gave him a sardonic smile.

"And in return? You do nothing without some payment, Hector. What will it be this time?"

"Well, well. I can see that despite Cyrus's little jab a minute ago, you're still a smart woman. Good for you. You can't afford to be dumb any more."

"Who do you want to pay back this time?" Cyrus asked. "I hope it doesn't involve killing anyone."

"It shouldn't do. Not if it turns out the way I expect it will."

He grinned at them both and sensed them recoiling. "But you never can tell. You must be prepared for the worst. Just in case."

He explained his plan. Told them what they had to do.

"Once it's complete, I'll have you on a boat or a train—-you tell me where you want to go and I'll see to it. But first, you've got to help me nail that Frenchman's ears to the wall."

Sixty-four

"Keep your wits about you and let me do the talking."

Officer Barney Carnahan nodded in relieved agreement. He was more than happy to allow Sebastian Russell to take the lead in interviewing one of the city's richest and most mysterious citizens, the Rich Widow of the Tenderloin.

Elizabeth Wenderhoven preferred her philanthropic activity to be private and anonymous, but her attendance at Mamie Bilouxie's funeral days ago had again sparked speculation in the local rags about her dealings with the city's poorest and most vulnerable people.

Barney knew that some questions

Sebastian wanted to ask touched on personal and delicate matters he'd never want to raise with such a lady.

He trailed behind the tall, well-muscled businessman up the path to the front door, thinking as he matched footstep for footstep that Sebastian still walked and talked more like the soldier he'd once been rather than the business manager for Basil Stockton's empire he'd become.

An attractive Spanish matron settled them in the drawing room while she went to find Mrs. Wenderhoven. She soon returned with fruit juice and glasses on a tray and the news that her mistress was joining them shortly.

The deputy's eyes scanned the walls with their gilt-framed paintings. He'd never been in a fine Nob Hill house like this one, and those paintings were like something you saw in museums. In front of the unlit fireplace stood big blue-and-white porcelain planters filled with live green ferns. He gazed around him, relieved not to be leading this investigation.

"Watch carefully and take notes," Sebastian said under his breath as the door opened and the Countess stepped into the room. She was about the same age as his mother, Barney thought, but there any similarity ended.

She swept her abundant brown hair on the top of her head, leaving some to fall in long curls around her face, which made her look younger than she probably was. Her eyes were sparkling and curious, as if she was expecting to learn something new. And when she spoke, the words flowed out like music, in perfect notes.

Sebastian stood, and Barney followed suit. "Countess."

"Mrs. Wenderhoven will do nicely," she interrupted, but she didn't sound annoyed. Amused, more like, Barney thought.

Sebastian gave a quick smile, which for a serious man like him was surprising to see.

"Mrs. Wenderhoven it is. My name is Sebastian Russell, and this is assistant police captain Barney Carnahan."

She held out her hand to each of them, her fingers lithe and light, swamped by his man's hand.

"Sir John's brother, I presume?"

Sebastian nodded. "The captain here represents the law in this matter, but I'm taking an interest because it has ramifications for our family business interests."

He gave another quick smile. "That, and because after the bitter war years I want to ensure that the world we fought for is the most just it can possibly be."

Elizabeth dipped her head. "Believe me, Mr. Russell, I'm fully in sympathy."

There was a moment of silence, as if some understanding passed between them. Barney surreptitiously pulled his pen and notebook out of his hip pocket.

"We would appreciate the opportunity to ask about Bully Pike's estate. I understand you are his executor?"

Elizabeth sank into a chair set opposite their sofa and assented. "I am."

"It's not an inconsequential matter, Mrs. Wenderhoven. I should warn you, some of the questions may be delicate. But lives are at stake, so I trust you'll understand."

"Bully's done and gone. He had no children, so I see no harm in telling you all I can. First, though, let's call Francesca for some tea."

As if she'd pushed a secret buzzer, the woman who answered the door returned with hot tea and biscuits.

"So you can say with certainty you did not arrange for the whale-tooth pendant to be sent to Cyrus? And you know of no bequest of that item?"

They had drunk hot tea, enjoyed fresh-baked oatmeal biscuits and got down to business. Elizabeth Wenderhoven spoke quietly and delivered her responses in a level voice, even when Carnahan expected that Sebastian's questions might shock her.

"I regret to confirm that yes, I believe Bully was conducting an affair with Cyrus's wife. They'd known one another many years and Bully considered it more than a light flirtation, let's put it that way.

"I was very close to Bully for a long time, that's how I came to be his executor. I respected his secrets and he told me almost everything. Well, I think he did."

She gave Sebastian a quick smile. "He'd reached a stage in life when he would have liked a wife to grow old with. I didn't want to marry again, and Misty isn't free to marry, so he came up short."

"And do you believe jealousy drove Cyrus to kill him?"

She stared into her teacup for a long time before answering.

"I honestly would never have thought him capable of that level of rage. It's very out of character for him to be violent. But I've sadly concluded that's the most likely explanation. He adored Misty his whole life, and she never gave him reason to be possessive before.

"She's always attracted a lot of male attention, yes. But I think he enjoyed having a desired wife, because he was secure that he possessed her. He and no one else. When she stepped over that boundary, it was a different story."

Sebastian twisted his mouth in regret. "He'll have guessed we're onto him. His silly attempt to implicate Leilani Manolo would never have worked for long—not when he's been seen with the necklace. And he put his wife in hospital with a vicious attack. If he's seeking an escape, where do you think he'd run to in the short term?"

Elizabeth searched the inside of her

teacup, as if divining the answer, and then gazed directly at Sebastian with sad eyes.

"Bully and Hector are excellent friends with William Ralston, the Bank of California man. He has a wonderful estate twenty miles south of here, at Belmont. A remarkable house set in two hundred acres of park.

"I stayed there often with Bully. The menfolk use it as a bit of a 'boys' retreat' when they want privacy. There are so many rooms you can occupy an entire wing, and no one would know you are there unless you want them to."

She stood, if she'd said all that was required of her.

"That's my guess, for what it's worth. Ralston Hall, or Belmont. It's known by both names. It would provide a perfect luxury hideout while they decide what to do next. William would be loath to think the worst of Cyrus. He'd welcome him as a guest in all innocence, as he has in years gone by.

"Everyone loves Misty, and I suspect she's been there often with Bully in recent times. She'd know the place. Try that. It takes about an hour on the San Jose train. It's gorgeous. And let's face it. Misty would never want to rough it."

Sixty-five

Charles Krug, one of the Golden State's best-liked and respected wine growers, had agreed to be the master of ceremonies for the Golden Gate Symposium finale, and as the ladies and gentlemen who'd paid $50 a head to sample the evening's selections over a fine dinner made their way into the Occidental ballroom, his steady presence lent the occasion much-needed gravitas.

A man further removed from the poisoned-wine disaster of a few nights ago couldn't be imagined. The German had enjoyed a reputation for making superior wine in Sonoma for nearly a decade, but he was even more highly valued for his unwavering integrity and encouragement of better wine quality and higher standards. As the wine commissioner for Napa County he was one of the industry's key men, and the elect group arriving in black-tie suits and sequined evening dresses knew it.

He was a serious, stocky man with a neat salt-and-pepper beard, close-trimmed hair and steady eyes framed by librarian-style steel-rimmed glasses. The Occidental's staff were scurrying helter-skelter, carrying out his commands under Sam Morley's watchful eye.

Tonight would prove very different from the debacle of a few days ago, Aristide was confident of that. The evening was scheduled to get under way by five p.m., but he'd arrived at least two hours early, on tenterhooks to satisfy himself nothing would go wrong with their entry this time. He'd pestered Will for reassurance, hung around the kitchen offering Sam assistance, and generally made a nuisance of himself, he had to admit.

Underlying all his pent-up anxiety about wine was an even deeper tension he hadn't been able to shake off since that awful scene this morning in the Market Street jail. He saw it all again in his mind's eye: a recoiling, frightened Leilani Manolo, disheveled and defenseless, her arm covered in angry bites.

She could barely bring herself to look at him. No matter that they'd been able to get her released immediately, she shouldn't have been there, and she probably wouldn't have been except for her association with him.

His sick shame at causing her undeserved distress threatened to swamp his eager anticipation for the coming awards. Lani would not be here to share them, and that took the shine off everything.

Because the state's "new" wine industry—post the Mission period—was only a decade old, and the varieties of grapes being grown and tested were wide, the finals were judged in three broad categories: still whites, sparkling wines, and reds. The grape varieties in each category were flexible—anything from Muscat of Alexandria to Golden Chasselas, from Black Malvoisie to Zinfandel. Vino d'Oro had entered in two of the three categories, the still whites and the reds. They were leaving the sparkling wines to experts like

Charlie Krug, who'd already got excellent reviews in local wine sheets.

The hotel waiters had opened the reds the judges would be tasting and poured them into unmarked bottles so the judges weren't influenced by labeling. Not only did this ensure that no one had an inkling of what they were tasting ahead of time, but it also gave the new vintages time to breathe and sediment to be decanted off.

With an hour to go they opened the still whites, poured them into plain carafes and put them in the hotel cooler. A few minutes before the tasting they would bring them out and put them in buckets of ice, some for the judges, the rest for guests who would eat their way through a full menu while the panel cleansed their palates with nibbles of bread rolls.

Behind the judges' dais were placed several champagne buckets on stands for them to spit the wine into.

With Charles Krug watching, Sam wrote out the names of all the wines on small pieces of paper, then placed them in a hat. Krug would ask Governor Hunt to draw the names out to determine the order in which they would taste the wines, with the sparkling whites first, followed by the still whites, and then the reds.

Only Krug would know that order until after it all was over.

As the judges filed in and took their seats at the high table, Aristide noted the scorecards, pencils, and two stemmed glasses already set at each place. Each judge was asked to rate the wines by four criteria.

By sight—for color and clarity. For

smell, for taste and "harmony"—a combination of the effect the drop had on all the senses. Each entry was marked out of twenty, and the results collected and counted—once again under Krug's keen eye—in two sessions. All of the whites first, followed by a break, announcement of the first round of winners and then the reds.

And then finally, the grand finale was underway.

"Not hungry, Aristide?" John Russell's eye-catching New Zealand wife Pania, known to every person in the room as the stage star Pania Hayes, cast a sympathetic eye at the bowl of French onion soup going cold in front of him.

The Russell clan had turned out in force, with Sebastian's wife Isabelle, and the youngest brother, Nathan, also

present with his wife Graysie, another
singer before she settled, like Pania,
into new motherhood. The only ones
absent were his sister Madeleine and
her husband Caleb. She was pregnant
with her first child and wasn't going out
at night.

Together they filled a table, with Will
Davenport taking the chair that might
have been for his escort, if he'd had
one.

Aristide gave Pania a rueful smile.
"I'm sure it's delicious, but I'm happy
to leave it."

"You'll be starving later," she teased.
"After you've won."

Truth was, he couldn't keep his
attention off what was happening at the
judging table. As the army of waiters
circled the room serving the paying
guests with Shrimp in Saffron Cream,

Veal Fricassée with Veal Meatballs and Oysters, Petits Pois de Paris, and the rest of a fulsome lineup, the judges were quietly working their way through the selections with serious faces, swirling the wine in the glass to catch the bouquet, leaning forward to take a good noseful of the aroma, and then working it in their mouths.

Wine tasting was a sober business. Sometimes Aristide would catch a grimace—some disliked edge or acidity a sensitive palate had detected—and at other times a raised eyebrow of appreciation. Something to the man's liking. Between wines the judges exchanged quiet comments. How he'd love to be close enough to eavesdrop.

Hector de Vile sat at a table with Governor Hunt and other wine commissioners while the Meadows, not surprisingly, were nowhere to be seen. He imagined Candy was already on a train to the East Coast, there to board an ocean liner to London or Paris. And good riddance to her.

And then Charles Krug was tapping a glass with a spoon and standing to make his first announcement.

"Ladies and gentlemen, we will now take a break before we serve dessert to give our judges a breather and a chance to sip some mineral water and recover their palates. But before we do, I've got our first round of eagerly awaited results."

His eyes behind the wire rims held a mischievous twinkle. Even the solemn Krug knew how to play a room.

"Let me explain: we've agreed to nominate one winner, and then the closest two runners-up in each category. Here we go. Top three entries in the sparkling wine class are: First place, Arpad Haraszthy at Buena Vista in Sonoma, followed by Victor Fauré from Mariano Vallejo's Sonoma vineyard, and Charles Krug, also from Sonoma.

"Seems like a win-win for Sonoma," Krug joked. "And no, as you can all see, I wasn't one of the judges."

The crowd, happily full of food and wine, laughed appreciatively. Aristide noticed out of the corner of his eye that de Vile had shot a triumphant glance toward the Russell table. He pretended not to notice. So the Buena Vista vineyard—if not the cooperative—would have something to boast about.

Krug brought out the second sheet of paper, with the next round of results, and Aristide's stomach tightened. Thank goodness he'd eaten nothing, or he might be heading for the bathroom at this moment.

"And now for the second category, the still whites." Krug adjusted his glasses, and glanced over at their table. He pushed them back up his nose and began reading.

"First place, White Muscat, Sir John Russell and Vino d'Oro. Runners-up, Jacob Schram from Mount Diamond with a Riesling Hock, and George West, from San Joaquin, with a Golden Chasselas."

Krug removed his glasses. "Let it be noted that George West abstained from judging in this category. Ten minutes, ladies and gentlemen, and then we'll resume our seats for dessert and the last category, the red wines."

Sixty-six

"Misty! What are you doing here?"

Lani's aunt stood in her hotel room doorway, her cheekbones highlighted a hectic rose-pink. Misty never got excited, so what was up?

"It's Cyrus. I need your help, dear child. Please. Come with me now. We've got to find him."

She wore a silvery-olive day gown trimmed with a subtly contrasting braid border and tiny mother-of-pearl buttons down the front. She twirled her matching foiled parasol on the hallway carpet, to emphasize urgency. Odd that she'd bothered with a parasol too, Lani thought. The afternoon was nearly over, so she could hardly expect hot sun.

"What do you mean, find Cyrus? Has he gone missing?"

Misty struck a languorous pose against the doorjamb, contradicting her anxiety of a few seconds ago.

"He's not at home. I don't know where he is. I'm worried. With everything that's been going on . . ." Her voice trailed off.

"Well, I can't say I'm surprised." Lani's voice was chiding, as if she were the adult and Misty the child. "After that stunt he pulled—what has gotten into him?"

"I don't know, Lani, but I need your help. Please!"

Lani stepped aside. "If I'm going out I'll need to grab a coat and change my shoes." She ushered Misty inside. "What are you proposing?"

"I thought we might visit Elizabeth. The Countess. She might know where he's gone."

This struck Lani as even more ridiculous than the idea that the Cyrus might have absconded without Misty. "Really? Why? How?"

"Well, she knows everything. Maybe Bully told her something . . ." Her voice trailed off again, uncharacteristically tentative.

"Bully? This gets weirder by the minute. What's Bully got to do with it? And why would Cyrus leave without you? We all know he's devoted to you."

"Let's talk about this in the cab. Get your coat. We can't waste another minute."

Lani searched Misty's face, trying to see beyond the veil of distraction playing across her classic features. And she considered her options.

Go on this merry jaunt with Misty, or stay here alone resisting the urge to go downstairs to the ballroom?

She cringed at the social faux pas that would amount to. Crashing a party to which she hadn't been invited and, worse, been expressly asked to stay away from.

"Wait there. I'll get my coat."

Misty draped her arm over her shoulder as they stepped into the street where a hack stood, waiting for them.

"I can't tell you how much I appreciate this, Lani. I really do."

They got in and the driver moved them off with no further instructions. Misty must have primed him before she came in to pick her up.

The cab proceeded up Market Street, the broad avenue where old and new

San Francisco stood shoulder to shoulder, with grand new blocks like Treadwell's standing opposite the frail wooden shells that survived from Gold Rush days twenty years ago.

Misty pulled down the blinds. "We don't want that dreadful wind."

She delved into her reticule and pulled out a silk scarf. "Here, put that over your nose if it's too unpleasant."

Lani had been here only a couple of weeks, but she'd heard about the notorious Market and Third Street corner that had been dubbed "Cape Horn" because of the nasty afternoon wind that whipped dust into pedestrian's faces. If you wanted to promenade Market Street's fancy shops, best do it in the morning before the wind got up.

"I'm fine." Lani settled back against

the seat. "Now tell me what's going on."

The cab lurched to the left. She heard the hack man cursing out another driver and, distracted from her own question, lifted the blind to see what was going on. They were outside the Turkish Baths near Fourth Street, and a moist hot steaminess laced with the fragrance of honeysuckle and gardenia replaced the air's dry dustiness.

"Smell that. Better than the dust."

The cab slowed and took a turn to the left by a red brick church. "St. Ignatius Church," she read from the board on the wall outside.

"Is this the right way? I thought you went further up Market Street to get to Pine Street, to Elizabeth's. And you turn right, not left."

She pulled back from the window.

Misty was pressing against her, a weird sheen in her eyes. She glanced down at the hand that had dug around in the bag for the scarf moments ago. Now it was holding an ebony-handled Remington double-barreled pocket pistol.

Lani started and banged her hip against the cab wall.

"Misty? For goodness' sake, what's going on?"

"Sit tight and everything will be fine. I have to make sure we both get there."

"Get where? Where are we going?"

"We're going for a brief train ride, but don't worry your head. Nothing bad will happen. The place we're going to is beautiful, Lani. You'll love it."

Lani stared at her old companion. Her green eyes had a moony glaze she'd never seen in them before. "You haven't been smoking opium, have you?"

Misty crowed. "No, you silly girl."

Lani leaned in. "Then it's the whiskey. I can smell it on you."

"Shut up, Lani."

"This is all Cyrus's idea, isn't it? He's not missing at all. You are taking me to him, whether or not I want to go."

She wriggled against the cab wall to gain a few more inches of breathing space from the gun barrel and flicked up the blind again. They were pulling into a train station.

The hack slowed and pulled up. "We're both going quietly in here, and getting on a train," Misty said. "Don't try anything stupid and you won't get hurt."

Lani stumbled out of the cab, still not believing what was happening. Misty had wrapped herself in a voluminous shawl which hid the gun in her hand. They were a fond mother and daughter, out for the afternoon.

Over the traffic noise and the chatter of the other passengers, Lani caught a garbled loudspeaker announcement from the platform.

"Central Pacific line. San Francisco to San Jose. Departing in five minutes. All aboard please."

Misty hugged her tighter. "See, I told you it would be fun. We're going somewhere really nice."

"Did you tell her?"

Well-wishers swamped Aristide, crowding their table, wanting to shake his hand, to congratulate Sir John on his foresight in hiring him, telling him they'd known all along that he'd win.

But much as he appreciated their good intentions, one thing was more important to him than any of this.

He'd kept a watch out for Will's return all the time he was accepting praise and attempting to engage. As soon as he saw the broker's slim form coming back into the ballroom, he slipped away from the knot gathered around Sir John.

Will shook his head. "No, I didn't see her. She doesn't appear to be in. I knocked several times, loudly, but no one answered. I guess she's out."

"Did you leave the note?"

Will tilted his head on one side, like a cheeky sparrow. "Does a dying man count his change? Of course I left the note. I followed your instructions to the T. I knew I'd hear it from you if I didn't."

Aristide had written Leilani a quick note, letting her know of his success and apologizing for not being able to uphold his invitation for her to be here.

Be assured, mademoiselle, this difficulty will blow over soon and then I look forward to enjoying more of your company, if you will consent to such a proposition. Yours admiringly, Aristide Laurent.

"Where did you leave it?"

"I slipped it under the door, as you suggested. She'll trip over it when she comes back."

Now Charles Krug was standing at the front again, chiming the glass with his determined spoon. "It's time, please, ladies and gentlemen. Resume your seats and we'll begin the second and final part of our Symposium tasting."

The judges returned to their seats and the room fell silent.

"As you're no doubt all aware, we categorize this section as red wines. They can be Bordeaux-style clarets, Zinfandels, anything made from any blend of grapes the vintner so desires. We are only interested in the final result. We're giving diners the option of sweet dessert wines extra to the tasting, so please, go ahead and enjoy the final courses while our judges deliberate."

Not in her room.

Was he being ridiculous worrying about her? Couldn't she go out if she wished? For all he knew she might be with her brother—he wasn't in evidence here either.

But no matter how much Aristide tried to convince himself, his danger gauge stayed on high alert. He couldn't quell a rising disquiet.

Cyrus May was a desperate man. If that hadn't been obvious when he was caught with the shark tooth, it was screaming from the rooftops after his bumbling attempt to plant the incriminating evidence on Lani. Would he leave it at that and run, or was he planning some sort of revenge?

The mild cramps that had started during the first round of tasting worsened as the judges sampled the red wines.

He leaned in to Sir John. "I've got to slip out for a moment. Stomach cramps."

When he returned ten minutes later, the chatter of diners and clink of cutlery had silenced. Charles Krug was back at his post at the head of the room.

"The Golden Gate Wine Symposium finale. The judges have spoken and these are their results. For best red wine, Aristide Laurent and Sir John Russell, and the Vino d'Oro Zinfandel, Sacramento. Runners-up—and here we have three names, as the judges considered they were too close to separate. Mariano Vallejo and Victor Fauré, Sonoma Claret from Zinfandel grapes; William and Eliza Hood, Cabernet Sauvignon from the Upper Sonoma Valley; and William Blackmore Rankin, for his Lexington Ranch Glenwood Zinfandel."

Krug turned his sights to the Russell table. "Congratulations, Sir John, Mr. Laurent. A clean sweep, and well deserved. We're all aware you've had your problems. It's good to see justice and hard work prevail. And to the runners-up, I think we've proven that California can produce top-quality wines. And a note of interest—all the finalists except Vino d'Oro are members of the Buena Vista Cooperative."

The diners clapped heartily and Aristide waited for the exhilaration of winning, the conqueror's surge of triumph, to lift him out of the doldrums.

The senator's brows pulled down in a stormy line. He raised his glass and dipped it sardonically toward their table, as if in a toast. He flashed a shifty glance around to check if anyone was watching, and then turned back to Aristide and drew the glass across his throat.

He was issuing an explicit threat, and Aristide's marrow melted under the malevolence of his stare. Lani wouldn't be returning to find his note tonight. Of that he was certain.

When he looked over to de Vile's table a few minutes later, the man had vanished. His eyes raked the room, but his distinguished figure was nowhere to be seen.

He wanted to sound an alarm, set up a search party, do something, anything. Except he didn't know what he should be doing, or where.

A helpless gnawing in his innards told him something dreadful was about to happen.

A man grabbed his hand, pumped congratulations. "Well done, Laurent. You've been through a lot, but now it's all been worthwhile."

And wasn't that the farthest thing from the truth?

Sixty-seven

The crowd in the big ballroom thinned out. The winning tables were the last to depart, the place-getters hovering in the afterglow of success as the waiters navigated around them cleaning up the party debris. Already the room had a stale smell of over-aerated wine and old tobacco. Sir John took Aristide's forearms in both hands. When he spoke his voice was steady and warm.

"It's been hell for you this last two weeks, Laurent, I understand that. But that's all behind us now. Here's to the opening of a whole new era for Vino d'Oro."

"Thank you, sir. It means a lot to me

to be vindicated."

Sebastian approached, his wife Isabella at his side. "Sorry to break up the party, brother, but we're off to bed. Great night, Aristide. Congrats once again."

As he turned to go Hector de Vile loomed into their space, a ghost from nowhere.

He thrust his hand out to John Russell. "Never say I'm a poor loser, Russell. Well done." He drew a bulky envelope out of his evening jacket and handed it to Sir John.

"Don't know how you scammed it, but you did." Aristide and John Russell were probably the only ones to hear the low sneer.

Russell jerked back his hand as if he'd palmed a hot branding iron, though he kept a firm grip on the envelope.

"Scammed it, de Vile? What a bad loser. You never play fair, do you?"

De Vile threw back his head and roared. "You're right there, Russell. But I'm not a bad loser, because I never lose."

He dodged around a champagne bucket, dipped his hand into his jacket once more and pulled out a piece of paper. "Aristide understands that, don't you, sonny?"

He pushed the note into Aristide's numb hand.

Then he leaned close and whispered, "Withdraw those wines from the contest within twenty-four hours or you'll never see her again. Use any excuse you like."

He looked up, eyes glittering, and continued his low rush of words.

"Any excuse—you can't fulfill the volumes required, you've come down with wine blight. I don't care what. Put yourself out of the running. *Or else.*"

Aristide glanced down at his frozen fingers. He didn't need to open the scrap to know it was the note Will left in Lani's door earlier that evening. The note assuring her everything would be fine.

"What the heck was that all about?" Sir John eyed the senator's retreating back. "What did he want?"

Aristide repeated the threat, word for word. He shook the paper in front of John's nose.

"This is a note from me Will left for Miss Manolo at the break. Telling her we'd won the whites and reassuring her we'd come through without another disaster."

John Russell stared at him for so long Aristide had time to register his feet were sore from standing. Then the older man swung to the door and hollered through cupped hands.

"Sebastian! Come back here." His quiet rock of a brother halted and turned, a question playing across the hard planes of his face.

"Something's come up."

Russell swiveled to Pania, standing patiently waiting for him to complete his farewells. "Darling, can you take Isabella home? We'll join you later."

She raised an imperious eyebrow.

"I know. How much later I can't say. Make sure you and Isabella stay safe. You know the drill. Answer to no one till we get back."

He kissed her on both cheeks and tapped her in the middle of her back as she turned to leave.

Then he drew his brother and Aristide

into a tight circle.

"Now for goodness' sake spit it out. What the heck is going on?"

Before Aristide could speak, Russell reared back, his hand up in arrest. "Hang on a minute." He grabbed the waiter who'd approached to remove the champagne bucket.

"Can you bring Sam Morley here? It's urgent. Get him right away."

The waiter flinched at the rasp in Russell's voice, then scuttled off like a frightened rabbit.

Aristide sympathized, but a rising indignation swamped his earlier fear. De Vile had gone too far. He'd lived too long in the woods to be scared by an owl.

They got the confirmation they were seeking when Sam Morgan arrived, his hand on Teddy's shoulder.

"Excellent that Teddy's here," John Russell said. "He might have seen something."

Sam shrugged. "Now his mum's gone he's spending more time with me at the hotel. He's quick and smart. Useful to have around."

John bent down and addressed the boy directly. "Teddy, have you seen Miss Manolo today? Did you see her go out anywhere this afternoon? Or did you see anyone go to her room?"

The boy jigged his right foot up and down as he gave Russell's question deep consideration. He thrust his hands into his pockets and his foot stilled.

"Didn't see anyone go to her room. But I did see her outside with that old lady who comes here all the time. The one with white hair. Worked for the

665

cove who got killed. That one."

"Misty. Has to be Misty," said Aristide

"And what were they doing?" asked John Russell. He'd reined in his impatience, and spoke to the boy as though they had all the time in the world.

"They got into a hack. Lani seemed all right. It was just the two of them."

"And about what time was this? Can you remember?"

"Around the same time everyone was arriving for the do. I was out to run errands. Lotsa people around."

Russell straightened up and addressed Aristide and Sebastian. "Sounds like around five o'clock. They were getting their insurance policy in place."

Sam spoke. "But why Misty? What's she got against the girl? I thought they were close."

666

"They might be close, but that husband of hers wants a way out. No one likes the prospect of the noose around his neck," Sebastian said. "Lani is de Vile's price for helping Cyrus escape."

He clapped his hands together in one volcanic thwack. "And I've got a lead on where they're going." His voice had taken on an excited edge, unlike his characteristic stoic moderation.

"De Vile will use any leverage he's got. You've seen how he works. He's obviously taking advantage of a desperate man. Maybe he's promised to get him off murder charges. You scratch my back . . . You know the rest."

Sebastian glanced around at the men. "Sit down and listen up. Just for a minute or two. Then we'll have to move fast."

He outlined his conversation with Elizabeth Wenderhoven in brief, clipped detail.

"She confirmed that Misty was having an affair with Bully. He confided in her. We always wondered if a jealous husband had the motive. I'm satisfied the evidence points that way. He killed Pike. And after that stupid business when he tried to blame Lani . . . He'll know we're onto him. And Mrs. Wenderhoven told me exactly where she thought they'd run away to."

All the heads came up in shock. Sam Morley, who'd remained standing with his hands resting on Teddy's shoulders, gave an excited yelp.

"They'll be headed to William Ralston's summer house down the Peninsula. He calls it Belmont. The Mays and de Vile go there often. Ralston's got so many rooms he hardly knows who's staying."

John Russell turned to Aristide. "Before we rush off on a rescue mission, Aristide, I want to check with you. This win is important to you, I know. Do you want us to risk all on a rescue that might end in death—for us or for the lady? Or would you prefer to accept de Vile's ultimatum? Withdraw from the win and trust he will return Miss Manolo unharmed?"

"You would give me that choice? I can't believe it." Aristide's chest pounded, fiery blood pumping at his temples.

He squared up to Sir John. "It's your wine, your company."

"Lives come first, Aristide. Every time. Wouldn't you agree?"

Aristide went hot and cold. For a few

seconds he considered brazening it out. Ignoring de Vile's threats. Clutching his prize to his chest, wallowing in the delight of gaining the recognition he'd sought all his life.

Then he thought of Candy, of her reckless disregard for others that had cost them their lives.

No. The ends did not justify the means. The prize that had once seemed like the crock of gold at the end of the rainbow had turned to ashes.

I am not anything like my father.

The refrain came roaring back into his head, but now it had the ring of conviction.

I am not like my father. Or like Candy Meadows.

"Thing is, Sir John, even if we did play his game . . . We could go public with a lot of lies and he still wouldn't return her unharmed. I appreciate the opportunity to make this choice. I'm touched you've the confidence in me to make the right one. But the wine is a secondary matter.

"We have to go after them. Is everyone agreed on that?"

Everyone, it seemed, did.

Sixty-eight

The brothers planned their assault on Belmont House like a military campaign, and Aristide couldn't decide who was the better soldier, Sebastian or John.

Within an hour they'd organized a rugged, all-weather coach and an experienced driver capable of driving through the night, called in assistant chief of police Barney Carnahan as the official arm of the law able to make any arrests, got survival supplies—food, water, blankets, and weapons—and they were on their way.

They'd underplayed the fact that the Manolo girl was possibly being held against her will and emphasized to

Officer Carnahan that Cyrus May was on the run from Bully's murder and should be taken in for questioning.

Trains ran four times a day to Belmont station south of the city, where William Ralston's fine Italianate mansion was located, but the last one for the day had left at six p.m. They calculated that Misty and Lani had probably been on that train—and they had no intention of waiting until morning to give chase.

Belmont was well known to the beau-monde set. Ralston, dubbed "the man who built California" because of his vision and drive, had made his money in Comstock silver and then set up the Bank of California with $5 million in capital. But that wasn't all. Soap, sugar, silk and furniture factories, wool mills, watch manufacturing and several magnificent hotels all added to his empire.

The impressive summer house he'd built in the country had originally been a modest Italianate villa owned by a Tuscan nobleman, the first Italian consul to San Francisco, Count Leonetto Cipriani, who'd imported his marble-slabbed 120-ton home in pieces from Europe and then reassembled it like a giant jigsaw puzzle. Ralston had taken over the two-story home and built out and up to create a four-story mansion, the 120-room White House of the West, where he courted Bank of California investors with lavish hospitality.

And this was where they were going. As the coach swayed and their knees banged in the cramped cabin, it amazed Aristide to see the other three drop off into sound sleep.

He, by comparison, drowsed off in ten-minute snatches and then started awake, terrorized by dreams of cut throats and poisoned wine. He recalled how close Cyrus had come to strangling the life out of Misty, and he prayed to a God he didn't believe in to ensure they'd arrive before he did the same thing to Lani.

His passion for conquering the world with his wine lay on dead coals. He wondered how he could ever have been so dumb as to think it would make his life complete.

Lani Manolo slept like a baby. Part of it was the exhaustion of trying to process everything that had happened. But an even bigger part, she suspected, was that Misty had slipped a sleeping draught into the hot chocolate she insisted on making before bedtime. The thudding hangover headache she woke up with when she'd drunk no alcohol at dinner confirmed her suspicion.

If I didn't know it before, I know it now. Don't trust Misty.

They'd arrived at the place Misty explained belonged to a rich banker friend of hers as the day was drawing in. William Ralston wasn't there, but his wife Elizabeth and their three children were, along with an army of servants who showed them to their rooms and made up their beds with practiced ease.

Elizabeth Fry Ralston—Lizzie to her close friends—was a delicate brunette and consummate hostess. She lived at Belmont all year round, while William traveled back and forth between their country house and the city one. He was in the city this weekend, but Mrs.

Ralston was unfazed by her unexpected guests. Given her husband's enthusiasm for company—he was the man who took a big party of his friends on their honeymoon—she and her well-trained household were used to catering for arrivals at all hours.

"He'll be home tonight or tomorrow at the latest," she said. "In the meantime, please make yourself at home. That's what he built this place for. Entertaining."

The situation bewildered Lani. Misty had abducted her at gunpoint, but she was enduring the most civilized confinement she could ever imagine. Misty had made it clear they would be together at all times, and she issued dire warnings about the consequences of running away. But she'd also reassured her if she did what she was told, she'd be fine.

Cyrus acted as if it was the most normal thing in the world for her to be joining them for a country weekend, and in different times it would have been. But she only had to observe Cyrus and Misty as they mooched around the library after their arrival to see that things were far from normal.

There was a brittle uncertainty in the way they addressed one other that had never been there before. Misty flinched sometimes when Cyrus made a quick movement, anticipating a blow. And Cyrus, no longer the relaxed, gregarious uncle of her childhood, took offense at the slightest thing.

Intense, almost fanatical interludes, where he sought reassurance from Misty on the weirdest range of fancies, interrupted his morose silences. That as a young man he'd ridden more thunderous waves than Bully. That his post as consul was about to be renewed for another five years. That they would spend Christmas in Paris. (It was the first Lani had heard of such a proposition.)

Misty replied in a warm affirmative to everything he said, because he lost his temper if she attempted to moderate or demur to his assertions. He'd jump up and pace the floor with irritated quick steps, twisting his fingers with a relentless fervor that, Lani imagined, reflected his inner turmoil.

Lani avoided being drawn into their tetchy squabbles, pretending to read a copy of *The Count of Monte Cristo* she'd found in the library.

Now in the early morning light she reached for the book, thinking she'd read another chapter before they rose for a late Sunday breakfast. She snapped on the bedside lamp. Misty had locked their room and put the key under her pillow before they'd gone to bed last night, so she didn't have much choice but to read.

It hadn't escaped her attention that she'd chosen a story about another wrongfully accused Frenchman. She hoped that at least one good thing had come out of this sorry mess, that Aristide had got his wish to see his wines launched spectacularly with a win at the Symposium.

Lani was tapping the head off her second boiled egg at the breakfast table set up in the sun parlor when a loud thumping at the front door interrupted their conversation.

The sun parlor, as Elizabeth Ralston had explained when they took their seats, was a reminder of William's youth working Mississippi river boats, the long enclosed veranda operating like a deck promenade, lined with floor-to-ceiling windows that faced onto ascending terraces planted with heliotrope, oleander, crape-myrtle, camellias, laurel, and lilac.

Elizabeth appeared distracted by the intrusion. "Oh, my goodness. Even William rarely turns up at this hour on a Sunday."

The serious Scot who was the Ralston's house manager was at the threshold in a flash. Cyrus and Misty, who unlike Lani sat with their backs to the windows, turned to watch.

"Hector."

Before any of them had a chance to

register the visitor's identity, Elizabeth Ralston was on her feet, her abundant, loosely braided, dark hair tumbling down her back.

"No one mentioned we were to have the pleasure of your company. William didn't say."

Their vivacious hostess had flushed a light pink as she swept toward the front door where the senator for California stood, hand poised on his tortoiseshell-headed cane, as if it was the most normal thing to turn up, uninvited, in the country at ten a.m. on a Sunday.

He leaned forward and kissed Mrs. Ralston lightly on both cheeks. "You've got some of my favorite people here, Lizzie. How could I stay away?"

The words sounded jocular, but the sweeping glance he made around the table was anything but. In the blink of an eye he registered that Cyrus had half-risen from his seat. Out of fear or friendship, Lani couldn't tell. Misty's restraining arm was at his elbow.

"Don't get up, Cyrus, old mate. We need not stand on ceremony."

His eyes flickered over Lani's face and moved on, as if he barely recognized her. Despite the warm veranda and the satisfaction of the meal, Lani tensed, as if caught in a cold rain.

Mrs. Ralston took de Vile's arm, her turquoise silk skirts whispering as she drew him to the table.

"Do come and sit down, Hector." She turned to the houseman. "Fresh coffee and croissants, Mr. Dunstan. As soon as Cook can organize them."

Sixty-nine

De Vile. Here. And not in the least surprised to see me seated at breakfast.

Lani examined her plate, saw the leftover smear of apricot jam and butter, and concentrated very hard on composing her features.

She would not reveal an instant of surprise or fear. She wouldn't try to alert her hostess to the strangeness of everything that was happening around her. Or let the senator think he'd won.

She heard de Vile's voice in her head, at Jack's over dinner. When was that? On Friday—barely two days ago.

"You'll regret this, Miss Manolo. Don't come whining to me then."

De Vile had put Cyrus up to this. Promised to help him escape, probably.

Elizabeth Ralston, ever the perfect hostess, was outlining the entertainment possibilities.

"You're most welcome to stroll in the greenhouses or the gardens. Even take a walk over the hill to William's grapevines if they are of interest. Closer to home we've got the bowling alley. And if your taste tends toward the hedonistic, we have lovely Turkish baths. Mrs. Dunstan would be happy to provide towels and lotions."

Misty was smiling and nodding, as if she really was here to enjoy a country weekend.

Lani's eyes snapped to the windows. The peninsula was a favorite destination because it was warmer and sunnier than the city, and today was no exception.

The camellia leaves shone a glossy green through the windows.

The sun parlor was like a tropical conservatory. Beyond the bushes, Lani caught a flicker of movement. A glimpse of a man's shoulder. The gardeners, no doubt. Or the chaps responsible for the Belmont butter, milk, and eggs they'd enjoyed at table. She tamped down the leap in her stomach, the unreasonable jolt of hope that rescue might be at hand.

If de Vile could make the journey, then couldn't Will? Or Kaleo? Or—dare she even hope for it?—Aristide Laurent.

She carefully directed her eyes back to the breakfast party, assembling her features into an expression of mild interest.

Cyrus was gazing at the floor, seemingly not aware of what was going on around him. Misty was tapping on the tablecloth, making some point to Mrs. Ralston. And de Vile? She feigned vagueness and glanced in his direction, to where he was sitting next to Cyrus, back to the windows.

He was watching her like a hawk.

By the heavens, she is beautiful, de Vile thought. Even more alluring than her mother, and more dangerous. Abigail had only wanted her own wild way. Fun and pleasure. This one, she had her genius under control.

But she will not win.

Cyrus sat next to him, lost in thought, a vacuum, barely present. He nudged him with his elbow, leaned over and spoke low.

"Buck up, Cyrus. Pay attention."

What a disappointment he'd turned

out to be. To fail so badly, so late in life. Everything he'd achieved, canceled out in one rash act. It was pathetic. He would be remembered as a cuckolded murderer, nothing else.

As soon as he'd entered Belmont's high-beamed sunny parlor de Vile saw that Misty was running things now. Cyrus was a lost man. Ending his misery would do him a favor.

He relaxed, sipped his coffee and engaged in a sliver of self-examination. Had he misjudged the Frenchman Laurent? Would he be willing to surrender his big dreams for this slip of a woman? A girl, really. Barely a woman. Even one as desirable as Leilani Manolo?

After a moment's hesitation, he answered in the negative. He was a playboy. On his reckoning, women were fairground dolls, only good for being set on a stick decked out in rainbow tulle. A dime a dozen.

He took another gulp of coffee and eased back into the conversation.

"I've got an interesting proposition for William when he gets back." He gave Elizabeth Ralston his practiced senator smile. The one with a hint of mystery, as if he'd got something unexpected up his sleeve. Because he always did.

Seventy

When rescue came, it didn't turn out at all the way Lani had hoped or imagined. Nothing like it.

They'd finished eating and loitered in the high-domed foyer at the foot of the grand staircase while the Mays debated how they'd spend the rest of their morning. Would they take up the invitation to tour the greenhouses? Investigate the grapes? Or explore the library?

They'd stuck close to her, Misty and Cyrus, always at her elbow. Cyrus wore a baggy hunting jacket in the fashionable, loose, English style, and from the distorted swing of the coat when he moved Lani knew he'd stowed a pistol in the big front pocket. If anyone else noticed the bulge, they were too polite to mention it.

She was bending down to pet the Ralston family dog Slinky, a sleek, musty little dachshund, when a gust of fresh air blew away the doggy odor with the cherry vanilla smell of heliotrope. She guessed that the front door had opened and instantly Cyrus had his arm across her throat, his gun at her temple.

He hauled her backwards up the grand stairs, step by painful step, his arm slick with sweat. Before they'd reached halfway, Lani was forced to follow his lead and take her own weight to reduce the choking pressure across her larynx.

Sebastian and the ginger cop who'd let her go two nights back came to a hard stop. They stood, guns drawn, tight-faced, at the foot of the stairs, staring up.

Cyrus's breath rasped at her ear, hot and damp, as they reached the top and he dragged her sideways.

Belmont's celebrated mezzanine rivaled the downstairs parlor in its originality of design. A series of Paris-inspired opera boxes looped around the atrium like a Renaissance garland, giving the occupants above an unobstructed view to the parlor below.

Gossip said the architectural detail was a fancy of Lizzie Ralston's, a concession from her rich husband as compensation because she didn't enjoy their magnificent country estate nearly as much as he did. Thigh-level molded columns fronted six open, arched boxes like stairwell balusters, so low it would be frighteningly easy for a man to throw someone over them.

Lani scrabbled at Cyrus's swinging coat, desperate to hold on to something that would stop her from falling, as they lurched into the box closest to the top of the stairs. Cyrus was panting and swaying. His male scent, a sharp cheesiness, was overpowering at such close range. The gun dug into her hairline.

"Cyrus," she hissed through clenched teeth. "Be careful."

Her head swam at the gaping space that opened between them and Sebastian and the others below. One hard push in the middle of her back and she'd be in flight.

Sebastian's voice boomed out, forceful and demanding. "Cyrus! Let her go. It's over."

Cyrus's arm slackened for a second and then pulled even harder.

"You're choking me," she croaked.

Cyrus ignored her. "I want safe passage," he boomed back. "I won't hurt her if you give us safe passage."

"Safe passage, Mr. May? That will only be possible after you've answered some questions in relation to the death of Bully Pike."

Sebastian glanced up the stairs. Lani wondered if she was missing something—was someone sneaking up them?

"Until we've had that talk, safe passage isn't a possibility."

Hector de Vile's baritone rang out. "Come on, Cyrus. Don't make things worse for yourself. You're already neck-deep in trouble."

"I'm in neck-deep? This is all *your*

fault. You're the one who said bring Lani."

"Nonsense!" barked de Vile. "Utter nonsense."

Cyrus was wheezing, his breath sawing in and out like a steam train. He swiped his gun hand across his forehead, mopping his temples with his sleeve, then moved the barrel to the base of her ear.

"If I hadn't been trying to warn Bully about the girl and her brother, none of this would have happened," he yelled. "I wouldn't have seen him with Misty. I'd have been none the wiser." He emitted a bitter laugh, then pointed the gun at de Vile, and fired.

Boom! In the closed space it echoed like a cannon. The crystal chandeliers tinkled. De Vile leapt back, the fine parquet floor splintered at his feet.

The gun was back to Lani's neck even as she recoiled.

"On no!" A woman's voice. Probably their hostess.

Cyrus didn't react. He'd lost himself in his story. "I had to tell Bully. As soon as I knew, I had to tell him."

"Tell him what, Mr. May. What was it Pike needed to know?" Sebastian's voice was steady, sympathetic, even.

There was a long silence. Cyrus edged them forwards, closer to the box balustrade. Lani's head swam, but her eyes were fixed on Misty's white, distraught face. At Misty, waving the Remington, the gun she'd had on the train.

"Don't, Cyrus! Don't say any more!" She was screaming at him, her eyes narrowed and intense.

Cyrus ducked back, clamping Lani more

tightly to him, his shield. "You've let me down, de Vile. You said you'd get us out of here. Instead you've brought the law."

Silence.

"I had to tell Bully about the kids. I had to. He had great hopes of Washington. If you'd found out about the kids, I knew it would all be over. You'd never do business with Bully again. I owed him. I had to warn him."

Kids? Warn him?

Lani's head was spinning.

What kids? Surely not her and Kaleo? But who else could it be?

"You deserve everything you've got coming to you, Cyrus," sneered de Vile. "Bully did too. What you both did was despicable."

Despicable?

De Vile's words flowed like treacle laced with arsenic. Cyrus was holding her so close the impact of each one was carried in a trembling, convulsive wave which began deep in Cyrus and scorched through her.

He dropped his arm from her throat, stepped right up to the balustrade and fired down.

Lani crumpled, deprived of her bulwark.

A man's cry, a commotion of voices, men's and women's, below.

She scrambled sideways, shifting crablike on her bottom, desperate to increase the distance between them before Cyrus turned back.

A man's heavy black boot came down on the folds of her skirt, pinning her to the floor. Her eyes were stuck open; she could not close them or turn away, even if it meant staring into the barrel of a gun.

Has Cyrus finally flipped? Am I next?

She got a fleeting glimpse of dark hair, a handsome profile, as a male figure rushed past.

Right up to Cyrus, who was still staring out at the scene below.

Aristide Laurent raised a gun and pressed it into Cyrus's neck. "Drop it."

John Russell was hot behind him. He stepped around Lani's sprawled form and was right there, reaching for Cyrus's gun arm.

A shot sounded, and Cyrus pitched forward, his gun hand still held high, braced by Russell.

Lani's ears rang from the blast. A hot metallic smell filled the box. Russell was covered in blood, holding Cyrus under the armpits, trying to find space to lay him down, calling for a doctor.

A second blast came from

downstairs, followed by a woman's prolonged screaming.

Lani lay on the floor, paralyzed, deafened. Her ears were ringing, muffling the noise from downstairs, and yet other senses were heightened. The rotten-egg smell of gun smoke. The wet, shiny speckle of rust-red on her sleeve. She dipped her finger on the dots and ran her tongue over it. Blood. Had she known that already, or was she surprised? She didn't know.

Then Aristide was standing beside her, leaning down. Speaking softly, he drew her to her feet.

The warmth of his body flowed into her and she discovered her legs were able to hold her, that she could stand under her own weight.

A hollow ache pulsed in the place where her heart used to be. "Is he going to die?"

Aristide shook his head, his eyes fixed on her face, burning with regret.

"Someone fired from downstairs. I'm not sure. It happened so fast."

"Is he going to die? Is Cyrus going to die?"

Cyrus had killed a man. Tried to blame her. But she didn't want him to die. Not their Cyrus. He was family.

"I don't know. The doctor hasn't come yet." Aristide's eyes skittered away. He'd answered her question.

"Can you help me downstairs? I want to see Misty."

His dark eyes, as deep as inky wells, fastened on hers again.

"That's not such a great idea, *ma cherie.* Let me find you a chair and a strong brandy."

Seventy-one

"So that's the story of the Hawaiian lovers, Ohi'a and Lehua. Did you enjoy that?"

Lani pressed her warm lips against Aristide's forehead and pulled back to gaze into his eyes.

He tucked a wayward curl behind her ear. "I don't want to be a jolly tree! I want to be a human and live forever. Preferably with you!"

His voice cracked, and he threw his head back into the wind and laughed to lighten the moment.

The stray dark lock she'd come to treasure blew across his face, and Lani's heart broke open. She would remember this moment, and know she had never loved him more.

"I have to go home, Aristide. My old hāina mother, Ani, she's ill. She's waiting for me and I don't know how much longer she'll be with us."

"Your godmother. I know." He kissed her on her cheek, nuzzled her ear, then stepped back and took her hand.

They were walking on the beach below Cliff House, the restaurant which was a hugely popular day trip up the coast from the city. They'd had a great lunch on the cliff top, gazing out over thirty miles of empty Pacific Ocean to the horizon. With full bellies and a sense of pleasant well-being they'd stepped out onto the beach for time alone in the fresh air.

In the month since the disastrous day at Belmont they'd repeated the conversation about Lani's return home more than once, and found no way to change the inevitable.

"Ohi'a and Lehua. They do have something to tell us, don't you think?"

"And what's that?"

Lani's cheeks grew hot. She could blame the energizing sea breeze for her blush, but she knew she would be lying.

She had got to know Aristide a lot better in the weeks since they'd buried Misty and Cyrus, but she still found being a woman—as distinct from being a friend—unfamiliar territory. Sometimes it seemed as if she was groping in a mist, walking by faith because she had no sight.

She had been explaining the Hawaiian approach to life, to help him understand why she was leaving tomorrow.

And she'd had a niggling sense that the traditional tale—about a devoted couple reunited by the gods after they had been separated by the jealous Pele, the volcano goddess—echoed something of what they were going through.

It was said that Pele desired the handsome young Ohi'a, but when he turned down her advances in favor of his beloved Lehua, she transformed into a raging column of fire and burned him to a crisp, leaving him an ugly, twisted tree. Lehua fell to her knees at the base of his tortured trunk, begging Pele to transform her into a tree too, so she could be with him forever.

The jealous Pele refused, but the other gods, seeing her devotion, changed her into the scarlet Lehua flower that lights up the Ohi'a tree in a year-round spectacular display. Tree and flower would never again be separated.

"It's said even today that when the Lehua blooms, the weather will be fair and sunny. But if you pick the flower, expect heavy rain, because Lehua still cannot bear to be separated from her love."

"It's a beautiful story, Lani, I'll give you that."

He stood and stared out to the breaker line, where the white foam lit up when it caught the sun.

"When you're gone, I'll come out here sometimes and imagine you—somewhere straight out there." He swept his arm wide. "Two thousand miles across the sea."

His face mocked despair. "How will I survive?"

"You'll survive. You've got all that

wine to make and ship to New York and Paris. You won't have time to think about anything else."

He kicked the sand, glancing up. "You're right. We start harvesting next week, so I will have something else to think about, hard as that might be to imagine."

She poked out her tongue.

The truth of it was they'd become almost inseparable in the weeks since Cyrus and Misty died. The days had been precious, because they both knew they would be ending soon.

In the hours following the Belmont debacle, Aristide was at her side whenever he could get away from the grapes. They'd become devoted friends, but they always tiptoed around the delicate topic of a lifetime commitment. They both understood it wouldn't be possible. Instead, they dealt with things moment-by-moment, day by day.

Milestone things. Like burying the "godparents" she had loved. Coming to terms with those final minutes of madness, when Misty had shot Cyrus and then turned her gun on herself.

She'd done it to save him from the ignominy of the hangman's noose, Lani was certain. She thought of it as an honorable act, Misty's way of trying to make up for her betrayal, stating as definitively as anyone could a determination to not live on without him. Cyrus's final shot was aimed at de Vile, but missed, merely taking up a bit more of Belmont's parquet. She almost wished he'd found his mark.

Aristide had been understanding about the one thing she had not been able to do, and that was to come to terms with the revelation that Hector de Vile was her biological father. She had refused to have anything to do with the man, despite his repeated requests to meet.

The mere thought of talking to the Machiavellian senator left her nauseous. He'd blackmailed the Mays into snatching her. He'd betrayed everyone he'd exploited, including the Meadows. And he'd been relentless in trying to destroy their business, never mind that he hadn't known it was his own children he was cutting off.

Lani shuddered, despite the warmth generated by walking.

They were fortunate that Will Davenport had shown himself capable of making decisions independent of de Vile's malevolent influence. She didn't know what it might have cost

Davenport, but together with Kaleo they'd worked out a new sugar contract that was beneficial for both parties.

They'd agreed that Kaleo would stay on to manage the Bay end of things while she made sure everything was in order back in Honolulu. It was what she was destined for, serving the family that relied on her.

Aristide reached for Lani's hand. "That wind's strengthening. Come on, let's get in the buggy and drive."

The Cliff House Road that ran west from Bush Street all the way up the coast was the broadest, hardest, and smoothest track of any in the state. A million dollars of horse flesh could flash by in a few hours on the highly fashionable trail.

They drove back to the city in melancholy silence, each locked up in their own reverie.

Lani watched the ocean, aware that tomorrow she'd be somewhere out there on the gray water heading home to her hāina mother Ani, to her half-sister Malia, to the plantations.

Aristide dropped her back at Elizabeth Wenderhoven's Nob Hill villa at twilight.

She wanted to preserve this moment, the image of her handsome Frenchman, the reins held light and secure in his gloved hand, his face glowing from a day of salt and spray, dark eyes burning with unexpressed emotion.

"Please don't come to the dock tomorrow," she said. "I couldn't bear it."

She turned away, not wanting him to see the tears.

He placed his finger gently on her

chin and turned her back to face him. "I will never forget you, Leilani Kamamalu Lilolilo Arnold. Now go and conquer your world."

He gently pressed his lips to her wet cheeks, right, and then left, with the lightest of chaste butterfly kisses. He gazed into her face, his eyes suspiciously bright. "And remember, even the bravest woman is allowed to cry sometimes."

He jumped down from the buggy and went around to her side to help her down.

He walked her in silence to the Countess's front door.

Pressed her elbow, a final mute goodbye.

And turned and walked away.

THE END

If you enjoyed *Tainted Fortune* you may also enjoy *Captive Heart*, A Hawaiian Christmas Novella, continuing Leilani and Aristide's adventures.

They thought they knew the meaning of sacrifice. But the hardest choice is yet to come.

Sugar heiress Leilani Manolo and French wine maker Aristide Laurent defied death and found magnetic attraction during a turbulent San Francisco winter, but they accepted a future together wasn't to be their destiny.

Leilani belongs in Honolulu heading the family business and caring for her dying *haina* mother and Aristide must fulfil his promise as an award-winning vintner for one of California's rising wine ventures.

But living apart is even harder than resigning themselves to permanent separation.

And when Aristide learns Leilani is being pressured into a 'dynastic' marriage with one of the Hawaiian King's senior advisors, he suspects bad family blood runs deep.

Aristide faces a torturous choice. Reveal the true extent of Lani's betrayal and risk life-long rejection, or accept the match and see her lose everything she holds dear.

FREE PREVIEW

Captive Heart, A Hawaiian Christmas Novella, Of Gold & Blood, Book #8.

Want to read more of *Captive Heart*? See a First chapter preview for FREE here:

www.jennywheeler.biz/book/captive-heart

Enjoy Tainted Fortune? You can make a big difference

Reviews are the most powerful tools in my kit when it comes to getting my books noticed. Much as I'd love it, I don't have the budget of a big publisher to buy billboard ads and other national advertising.

But I have the promise of something more powerful—something publishers envy.

And that's a committed and loyal bunch of readers.

Honest reviews of my books help them gain the attention of others who might appreciate them too.

If you've enjoyed this book bundle, I would be grateful if you could spend a few minutes leaving a review (it can be as short as you like) on the book's Amazon page. You can jump right to the page by clicking below.

Post Your Reviews Here:
Amazon: https://geni.us/lSETk
Goodreads: https://bit.ly/33nWzd5

Thank you very much
Jenny Wheeler

ACKNOWLEDGMENTS

Tainted Fortune was begun right at the start of the crazy Covid 19 pandemic that has swept our world, and so occasionally it was hard to focus on the 19th century when contemporary drama and confusion were evident everywhere. It also curtailed my ability to draw on the National Library Interloan facility, which closed down due to the lockdowns instituted in many places.

However, with access to digital material and wonderful help once again from the Auckland Libraries staff when they re-opened, I was able to access colorful detail about 1870s San

Francisco which I hope gives the book "true terroir." (Wine does feature rather prominently, after all.)

Thank you to the wonderfully loyal readers who continue to support my work—and give me feedback on decisions on things like cover and title selection through my newsletter. In lockdown writing is even more isolating than it usually is, and it really helps lift the spirits to know your readers are taking notice.

Finally, thank you once again to the professional skills of editor Stephen Stratford in Auckland, proof editor Stephanie Parent in the US and Polgarus Studios in Tasmania for getting *Tainted Fortune* into shape for sharing with a wider audience. – Jenny Wheeler

ABOUT THE AUTHOR

Jenny Wheeler is the author of the Of Gold & Blood Old California mystery series:

Poisoned Legacy #1
Brother Betrayed #2
Double Jeopardy #3
Tangled Destiny #4 (Christmas novella and Prequel)
Unbridled Vengeance #5
Hope Redeemed #6
Tainted Fortune Book #7 (September 2020)
Captive Heart – A Hawaiian Christmas Novella (November 2020)

Boxed Set/Book Bundle Of Gold &
Blood, Series 1 Books 1 – 3
Boxed Set/ Book Bundle Of Gold &
Blood Series 2 Books 1 & 4

Jenny's online home is at
jennywheeler.biz or email
Jenny@jennywheeler.biz

You can connect with Jenny on:
Facebook: @JennyWheeler.Biz
Twitter: @Jenny_Biz
Instagram: @jennysbingereading
Pinterest
https://www.pinterest.nz/Jennywheeler
books